Spirit of the Herd

Spirit of the Herd

A STORY OF SECOND CHANCES

SALLY BORDEN BUTEAU

authorHOUSE®

AuthorHouse™
1663 Liberty Drive
Bloomington, IN 47403
www.authorhouse.com
Phone: 1-800-839-8640

Published by AuthorHouse   02/13/2013

ISBN: 978-1-4772-8953-2 (sc)
ISBN: 978-1-4772-8952-5 (hc)
ISBN: 978-1-4772-8954-9 (e)

Library of Congress Control Number: 2012921251

For Anna and Kelsey and Their Beautiful Mares
Heads Up Penny and Allegro

With gratitude to Pam, Bryan and Hailey LaFave at Stonegate Stable and all the creatures who pass throug its barn doors: human, equine, canine and fowl (with apologies to Larry).

Chapter One

The sun moved across the curtains, sending the first rays of light into Fen's room. She woke slowly, stretching her arms over her head, and turned to look at the horse clock sitting on the small table next to her bed.

"Eight o'clock!" Fen cried. She sat up quickly and looked around for her clothes. They were jumbled in a heap on the floor, as usual. "Oh, no! They're taking attendance and I'm still in my pajamas! I'm dead! Why didn't Mom wake me up?"

Fen fell back onto the bed, quickly deciding she would pretend to be sick. As she lay there, she heard the funny, off-key humming of her little brother, Alex, outside her door. Suddenly, she relaxed, remembering it was the first day of April vacation.

"Phew! Thank goodness for Alex. He always knows what day it is."

Fen got up and went to the window. She pulled it open and stuck her head outside to catch the chilly spring breeze floating by. The sun was already filling the valley and lighting up the snow on the far mountains. Their peaks were so high and jagged that it seemed to Fen they must be void of life. But her father had told her about all the plants that grew and animals that walked on those perilous peaks. He told her stories of his trips through the mountain passes and being awed by the beauty that surrounded him. He described the animals, wildflowers and the trees covered in sparkling snow, even in the height of summer. But his favorite scene from the top of those peaks was the view of the meadows below that surrounded the home he had built with his own two hands.

When Fen was thirteen, she had pleaded with her father to take her on a trail ride through those mountains. Mack had promised Fen that, when she turned fifteen, he would take her on a week-long expedition through the rocky peaks, just as his father had done with him. Two years had seemed like an eternity to Fen, especially since her seventh grade year at John Muir Middle School had turned out to be one long disaster and this year had been no better. She had hoped she would find friends in eighth grade, but she hadn't and it made her feel like an outcast pony at the bottom of a herd's pecking order.

Although Fen was a smart student, earning good grades in the advanced placement classes, she considered school a prison sentence. All she ever wanted to do was ride her horses out on the wide open range and along the wooded trails that surrounded their ranch. During the spring and summer when other kids were playing baseball and swimming, Fen's favorite place was the arena, barrel racing and roping cattle.

When Fen complained to her father about school, he was not sympathetic. Mack hadn't been given the chance to finish high school because his family was so poor he had to get a full-time job to pay the bills. Fen's mother, Renee, had gone to law school and become a successful attorney. She knew the value of a good education. Between Renee's college degrees and Mack's strong work ethic and business sense, they had built a working ranch, buying, training, breeding and selling horses. Fen assumed she would inherit the ranch and wouldn't need a formal education.

"Why do I have to go to school?" Fen had asked her parents at the end of a particularly bad day.

Math class had been so boring she had drifted off to sleep and fallen out of her chair. She had let out a yelp and suddenly reached out, wildly swinging an arm in the air. Her instinctive grab for the reins in her dream, quickly melted into the reality of a classmate's pant leg. It had startled him and her and the entire class went into gales of laughter. With all the commotion, the teacher had lost his place in the lesson and decided to end class for the day.

The teacher had reprimanded Fen for her lack of commitment to academic work, when she had so much potential. She had heard the speech before. But Fen knew that any responses she had thought to say would be considered rude or impertinent. If you tell me something new, I'll listen. If you teach me something I don't already know, I'll be interested. If you let me tell you what I really think, I'll participate.

"Why didn't one of your classmates wake you up before you fell over, for Pete's sake?" Fen's mother had asked about the incident.

"Nobody likes me that much, Mom. They were all waiting for it to happen! Mr. Finnigan had to end the class and send everybody out for a 'movement break'. It was so humiliating! I'd much rather muck twenty stalls a day than go back to math class or any class for that matter."

"Then mucking stalls will be the only thing you'll be able to do for the rest of your life," Mack had responded with a stern look. "Now go do your homework and then you can muck those twenty stalls that are waiting for you out back."

Fen sighed, remembering the conversation. She shivered in the cool air and closed the bedroom window. Pulling on her plush, purple bathrobe made her feel better. Fen opened the door to find Alex sitting on the floor. He sat outside her door every morning when school was not in session.

Alex had turned six this year and now attended a private school for children with special needs. His legs were splayed out and he was bouncing a small, red, rubber ball in the space between them, using one finger to keep the ball in motion. He never missed a beat and the ball made a rhythmical, "bonk", on the wooden floor that would go on for hours, if he was left uninterrupted.

"Good morning, Alex." Fen knelt down beside her brother.

She waited for a response, but Alex continued to bounce the ball and hum. Fen knew never to take the ball away because her brother's tantrums were immediate and fierce.

"Alex. Stop bouncing the ball, please."

Alex stopped the bouncing by putting his finger on the ball as it hit the floor. He stared at his finger and continued humming, gently rocking back and forth.

"Good morning, Alex," Fen said, again. She gently put her finger under his chin and he instinctively pulled his head up. He didn't look at her, but let his gaze fall somewhere over her left shoulder. Fen pulled her finger away and Alex went back to bouncing his ball.

When her brother had been diagnosed with Autism three years ago, Fen had been told to continue talking to Alex and encouraging him to look in her direction when he was calm. His teachers told Fen it was difficult for Alex to look people in the eye and his repetitive activities, like ball bouncing, helped to keep him calm. His repetitive behaviors did seem to give him peace, but Fen thought it wasn't helping him to learn or be part of the family. She thought he must be lonely, staying inside his own mind so much of the time.

When Alex became agitated, Fen often took him out to see the horses in their pastures. At the end of the day, it was their ritual to visit the horses in the paddocks before they were turned in for their evening grain. Having schedules and routines kept Alex happy and he loved grooming the horses and stroking their soft noses. Animals always quieted when Alex was around. The horses nuzzled his clothes and face and stood still and relaxed when he touched them. It occurred to Fen more than once that she and her little brother had something very important in common. They both felt more comfortable with horses than people.

One of Alex's teachers had told Fen that the horses and Alex understood each other. Both of them faced the world in a constant state of fear, always alert for danger. Alex's repetitive behaviors, like humming and ball bouncing, were his way of avoiding social interaction, protecting himself from a confusing and unpredictable world. Fen wondered why Alex's teachers didn't encourage him to do what horses do. Horses didn't isolate themselves to become vulnerable and lonely. They sought togetherness in a herd, finding peace in the shelter of each other.

Fen knew that when horses paced in pens, cribbed on their stall walls or developed repetitive motions, like head swinging, it was because they were stressed. All they needed was the company of other horses, physical activity and attention from people to pull them out of their boredom and unhappiness. In a moment of frustration, Fen had tried to explain this to one of Alex's teachers. She thought her words hadn't made a difference, until she was with her mother at pick-up time the next week and noticed that Alex had been moved to a larger play group in the afternoon.

Fen understood that horses were prey animals and that fear was a good instinct to have, but knowing that Alex lived with constant anxiety made her sad. Fen was fearless and she knew her lack of caution had gotten her into plenty of trouble; but it also made her a great rider and riding was her passion, as well as her source of pride. She could already keep up with her father and his ranch hands, as well as anybody else who wanted to take her on, in or out of the ring.

Fen looked down at Alex and sighed. Her brother never spoke a meaningful word, but the teachers said he was making nice progress in school. She briefly wondered what they considered progress when he was six years old and couldn't or wouldn't say his sister's name. Alex would often mumble to himself, but it sounded like a jumble of sounds to Fen. She always said something back, hoping one day it would actually become a conversation.

Sometimes Alex would repeat what someone else said, but only in his "robot voice", as Fen called it. The teachers had explained to her that when he used that voice it meant he didn't really understand the words. They called it, echolalia, and, indeed, it did sound like a hollow, haunting echo to Fen. It was curious and saddening to her that horses could communicate with each other and people without words. But her little brother, who had a voice and even had words, couldn't seem to communicate with anyone at all.

Fen went downstairs and made bacon and eggs, knowing that her mother was already at work and her father would be out checking the border fences. He checked them every other morning to make sure they were in good shape and it gave him a chance to see that all of his horses were safe. Cougars were rarely seen, but there were bears around now that hibernation was over. Deer were also a problem. Fen had watched these skittish animals as they fled from predators. In their flight for life they would misjudge the height of a fence, seeing it at the last moment. The deer usually got away from the torn up wires and posts, but it made more work for her father and his busy ranch hands. It seemed like they were always fixing fence line somewhere on the large property.

At the smell of breakfast, Alex shuffled down the steps and sat at the table to eat. He carefully broke each piece of food into small pieces on his plate before eating them. As Fen and her brother sat quietly munching together, the kitchen door opened.

"Hello, my dears!" Rosie's cheery voice broke the quiet.

Rosie was followed by her son, Clancy, Fen's best friend. Fen found the company of girls confusing, complicated and often hurtful, so her childhood friend continued to be her only friend, even though he was a boy and two years older. Although he was sixteen, Clancy had been retained a year, so he was in ninth grade at the middle school.

Rosie was Alex's day-care provider when school was not in session. Fen loved Rosie. She was tall and robust with a head full of beautiful, golden curls that had just a twinge of grey around the ends. Rosie was gentle and sensitive. Her efficient manner and calm nature were perfect for Alex. They baked together, worked on craft projects, took walks and played on the playground equipment and obstacle course that Mack and Clancy had built for Alex.

"Hey, Fen! Hey, Alex!" Clancy said, smiling at Fen.

Clancy sat next to Alex who was chewing his last piece of egg. Clancy picked up the boy's glass of orange juice and put it next to his own face. Alex looked at the glass and Clancy moved his face to get into Alex's line of vision.

"Good morning!" Clancy said, again.

"Good morning," Alex repeated in his echolalic voice. He took his glass from Clancy, put it back on the table and looked down at his empty plate.

Fen sighed. She looked at Clancy and shrugged her shoulders. It always discouraged her when Alex ignored the attention of the people who loved him. But Clancy never got impatient with the boy's lack of emotional response.

"He is who he is, Fen, just like you and me. He'll get as far as he can go and that's good enough." Clancy smiled and picked up a piece of bacon.

Fen marveled at her friend's good nature, despite his difficult past. Clancy smiled a lot with the kind of face that smiled all over, just like his mother. But he carried his father's coloring and features, reminding them that, although Hal was gone, part of him was still walking with them. Clancy's brown eyes twinkled and his cheeks glowed against skin that reminded Fen of cinnamon. He was lean and tall for sixteen and his head was covered with thick, black curls.

Although Clancy was usually a happy-go-lucky guy, Fen had seen his smiling face quickly turn as dark as the thunderclouds that swept over their valley, covering the vast, blue Montana sky without warning. Anyone who tried to hurt Fen or Alex or abuse an animal, paid the price with Clancy's fists. His temper had gotten him into trouble more than a few times, but he never admitted regret for protecting what he cared about.

"Hey," Clancy said to Fen. "Wanna take a ride up to Riverbend sometime? I heard that cougar tracks have been seen around there recently. If you weren't such a lazy cowgirl, sleeping in till nine o'clock, maybe we could have seen the cat ourselves this morning." He winked at Fen.

"It was eight o'clock," Fen scowled. "Just give me ten minutes and I'll be tacked up and ready to go!" she exclaimed, heading for the back door.

"Uh, Fen?" Rosie said, quietly. "Don't you think you should change out of your p.j.s?"

"It's too late now, anyway," Clancy sighed. "I've got chores to do and a bunch of homework to make up for school. And it's all due tomorrow." Clancy looked away from his mother's frown and rolled his eyes at Fen. "Let's plan for tomorrow afternoon. I'll come over when I'm finished fixing Mrs. Bixby's fence." Clancy's face turned a slight shade of red, while his mother crossed her arms over her chest.

"So what happened to Mrs. Bixby's fence, Clance?" Fen asked, taking her last bite of toast. She smiled at Rosie's scowl, knowing there must be a good story behind it. "Well?"

"Ugh," Clancy answered. "I thought the whole town had heard by now. You have been in bed a long time." He shrugged. "I was riding Bandit and he spooked at something. He bolted, so I let him go, thinking maybe he knew something I didn't, like there might be a cougar waiting in a tree?" Clancy glared at his mother, but now it was her turn to do the eye-rolling. She had heard that excuse more than once in the telling of the story.

"Anyway," Clancy continued. "We galloped for awhile and then, suddenly, I realized we were heading for Mrs. Bixby's fence. You can't see the darn thing. It's one of those new-fangled, flimsy pieces of junk people use so you can't see it. How stupid is that? A fence is supposed to be seen so things don't run into it! So, over we went, only, well, we didn't quite make it and Bandit basically ripped the whole fence line right out of the ground."

"Yikes, Clancy!" Fen exclaimed, in mock distress. "Were you and Bandit okay?"

"Sure. When Bandit's in a full-out gallop, his weight and momentum turn him into a small freight train. That fence might as well have been a bunch of toothpicks with dental floss in between," Clancy griped. "But, she wants it put back up, so there goes my afternoon." He sighed and drank the last of Fen's orange juice.

"Well, you better get to it." Rosie slapped Clancy's leg. "Alex and I have some fun things to do and I'm sure Miss Sleep-Until-Noon Fen, here, has some chores on her list, too."

"It was eight o'clock!" Fen exclaimed again, indignantly.

Rosie helped Alex clean up the table and they started washing the dishes. It was a chore he hated. Whenever water poured from a faucet, Alex put his hands over his ears, shrieked and rocked back and forth. The sudden sound and motion threw him into a panic. But Rosie had learned to turn the water on gradually, letting a steady drip slowly turn into a light flow so they could get the task done in peace. Fen put her dishes on the counter and started for the stairs. Clancy got up, gave Rosie a hug and headed for the door. He stopped and turned around with a big grin on his face.

"By the way, cowgirl, I also heard from one of Red Drysdale's ranch hands that he saw tracks of a wild herd, just north of Riverbend."

Clancy hopped out the door and ran for his truck before Fen could chase him down. He knew how much she loved to catch a glimpse of the wild ones. Fen ran across the kitchen and started out the back door, desperate for more information.

"Pajamas?" Rosie gently reminded the eager girl.

But Fen had already stopped. She knew she couldn't catch Clancy and quickly remembered they had a trail ride planned for the next afternoon. She gave Rosie a kiss and went up the stairs to get dressed, excited about their upcoming adventure. A trail ride with Clancy always proved to be exciting and a bit dangerous, which was Fen's idea of the best kind of day. The chance to see a cougar was good enough, but the thought of watching a wild herd made her heart pound, like the hooves of the horses she heard every night in her dreams.

Chapter Two

It was dawn and soft raindrops fell steadily on the horse's withers. The dappled gray mare was resting alone at the edge of field and forest, her body lying on the wet grass, but her head up and alert. The previous night had been terrifying and she had hardly slept after her escape.

In the darkness, a cougar had slunk into the wild herd. The cat had watched the horses from the shrubs surrounding their grassy clearing and noticed this heavy mare who moved more slowly than the others. She would be the easiest target. But the large, dun stallion who protected the herd, caught the scent of the cougar just in time. He had quickly roused the mares and yearlings from dozing and grazing. They fled in a stampede of pounding hooves and whirling tails, following their well worn path from the clearing to the river.

The stallion had stayed and stood his ground, knowing the herd would flee to the river, their place of refuge. He reared up and flailed his front hooves. His tawny body glowed in the last rays of sun and his black mane and tail tossed in the breeze. The black stripe down his back accentuated his large barrel, flanks and rump. He snorted and squealed at the persistent cat who dashed about, waiting for a chance to jump on the horse's neck.

The cougar weaved and dodged, while the stallion wheeled about, kicking with his hind feet. The cat slowed momentarily, cautiously slinking around the bucking horse. The stallion saw a chance to stop and catch his breath, waiting for the animal's next attack. But the horse paused one moment too long and the cougar leaped onto the stallion's neck.

The cougar's claws dug into the horse's skin, but with one toss of the stallion's large head, the cat was flung to the ground. Claw marks remained on the horse's neck, blood starting to drip from the wounds. The sudden pain sparked a surge of adrenaline and instinctive power. As the cat made another leap for the stallion's back, the horse spun around and kicked. The impact of his heavy hoof on the cat's chest catapulted the animal through the air and onto its back. It writhed for a moment and the big horse reared over it, ready to stomp the life from its predator. But the cougar rolled out of the way, struggled to its feet and loped unsteadily back into the woods. The stallion snorted and stomped, then quickly turned and galloped down the brushy trail to catch up with his herd.

The stallion's alpha mare, big and slow, had tried to keep up with the fleeing horses, but soon found herself wandering off the path in a state of confused exhaustion. Finally stopping to rest at the edge of a field, she lay down, quickly falling asleep. The mare woke up in the early morning light, her body already moist with dew and now sodden from the rain. It was quiet, except for the scratching of a chipmunk who was running up and down the large tree behind her and the call of a red-tailed hawk, soaring overhead.

The mare was not used to quiet, living in a herd where there was constant motion of hooves and bodies as the horses moved around each other for the best grazing spots. Snorts, squeals, nickers and whinnies were frequently heard as the horses interacted, strengthening their bonds with each other. The quiet made the mare uneasy and she kept her ears pricked and nostrils flared, ready to escape at a moment's notice. She knew the cougar's territory was wide and he would be hungry after the long winter. She knew her separation from the herd would not go undetected by the big cat.

During the last hours of night, the cougar had rested for a bit, recovering from the stallion's kick. But he had taken advantage of the last bit of darkness before dawn to start tracking the horses. He had begun to make a large loop around a grove of trees, following the tracks of the herd, when his nose had picked up the scent of one horse who had taken its own path. He knew it must be the slow mare he had watched the night before. She was either old or sick and, thus, perfect prey. He changed direction and headed off in search of the lone horse and a certain meal.

The mare was neither old nor sick, but heavy with foal. As with all mares, the ability to hold off giving birth had allowed her to escape the cougar, but she could feel the foal's movement in her belly and knew it was time to prepare. The pregnant mare needed the herd for protection, especially with the cougar probably still in the area, but she did not have the time nor the energy to find them. The rain fell harder, making her gray dapples look like dark blotches on her white body.

The mare put her front hooves on the ground and slowly rose, letting out a snort. Heaving her body up took great effort, but she needed shelter from the rain and camouflage from predators. She walked to a large balsam tree at the edge of the woods. Its branches hung low. She ducked her head under and stood against the trunk, well hidden and out of the pelting rain. Her front legs crumpled and her body fell to the ground. Her barrel heaved and she let out a long, soft sigh. Her breath floated from flared nostrils, creating tendrils of steam in the chilly morning air.

To her relief, the rain finally slowed and then stopped. The sun's rays splashed through the dispersing clouds and the dark morning suddenly changed to a glowing day as it often did in the valleys and mountains of the west. As the mare rested, the sun took its time rising over the hills to finally flood the valley with light and heat. The mare chose to stay hidden under the tall tree and let the dappled light warm her body.

A few miles away, the rest of the herd grazed in the sun by the great river that flowed through the lush valley. The stallion wandered amongst the horses, looking for his mare who was ready to foal. He wondered if the cougar had found her and made the kill. There was nothing he could do but wait for her return or find the remains of her carcass.

The other mares, a paint, a chestnut, an appaloosa, a blue roan and a young grey, were aware of the alpha mare's absence and approached the stallion for comfort. He was grumpy and pinned his ears, warning them to keep their distance. As the mares shyly came closer, he stretched his head out and headed for them, driving them away. They knew if they got too close he would charge, bite or kick them. The mares wisely chose to return to their frolicking foals, splashing at the river's edge.

During the last few years the stallion had worked to breed with the mares and protect their foals. It was a small herd and he knew that safety and strength came only in large numbers. Wild horses were becoming scarce as the men on horseback rounded them up and drove them into large pens. The stallion had watched it happen to other herds. Just before winter his own herd had to make a desperate run for safety, barely outrunning the men on horses.

The stallion pricked his ears and put his large nose up to catch the breeze. His nostrils flared, inviting the smallest scent of his lost mare. He would have to guide his horses upriver to find her, knowing the mare's instinct would be to seek the water as an escape route. But he would wait to prod his herd along, knowing the horses needed to rest and graze after last night's ambush by the cougar.

Under the balsam tree, the mare's belly was writhing. It contracted and expanded with each movement her foal made. The pain came and went in waves as the baby continued to push then rest, push then rest on its journey down the birth canal. Finally, a head appeared. Slowly, the rest of the body slid out and plopped gently onto the soft mat of pine needles at the base of the tree. Its heavy boughs sheltered the new mother and her baby from the glaring noonday sun.

The small filly was chestnut colored. Her only marking was a white teardrop between her large, dark eyes. The mare licked her foal from nose to rump, her warm breath drying the baby's skin. The foal nuzzled her mother's gray nose and pink nostrils. She let out a tiny whinny.

The mare nickered back. They lay together, content in each other's presence.

It was important to get the foal to her feet as soon as possible. The mare nudged her baby's back and neck, encouraging her to stand. The filly wobbled and fell. She quickly rose, only to crumple again into a heap on the ground. For a time, the filly continued to stand, wobble and fall, resting at her mother's feet when she became too tired.

The mare finally urged her foal to stay upright by walking a small distance away and turning to offer her teats to the hungry filly. It was too tempting to the newborn. She stood up again and took careful steps, swaying to and fro as she followed her mother. The milk was sweet and delicious and the baby suckled hard and strong. The new mother nibbled on the fresh spring grass, now dry with the warm sun.

Although the mare was content with the birth of her foal, she knew they were both in grave danger. The cougar, as well as other predators, were never far away, waiting for twilight to make their kill. She needed to find the herd who had probably taken their usual flight to the river for safety. She knew the way, but needed her foal to keep up and that was a lot to expect of a newborn. By mid-afternoon, with the sun sliding towards the distant mountains, the mother and foal began their slow journey downriver. Next to the rolling waters, they followed the path that thousands of animals had travelled for hundreds of years.

Only a few miles away, the stallion knew he had to get the herd moving out of the cougar's territory. He hoped his mare was alive and with foal. He wondered if the baby had strength enough to make the trip, following its mother at such a young age. Would the cougar find them in their vulnerable state and kill them both?

He knew his mare was strong and would protect her baby at all costs. He had watched her defend twin colts three years ago from a pack of wolves so he knew she had stamina and a fierce temperament when tested. The other females never questioned this alpha mare's top rank in the herd. Although she was gentle and nurturing with the young, she defended her position with confidence and pride.

The herd heeded the stallion's nudges and snorts as he efficiently moved his horses to the path that followed the river. They moved along at a steady pace, the yearlings strong enough to keep up. With no young foals to slow them down, they could make good time before darkness fell. The stallion couldn't know if he had chosen the right direction. He couldn't know if the mare had crossed the river during her escape. He could only follow his instinct, look for her tracks and wait to pick up her scent.

As the sun slowly slid on its arc across the sky, the cougar slept on the branch of a tree, knowing that prey was well within his reach. He hadn't found the lone horse but instinct told she couldn't be far. He knew the herd was at the river but he wasn't interested in taking the journey there, only to face the stallion again and watch his prey swim for safety to the other side. The mare was an easy target and he would patiently wait for dusk to begin trailing her. He went back to sleep, waiting for the coming of nightfall and the cover of darkness, dreaming of the sweet taste of fresh meat that awaited him.

Chapter Three

Fen brushed her long, blond hair and pulled it back into a loose ponytail. She threw on a t-shirt, sweatshirt and jeans and went to the bathroom to brush her teeth. Fen could hear Alex and Rosie in the kitchen making bread dough as she headed for the barn to do her chores. Fen's father didn't have many rules, but he always expected the chores to be done before she could ride.

It took a few hours to muck out the stalls, shoveling the manure into the bucket of the tractor and dumping it onto the big compost pile out back. Fen refilled the stalls with fresh bedding and swept all the aisles and small rooms where feed, tack and tools were kept. Fen had learned to muck stalls and drive the farm machines when she was eight, just old enough to reach all of the necessary pedals and tools. Boss, the farm dog, loved to slow her down by jumping in front of any moving vehicle until Fen let him hop on for a ride.

Boss had wandered into their yard when Fen was five. He was small and skinny, muddy, matted and covered in fleas. Fen's father said if she cleaned him up and promised to keep him fed and watered, the "mangy looking dog" could stay. After a good washing, they could see he was part Beagle, part Australian Shepherd and remnants of some other small breed they couldn't identify. His four paws were black as if he were wearing socks. One of his soft ears drooped while the other stood straight up, as though he would just as soon take a nap as he would a long run in the woods. It all depended on what everybody else was doing.

It was clear from the beginning that Boss wanted to be part of a family, as well as a working animal. He proved to be a great herding dog and was useful when the horses needed to be turned into their paddocks at dusk. But he was also a loving animal, who spent hours snuggling in Alex's lap by the woodstove when the winter winds howled down off the mountains and across their homestead.

Boss followed Fen around as she did her chores, occasionally finding a chipmunk hole to dig out. He was fun to watch but not much help getting jobs done and Fen had more work than usual because Pete, Mack's head ranch hand, had gone on a trip to Cheyenne, Wyoming. Things weren't the same without Pete around. Fen loved Pete and the family depended on him for the smooth running of the ranch. Fortunately, he was due back late tonight.

Mack did have two other ranch hands, Buck and Frank. Fen liked Buck. He was tall and lean with blond, wispy hair and deep, blue eyes. He was quiet, not likely to engage in long conversations, but he was gentle with the horses and Mack hired him because of it. Buck knew how to train them using the natural horsemanship way, rather than the traditional methods of "breaking" a horse that Fen had seen other cowboys practice.

Buck had helped Fen train her own two horses. Sundancer was a fourteen-two hand palomino. She called him Scoot. He was small, quick, smart and the best barrel racer around. Her other horse, Ebony, was a sixteen-two hand Percheron Quarter Horse cross. He was big, strong and black as night. She called him Hack because that was his favorite thing to do. Fen and Hack would happily stay out all day, wandering the wooded trails and galloping across the range. He could run down any horse, even when Fen gave her opponent a head start, and it took all Fen's strength to pull Hack down to an easy jog when the race was done. Fen owed her horsing skills to Buck who had been a patient teacher with her and her equine partners.

Buck had been a loyal ranch hand for years, working from sunrise to sundown, doing whatever was needed. He was so important to the success of the ranch that when his first baby was born a year ago,

Fen's father had cut back on Buck's hours, but given him a raise. Mack also gave Buck a horse every two years that he could train and sell. Fen spent many hours watching Buck train the horses on the ranch and spent just as much time copying his exercises on her own two geldings.

The other ranch hand, Frank, was a different story. He gave Fen the willies. He was short and squat with dark hair and squinty eyes that never seemed to look at anyone. He had stopped at their ranch five months ago looking for work, just when Mack, Buck and Pete were all at the point of exhaustion from keeping up with the chores and obligations of a ranching business. Mack had hired Frank without asking for references and gave him one of the old cottages on the hill to live in. It was musty, dank and drafty in the winter, but Frank seemed indifferent to physical comforts. Fen had peeked in the windows of his cabin once, shortly after he had moved in. She couldn't believe anybody could be sloppier than her or messier than Clancy, but Frank's place looked like one notch above a pig sty.

Although Frank didn't mind living in squalor, Fen noticed that he certainly enjoyed eating. He wolfed down her mother's meals as if he was a starving, stray dog. It surprised Fen that Renee didn't seem to mind the way Frank stuffed food in his mouth, washed it down with milk and talked, all at the same time. Fen knew she certainly couldn't get away with that kind of behavior at the table. But Fen assumed her mother was flattered by Frank's enthusiasm for her food, even if a little put off by his nasty table manners.

Fen had long since learned it was her mother's way to see the one good aspect of a person or situation when Fen could only seem to focus on what was bad. Every now and then Renee would remind Fen of her tendency to see the negative aspect of someone or something. During one of those conversations, Fen felt particularly scolded by her mother.

"Fen, I think you inherited your father's predisposition to see the glass as half empty, instead of half full."

"What do you mean? What about a glass?" Fen asked. She was feeling grumpy after spending money on a used saddle that turned out to be too small for Scooter.

"It's an expression that people use," Renee replied. "It means that you see what you don't have, instead of what you do have. You focus on the negative aspect of a situation, instead of on the positive."

"What I have, Mother, is a useless saddle and not enough money left to get another one. What is positive about that?" Fen retorted.

"Well, you have a little brother who goes to preschool. They have a pony that can't be ridden because the teachers can't afford to buy a new saddle and nobody has a used one that is small enough for him. You could sell them your saddle at a price they can afford. You will get back some of the money you lost, the kids will be able to ride and that bored, fat pony will get slim and happy. Furthermore, the teachers won't continue to be teased by the local ranchers for having a 'hayburner' in their schoolyard. Everybody wins from your bad purchase of a perfectly good saddle!"

"Mom!" Fen had scolded her mother. "You know how much I hate the word 'hayburner'. That's what they called Sir Prize!"

"Yes!" Renee exclaimed. "To you, Sir Prize is my beautiful, elegant, loving Thoroughbred. To the race horse people, she was just a 'hayburner' ready for the slaughterhouse. That's what I'm talking about! And this whole ranch started because of Sir Prize. And this ranch has turned into a very big glass that's so full it's running over the edges and making a mess everywhere! There's always too much to do and not enough time or people to do it all. But it's a big, beautiful mess and it's home and it's all good, my dear."

And Renee was right. She and Mack had started the McCullough Ranch twenty years ago and it was still running strong. They bought, trained, bred and sold horses from anywhere Mack could find them. Mack had hired Pete fifteen years ago because there was too much work for two people to do. His only instructions were that the horses couldn't be mistreated and they couldn't be taken from the wild. Fen was proud of her father's decision to let the free horses stay that way. There were so many horses all over the country that needed to be trained and sold to good homes that Mack, Renee and Fen felt there was no need to take away a wild animal's freedom.

Pete felt the same way, including himself as an animal in need of freedom. He had built a log cabin along the river that ran through the property, living alone at the age of forty. His only companion was a big wolf-dog. He had found her as a pup, trapped in a den, while a forest fire raged across hundreds of acres that surrounded the McCulloughs' property. While helping to fight the fire, Pete heard her whimpers and dragged the scared animal out of an abandoned cave. He called her Phoenix. Her name came from the mythical story of a bird that had risen from the pile of ashes left after a pillar of fire had burned itself out. Each evening, just as the moon rose over the mountains, Phoenix would start howling by Pete's cabin door. Pete would join in and, before long, a distant howl of the wild wolves could be heard echoing off the mountains and across the starry sky.

Phoenix and Boss had become playmates on the ranch, but the wolf-dog had gone with Pete to Cheyenne, leaving Boss to shadow Fen during her chores this morning. Today, like most days, Fen felt a sense of pride and accomplishment when the last job on the list was checked off. But she was always happy to hang up the shovel and put the tractor away in its shed. She leaned on a fence, watching the horses graze in the pasture. The sweet, fresh air of spring rolled across the meadow grass and through the trees surrounding her home. Later in the day there would be more jobs to do, but for now, Fen was free to ride. She went to the gate of the east pasture and called for Scoot.

"Hey, Scoot! It's time to ride ole' buddy!" The horse looked up from grazing and pricked his ears. "Come on, now. Too much eating isn't good for a barrel racer!"

As usual, Scoot took his time getting to the gate, snatching a few more bites of grass on his way. Fen opened the gate and threw the lead rope over the horse's neck, being careful to latch the gate behind her.

Horse and rider went into the barn and tacked up. Fen didn't know who loved the barrels more, Scoot or her. They spent half an hour warming up in the ring. They practiced doing patterns, transitions and ten and twenty meter circles at different gaits. When Scoot started tossing his head and yanking on the reins, Fen knew he felt like she did at school. It was time to have some fun. They left the ring and Fen turned Scoot around to face the open gate. Scoot was pawing the ground, anticipating the next move, but Fen made him halt and square up. He couldn't go until she gave the signal. When Fen was ready, she held up one hand like a pistol.

"BANG!" Fen shouted.

Scoot took off at a full gallop. He cut around the first barrel, missing it by an inch. He charged for the second barrel across the ring and spun around it with ease. Fen headed him down the middle of the ring for the last barrel. His tail and mane were streaming out behind as he raced for the end of the arena. He whirled around the last barrel, straightened up and stretched out for the gallop to the gate. The girl and her horse spent the next fifteen minutes practicing technique and speed. Each time Fen brought Scoot out of the gate for another round, he snorted and pawed the ground for more. Fen knew they could both go on for hours, given enough daylight and food. But she didn't like barrel racing in the dark and Scoot always got anxious for his left-over pizza or donut or whatever treat she had brought him. Finally, when Scooter's stomach started grumbling and the light started to fade, Fen decided it was time for the last circuit. As they rounded the last barrel and headed for the finish line, Fen quickly checked her watch. It turned out to be their record time for the day.

"Yahoo!" Fen yelled. They flew out of the ring and across the driveway to the front yard where Scoot came to a perfect sliding stop. Fen was so excited she gave Scoot a cue to do their favorite trick, a dramatic rear with a whinny. It always made her feel like she was in the movies.

The air was beginning to get moist and chilly as Fen walked Scooter back to the ring for his cool-down. She watched the sun slide towards the western hilltop, enjoying the last rays of golden light dance off Scoot's gleaming coat. Fen looked up at Frank's shack on the hill, now dark, hidden in the shadow of the great mountains surrounding it. Suddenly, she shivered as if fingers were running down her spine. She was glad it was time to start the evening chores. Fen stopped at the water trough to let Scoot take a little drink before leading him to the barn. After his tack was put away, Fen gave him a treat.

"You deserve it, Scoot. You're the best barrel racer, anywhere. People think that new girl from Kentucky is going to give us a run for our money at the big rodeo in June, but don't listen to that nonsense. She's a dressage rider wearing western clothes, learning to do rodeo from a book. We're the real deal, ole' chum." Fen slapped the horse on his rump and he went into his stall for grain.

Fen started turning the other horses in for their evening meal. Frank and Buck showed up soon after, having rounded up the rest of the herd from the outer pastures. They finished putting the horses in their stalls and grained them in silence. When Frank wasn't around, Fen liked to talk to Buck. He seemed to enjoy her company, although she often felt like she was having a conversation with herself. Sometimes it reminded Fen of her attempts to get Alex to talk.

Buck had always been kind to Alex. He encouraged the boy to groom and grain the horses. He showed him how to pick hooves, bandage wounds and treat other ailments the horses developed. Alex was smart and remembered everything Buck showed him. When Buck wasn't around, Alex often treated a horse's problem, remembering what medicine to use and how to figure out the correct dosage, as well as knowing how to wrap injuries while keeping the horse calm.

Fen had spent so much time doing chores and riding Scoot that her practice with Hack would have to wait till morning. He was her drill team horse this year and she needed to practice the routine for the upcoming rodeo. Clara Perkins, the dressage girl from Kentucky, had joined the team again this year with her elegant, chestnut, Thoroughbred stallion. He was almost sixteen hands, slender and stately, with a perfect blaze down his nose.

Last August, Fen had sat next to Clara on the bleachers, watching the roping competitions at the final rodeo of the year. Clara had ridden earlier in the day in the drill team performance, which Fen had never done. Clara had recently moved to the area and Fen could see what a good rider she was. As they sat in the audience, Fen had tried to strike up a conversation with her. The other girls she knew were all interested in boys, going to parties and hanging out at the mall, things Fen had no use for. She was hoping to find one girl she could talk to at school.

Unfortunately, Fen quickly found out that Clara seemed to be more interested in watching the boys than talking to her. After Fen had chatted for a few minutes with no response from Clara, the older girl finally asked a question.

"How come your name is 'Fen'? It's kind of, um, different."

Fen hesitated. Nobody had ever asked her about her name before because she was born and raised there. Everyone knew the story and had taken her name for granted. She had never had to explain her own name to someone.

"Well," Fen paused. "A fen is a marshy area and my mother likes marshes because they're great habitat for plants and animals. You know, they're full of life. Besides, if you add another 'n' to my name, it's my mother's maiden name."

"Oh. How sweet," Clara had said in a condescending voice and looked away.

Fen flushed with embarrassment and decided that this was just another girl, like all the rest she knew. That was the last time Fen and Clara had spoken. Neither of them could have known that they would have plenty to say to each other in the future. And neither of them could have known how similar they really were. They were both competitive. They each felt like they had something to prove and they both had a stubborn streak a mile wide. But the most important thing they shared had nothing to do with competition, willfulness or pride. They shared a love of wild horses and both would do anything to keep them wild.

Chapter Four

The chores were done and Fen headed to the house. Her mother pulled up in their jeep, stepping out in high heels, wearing a burgundy suit and white shirt. Renee always looked crisp, clean and "well-put-together" as Fen's father always said. Being a lawyer, she felt the need to keep up a professional appearance in the office, even though she could be caught mucking stalls on the weekends.

"Hey, Mom!" Fen called.

"Hey, sweetie! What's up?"

"Oh, I just finished chores. I rode Scoot today. He did great! I saw Clancy this morning. He's going to take me on a hack tomorrow up towards Riverbend. I guess someone spotted cougar tracks and hoof prints from the wild herd!"

"Great," Renee answered, sarcastically. "So, I get to spend the day worrying about whatever antics Clancy has up his sleeve. That boy is irresponsible, Fen. I love him but he has a knack for finding trouble."

"And fun," Fen replied with a grin.

"Ugh," Renee responded. "Well, I guess I chased a few of those fellows myself when I was young. But I didn't marry one, so just remember that, young lady!"

"Mom! I'm fourteen, for Pete's sake. Besides, I'm not chasing Clancy. He's my friend."

"I know. I know. And I do like him. He's helped your father and a lot of other people in this town. Since his dad died, he's repaid all the help the community gave them when he and his mom needed support. He's got a good heart and strong hands. That's all a man really needs."

An hour later, Fen, Alex and her parents were sitting down for dinner. Frank had gone to town, Buck had gone home to be with his family and Pete had called to say he was on his way home from Cheyenne.

"I hope Frank gets back from town in time to turn out," Mack said. "Last time he went to town he was late and Pete and I ended up doing all the mucking and feeding."

"Besides," Fen added. "He stunk."

"Fen." Renee looked at her daughter with a steady gaze.

Fen knew what that look meant. It was time to change the conversation. She often said things that got her into trouble, but sometimes she couldn't help speaking the truth, anyway. "I'm sorry, Mom, but it's true. He drinks too much alcohol and he gives me the creeps."

"Fen." This time her father spoke up. "He needed a job and he does pretty good work. He just has a few vices, that's all."

"Yeah, like drinking too much and giving the horses the wrong amount of grain and yanking on their reins because he can't remember to use the word whoa."

"Whoa," repeated Alex. He had been rocking and humming while Fen and her parents had been eating.

"Alex, honey," Renee said. "You need to eat your dinner. It's your favorite. It's macaroni and cheese with ham and peas."

"Cheese with ham and peas," Alex repeated, still rocking back and forth, staring at his plate.

"Oh," Fen said. "I know what's wrong with Alex. Pete's gone. I'll be right back."

Fen jogged up the stairs, went to Alex's room and returned with the framed photo of Pete that Alex kept by his bed. When Pete was gone, Alex was always distracted at dinner. One evening, Fen discovered that putting Pete's photo at his place at the table seemed to calm Alex.

"Pete will be back tonight, Alex," Fen said, putting the photo where Pete's plate would be.

"Back tonight, Alex," he replied.

Fen watched her brother pick up his spoon and eat, putting his utensil down between each mouthful, as he always did. Fen looked at her father who was staring at his perplexing son with a furrowed brow. Mack loved his son deeply, even though Alex was a complete mystery to him. Mack turned to Fen and smiled.

"So, I hear you have big plans with Clancy tomorrow." He smiled at Renee who rolled her eyes. "Just remember to practice for the rodeo before you go, particularly the drill team thing. It's coming up soon and that big brute of an animal you call a horse could use some schooling."

"I will, Dad. Can I be excused? I think I should start turning the horses out now. With Pete gone, it's going to take longer."

"You can wait for Frank, honey," Renee said.

"I'd rather not, thanks. Alex and I can do it ourselves. Come on, Alex. It's time to see the horses!"

Alex got up and went to the door to put on his jacket and gloves. He didn't like getting his hands dirty. He followed Fen out the door to the paddock. Fen came around the corner and was surprised to see Frank already in the stall with Paddy, one of their big draft horses. He was yanking on her halter and cursing the horse for not moving.

"What are you doing?" Fen asked, angrily.

"What does it look like? I'm trying to get this stupid animal out."

"She's not the stupid one and that's not the way to do it," Fen snapped.

"Now don't be interferin', sweetie. I've been around horses a lot longer than you have and I know how to handle it."

"Then why isn't Paddy moving?" Fen asked, sarcastically.

Frank stopped yanking long enough to give Fen a nasty look.

"Alex?" Fen asked, turning to her brother. "Can you go out to the paddock, please, and get Paddy out of her stall?"

Alex walked out to the paddock and stood in front of Paddy's open stall door. Paddy slowly walked towards Alex and put her head down to sniff his coat. Alex stroked the big horse's nose and rubbed her ears. He turned around and Paddy slowly followed the boy out into the pen. Fen noticed that the horse was limping. She brushed by Frank as she walked through Paddy's stall to the paddock. She stopped Paddy and picked up her hind foot. Fen pulled a hoof pick from her back pocket and worked a large rock out of the horse's huge hoof. Paddy continued to follow Alex, now with an easy stride, the limp gone. Fen glared at Frank as she came back through the stall to the aisle.

Alex and Fen continued to lead the horses out into the paddock, leaving the stall doors open in case they wanted shelter during the night. Frank put some tools away and began rolling a cigarette.

"My father doesn't let people smoke on the property," Fen said.

"I ain't smokin' it. I'm just rollin' it," Frank replied.

"Come on, Alex. Let's go inside. It's time for bed."

Alex followed Fen down the aisle of the barn, his sister seething with anger. Who did Frank think he was? He ordered her around like she was ignorant, sat on his scrawny bottom while she and Alex did all the work and then had the nerve to roll a cigarette around all that dry hay and their beautiful horses. Fen was kicking pebbles, smacking the walls of the barn and was so lost in her own thoughts that she almost bumped into Pete, who was coming through the door of the barn.

"Pete! You're back early!" Fen gave the big man a huge hug and then leaned down to give Phoenix a quick rub down, stroking behind her tall ears and under her chin.

Pete was a tall, beefy man with curly, blond hair and a bushy beard. His smile was broad as he picked Fen up off her feet and returned the hug. He knew better than to hug Alex, so he put his hand up for a high-five.

"Hey, buddy! Good to see you!" Pete said.

Alex looked at the ground and hummed to himself. He was calm and quiet in Pete's presence, but not yet willing to make physical contact with him. Alex only practiced the high-five gesture with his speech teacher at school, but Pete kept trying anyway. When Alex didn't respond Pete just shrugged and put his hand down. He looked at Fen.

"Well, you know how much I love the city," Pete said, sarcastically. "I couldn't wait to get home."

"Cheyenne is not exactly a teeming metropolis, Pete," Fen reminded him.

"Big enough for this cowboy, Miss Webster Dictionary, using big words on a backwoods ranch hand," he retorted. "Besides, I missed you guys."

Strong hands and a big heart: that's what her mom had said about good men and that was Pete. Fen briefly wondered why Pete and Rosie hadn't shown any interest in each other. Clancy's dad had been killed more than two years ago, long enough that Fen would have thought Rosie might be ready to start thinking about dating again. Rosie and Pete were about the same age, had no partners and they saw each other a lot on the McCulloughs' ranch and at community events. But Fen quickly decided that grown-ups were too complicated for her to understand. Besides, right now she had bigger fish to fry.

"Pete, Frank was yanking on Paddy's halter, trying to get her out of her stall. She had a rock in her hoof, which is why she wouldn't move. He's rough around the horses and Scoot and Hack are nervous around him. I think he makes Alex upset, too, the way he treats the horses. Alex has to go in and get to bed, but I'd like to talk to you more about it when you have time."

"Of course, Fen. We'll talk about it tonight. Say, I hear you and Clancy are tracking horses and cougars tomorrow!" Pete grinned. "Better take a big rifle and a bag to bring him home!"

Fen laughed, knowing that Pete would never want a cougar shot or bagged. She and Alex started walking toward the house as Pete walked through the barn and rounded the corner to the stalls. Fen remembered she hadn't returned the hoof pick to the grooming shelf. Knowing her father's compulsion to keep a barn orderly and organized, she told Alex to go into the house while she headed back to the barn. But hearing Pete's voice raised in anger, Fen stopped at the corner to stay out of sight.

"I never want to see a cigarette around this barn again, lit or not. You got that Frank?"

"Yes sir," Frank said, imitating a soldier's quick response. "By the way, that girl and her brother interrupt me in my work. They need to steer clear of the barn when I'm workin'. I don't want to be held responsible when that freaky kid gets hurt and . . ." Frank's words were cut off as Fen heard a body get slammed against a wall.

"Let's get some things straight, Frank." Pete's voice was calm, slow and quiet, but full of pent up anger. "There are some things you will never do again at this ranch. You will never call Alex a freak. You will never tell me how to run this stable. You will never come here late. You will never come here with alcohol on your breath. And you will never yank on our horses. I'm not blind, deaf or stupid, Frank. I know what's been going on. You better watch yourself or I'll have you fired with just one word to Mr. McCullough. You got all that or do I need to repeat any of it?" Fen heard Frank's body get pushed against the wall again.

"No. I got it," Frank said. "I'm just wonderin' why, if you hate me so much and think you know what's goin' on, why ain't you got rid of me yet?" Frank's tone was coy, but his voice shaky.

"I got my reasons," Pete responded. "But if I need to, I'd rather have only one good ranch hand in Buck, than have to use my two hands to throw you off this property. You get my meaning?"

Fen didn't wait to hear a response. She quickly ran to the house, pausing on the porch to take a breath before going in. It would only lead to complications for Pete if her parents suspected anything was wrong. She also knew that avoiding the confrontation between the two men was more important than returning a hoof pick to the barn, which was full of boiling steam from Pete's anger and Frank's bitter breath, full of jealousy and spite.

Fen could only hope that Pete would finally do something about Frank before everything her parents had worked so hard to create blew up in a terrible mess. Rosie had once told Fen that feelings of spite, bitterness, hatred and jealousy had the power to create human storms more fierce than any found in the wild winds, wave currents and lunar cycles of the world. Fen knew that Frank carried these feelings like sacks of sand over each shoulder and he had to go. He could never be part of the "beautiful mess" her mother had once described to her, the home that Pete, Buck and her family had tended with such loving care for so long.

Chapter Five

The mare and her filly had made slow but steady progress as they journeyed along the river. Sometimes the filly needed to stop and rest, flopping down in the grass beside the trodden path. She would often nudge her mother's haunches for a snack, slurping and smacking as the milk filled her mouth and belly. The mare took these opportunities to graze and rest. Giving birth and having a newborn was not an easy task and without a herd it was all the more difficult. Usually, she would have other mares and the stallion to rely on for protection and care-giving, so that she could rest and graze to get her strength back.

By dusk, the mare knew she had to find protection for her baby. Knowing the cougar could easily follow her scent by land, she decided to cross the river and find shelter on the other side. She found a shallow part of the river where rocks, gravel, mud and sticks had created a narrow land bridge with a foot or two of water running over it. As she stepped into the water and started to cross, the mare looked back to make sure her baby was following. But the filly was not interested in this part of the expedition. She whinnied and backed up onto the riverbank. Her mother turned around and nickered, tossing her head to the foal as encouragement to follow her.

The current was fairly slow at this point in the river, but the splashing and whirling of the water scared the newborn. Flaring her little nostrils and stomping her tiny hooves, she took her first step into the swirls of liquid at her feet. She found that she liked the coolness and the feel of water lapping against her legs. Tentatively, the filly took more steps, finally reaching her mother's side. The mare nickered her approval and the two continued to cross the river.

The stallion had decided to rest his herd for the night. He had no scent of his mare yet, but felt he was heading in the right direction. While the horses were grazing and finding their own places to rest, the stallion walked within the herd to make sure all was well. He smelled the air currents for possible danger and looked through the trees and shrubs for any predators. Satisfied that they were safe for now, he started to graze.

Suddenly, the horse heard a ruckus behind a copse of birch trees. There was a squeal and then a loud snort. The stallion loped around the trees to see two females, his appaloosa and chestnut, in competition. They were kicking and biting, whirling around to get at each other's necks and rumps. They reared up at the same time and the chestnut started falling over backwards. She stumbled, but regained her footing and made a quick dash to get away from the appaloosa's hooves. They continued squealing, snorting and panting as the two mares chased each other into a small clearing where the other horses had stopped to watch the scene.

The stallion burst into the middle of the fight. He jumped at the appaloosa and bit her neck. He ran at the chestnut and kicked her in the haunches. The two mares stopped and drew back. The stallion was in no mood for competitive females. With the alpha mare gone the other females were already vying for top position. It was important for the stallion to stop these squabbles. It would loosen the bond between the horses and make them all feel uncertain about the hierarchy of the herd.

Each horse knew his or her rank in the pack. If one position was tested, they might all attempt to raise their own rank. The stallion could not afford conflict in his herd, not now, not when he was trying to find the alpha mare who would make everything right again. He knew she was out there. If they couldn't find her in two days, then he would let the other mares test their strength and stamina against each other.

The mares had quickly gotten the stallion's message and they all went back to grazing and sleeping. After tussling a bit in mock battle, the foals lay down together and went to sleep. Their tails whipped against the first hatch of spring flies and their noses and ears twitched continuously, instinctively keeping their senses alert for danger.

Before the stallion returned to grazing, he took one last look up the river. He watched the current, the water swift and deep at this bend in the waterway. They had walked a long way and had no sign of the mare. The stallion was concerned that she might have attempted to cross the river to lead the cougar off her scent. But the river was fast and cold and the foal, if there was one, would struggle against the current and become chilled and exhausted. The stallion decided he would cross the water in the early morning light and quickly travel the path, both up and down the river, to make sure he hadn't passed them.

The foal and her mother were almost to the other side of the wide river, when suddenly, the filly's front legs crumpled under her and she rolled onto her side, back legs kicking wildly in the air. The mare quickly turned around and plowed back through the river, splashing water in all directions. She put her large nose under her baby's back and tried to push her upright. But one of the filly's front hooves had become wedged under a log. The mare knew that if her foal twisted and turned too much, she could easily break a leg. A horse with a broken leg wouldn't last a day in the wild.

The mare tried to roll the log off the foal's leg, but it was heavy with water and she couldn't budge it. She nickered at her baby, trying to comfort her. The foal had to stop flailing or she would break her leg for sure. The water was frigid this time of year and the filly wouldn't last long in the cold. The mare continued to try to move the log, stopping to rest and nuzzle her foal who was becoming increasingly desperate, struggling to free herself.

Time went by as mare and foal fought to get out of the river. The filly began to lose strength from her struggle and the cold. She stopped moving and put her head down on a rock jutting up out of the water. Her eyes were calm, but her breathing labored as if she was giving up the fight. The mare nickered and licked her baby's face, trying to encourage her not to give up. The filly's breath became slow and even as though she was either trying to save her strength or was giving her life up to the frigid water. The baby became still and closed her eyes. The mare had been frantic in her efforts to free the foal, but now realized that she was losing the fight to save her filly's life.

Suddenly, there was a rustle in the bushes across the river where the mare and foal had first stepped into the water. The cougar or a wolf had hunted them down and the mare had lost her chance to escape. She looked up, snorting and pawing at the water. She pulled herself up to full height and let out a loud whinny. She needed help and if the herd was anywhere near, they would hear her and come. If not, her foal would die.

When she heard the noise across the river, the filly opened her eyes. She was too young to know what to fear, but the feeling of fear had been bred into her ancestors from the beginning of time and was part of her own breath and bone. The foal looked at her mother in desperation, knowing that the mare should escape, which is what instinct told them to do. The filly would be abandoned to face what she feared alone. But the mare was not willing to leave her baby, who was still breathing and aware of her mother's presence. If she had to die fighting for her baby's life, she would.

Listening to the animal in the bushes across the river, the mare stood still, wishing for her rescue, hoping her stallion was close and had heard her cries for help. She tensed, knowing that her hope would soon turn into a battle with a stalking predator and she needed to be ready to move with speed and power. That's how it was for a lone horse in the wild, especially one followed by a vulnerable foal. Even if the mare did kill their predator, her filly would die, trapped in the water where she had given up all strength and hope.

Chapter Six

After his confrontation with Frank in the barn, Pete had decided to take an evening ride. He had never liked the guy since the day he strolled up the driveway, looking for a job. But he knew Mack needed the help, so Frank was hired. With Buck working fewer hours to spend more time with his family, there was always too much work to be done. Besides, Pete was only the head ranch hand and never questioned his boss's judgment. He respected Mack too much and knew the man made decisions based on good reasoning.

On the other hand, Pete and Buck spent more time with Frank than Mack did and saw what the guy was really like when the boss wasn't around. Mack was too busy with paperwork, financial matters, traveling to auctions and making sure the operation was running smoothly to spend time worrying about how his ranch hands were doing. That was Pete's job. Buck and Pete both knew that Frank had to go. He was unreliable, drank too much and made the horses and kids nervous. Buck was hoping Pete would talk to Mack, but Pete wasn't sure how to go about it.

When Pete was uncertain about what to do, taking a trail ride always seemed to clear his head. Pete wasn't used to feeling unsettled about things. From his perspective, life was usually pretty simple and clear. His last tough decision was leaving his one and only girlfriend, twenty years ago. He had loved her, but she was a city girl. He knew she wouldn't be content living on the range, putting up with his cowboy ways. There was another woman he had fallen in love with, but she had married a man from out of town before Pete had the courage to make his own feelings known.

Like most cowboys, Pete liked to think of himself as a man who didn't dote on memories or wallow in his feelings about things. He watched the horizon as the sky turned red and the stars began to flicker overhead. It was a lovely night and he was glad to be out of the city and back on the range where he belonged. He hummed a little tune and stroked Traveller's mane. He had named his large, paint stallion after the horse ridden by Robert E. Lee, who had fought for the south in the Civil War.

Pete never cared about politics. After all, he thought, it wasn't the horse's fault that General Lee had lead people into battle who believed they had the right to make men their slaves. He just knew that his own Traveller had the same spunk, stamina and devotion that Lee's horse must have had. But all this musing was not doing Pete much good about dealing with his problem at hand. Frank.

Pete had talked to Mack about Frank's rough way with the horses and his careless habits with equipment, but both men knew they couldn't afford to lose another ranch hand. It was hard enough getting all the work done with four men. Mack was considering hiring another hand, but wanted to find one like Buck who could train the horses using the natural horsemanship techniques. After watching Buck and the horses he trained, Mack could see that the traditional techniques were unnecessarily rough and not as effective in establishing a true bond between horse and rider.

Mack had watched his daughter use Buck's methods to train her two horses. No horseman could say they had a stronger bond with their horse than Fen had with hers. Not only was Mack impressed with the horses Buck had trained, but he also got twice the money for them than he had in the old days, using the traditional training methods. The horses had a gentle, giving way about them and people were willing to pay a higher price for a horse with a nice temperament and a willingness to please.

It was possible that any further discussion with Mack about Frank could lead to an argument. Pete didn't like conflict. Coming to blows with the boss about another ranch hand was not what Pete wanted to do. But Pete and Buck had discussed the situation and they both felt strongly about the horses. They knew Frank's presence disturbed the herd and really bothered Fen and Alex. You could see it in the boy's eyes and body motions, always wary and cautious around Frank. Fen was much less subtle about her feelings. She took every chance to glare at Frank, bump into him "by mistake" or hide his tools so he couldn't get work done in a timely fashion, the way her father demanded.

Pete thought it was amusing that Fen found sneaky ways to slow Frank down or get him into trouble. On numerous occasions, Pete had secretly watched Fen play pranks on the mistrusted ranch hand. She siphoned gas out of tractors, pulled out important engine parts and relocated equipment in abandoned, overgrown sheds where Frank would never think to look.

"Yup. That Fen is a stubborn filly who's gonna grow up into one difficult mare." Pete let out a laugh in the quiet evening air.

Suddenly, Pete heard a splash and a squeal around the bend in the river. He quickened his pace to a jog, drawing his firearm in case he had spooked a bear, cougar or maybe a wolf. The bushes by the river were too high to see over, so Pete stood tall in his saddle. As they came around a copse of birch trees by the river's edge, he slowed Traveller back down to a walk.

In the dimming light, Pete could see a horse standing in the water, dipping its head up and down. As Pete and Traveller came into a small clearing at the riverbank, the horse picked its head up. Pete dismounted and tied Traveller to a tree. Walking down the slope to the river, he could see the problem. Thank goodness Phoenix had followed him around all day and was more interested in lying on the porch with Boss than going on a trail ride tonight.

"Now, hold on there, little lady," Pete said softly to the mare. "I can see you have a dilemma. Don't you worry, though, cause ole' Pete's gonna help you and your foal out. Just don't kill me in the process, ya hear?"

The horse snorted and stepped forward. Pete stepped back. The horse stepped back. Pete moved forward. The horse moved forward and pawed the water, snorting and throwing her head as a threat. Pete stepped back and the horse backed up. The mare was threatening and then retreating and Pete was trying to see how close he could get without being charged. Normally, a wild horse would run at the sight of a man, but clearly this one was not going to abandon her baby. The man and horse stepped up and back a few more times.

"Now we can dance like this all night, my friend, but in the meantime your baby isn't gonna make it. Neither one of us wants that. So why don't you just let me get a little closer." Pete spoke in a slow, calm voice to the mare as he moved towards the foal. "How come Buck is never around when I really need him. He'd have you munching grass out of his hand and nickering in his ear by now so I could get your little one out of trouble."

Pete kept talking quietly and moving slowly, step by step, until he was a few yards from the mare. He knew he was well within striking distance of her hooves. She could rear up and come down on him. She could turn and kick out with her hind feet. Pete knew the mare could kill him with one well placed strike of her hoof.

Pete waited, breathing slowly and steadily, judging the situation. He could see the foal's leg was trapped under a large, water-soaked log. He was pretty sure he could lift it, but he would have to do it in one easy move. The mare was not going to give him much time to get the job done. The log might have broken the foal's leg, which meant he would have to put it down. He wasn't even sure the baby was still alive. Its head was resting quietly on a rock and its eyes were closed.

The mare and the man watched each other for a few minutes. The horse stopped snorting and stomping. Pete knew that a mare and her foal would not be left alone for this long if a stallion and his herd were around. As Pete took another step towards the log, the mare slowly stepped back and over, giving Pete room to get both of his big hands around the heavy log. It took all of his strength to lift it up and toss it away. The mare was startled and jumped for the bank, but quickly turned back towards her filly.

The foal opened her eyes and stirred. She tried to move her legs but the cold water had made them numb. Pete gently put one hand under the baby's belly and one on her back. He lifted her up slowly and carried her to the shore. He backed up into the river, watching the foal begin to move, wiggling and squirming with effort. The mare breathed over her baby and nuzzled her body and legs. It wasn't long before the filly was flailing around, struggling to get up. The mare nickered to the filly as she got to her feet and wobbled about, hiding behind her mother's legs. Pete was glad to see the foal's legs worked just fine, once they had warmed up. The mare looked at Pete and snorted.

"You are quite welcome, ma'am," he said, cheerfully and tipped his cowboy hat.

The horses trotted off into the woods and Pete wobbled across the river, back to Traveller. The whole experience had made him a little shaky in the knees, but he managed to mount his horse and turn him in the direction of home. He hoped the mare and foal were on their way back to a herd and not wandering, easy prey with the coming of night. Their herd was their home and Pete knew that no creature can survive without a home.

Home. Pete had never really had a home before he met Mack and Renee. He had been there when Fen and Alex had been born at home. Pete had always enjoyed spending time with the kids and he was proud of them, as different as they were from each other. He had been amazed, watching Buck's success with the horses and felt proud, seeing the business prosper. Pete knew what he had to do about Frank. He was not going to let Frank destroy the home they had all found at the McCulloughs' ranch.

Pete was shivering from nerves and the cold river water, which had soaked his shirt and jeans and seeped down into his boots, sloshing around his toes. He looked down at his pants, dirty and sodden.

"Dang. I just washed these pants. Now ya see, Traveller. That's why washing clothes is a waste of time. They just get dirty again, anyhow." Pete sighed and gently squeezed his legs, prodding his horse into a gentle lope. "It's funny, ole' boy, how things just seem to work out. I have a problem and so I set out to find a solution and I end up fixing someone else's problem. Huh. Well, maybe someone is workin' out my problem right now and I don't even know it."

Pete's problem did have a solution and it was going to be worked out without his help, but it would come to him in a roundabout kind of way. The solution was to come from one persistent girl and one hot-tempered horse, who happened to be on his way to the McCulloughs' ranch, due to arrive the very next morning.

Chapter Seven

"**H**ey! Who let you in here, you mangy dog?" Fen laughed, hugging Boss who had jumped on the bed and was licking her face all over. Boss usually slept cuddled next to Alex, but the boy had woken up early and was eating breakfast with Rosie. "Wow! I must be late if Alex is downstairs already."

"Hi, Rosie! Hey, Alex. Where's Mom? I thought she was staying home this morning," Fen said. She popped two pieces of bread in the toaster and went to the cabinet for the cinnamon.

"Oh, they called her into the office," Rosie replied. "They've got a tough case that needs good negotiating skills. They rely on your mother to bail them out of sticky situations. She's quite a good lawyer, you know."

"They rely on her too much as far as I'm concerned. Don't they know she's a mother, too, and we rely on her just as much?" Fen scowled as she buttered her toast.

"I know, Fen. It's been hard on you and Alex. Have you talked to her about it?"

"No. I don't want to make her feel guilty and I know her work is important to her."

"Well, you are far more important to her than any job. It might help if you let her know how you feel."

"Thanks, Rosie. I'll keep it in mind." Fen quickly ate her toast, grabbed a granola bar from the snack basket and headed for the door.

"Where are you off to in such a hurry?" Rosie asked. She watched Fen glug down some orange juice from the container sitting on the counter. It was a habit Renee prohibited, but Rosie kept everyone's small vices to herself.

"I have chores to do and then I've got to get to work on Hack. The rodeo is barely two months away and we have to practice the drill team performance. Neither of us has a clue what the routine looks like. I can read the map Stan gave me, but, well, Hack has some trouble interpreting the signs and arrows."

"Honey, I don't think that horse knows his right from his left or his poll from his hindquarters," Rosie laughed.

"Hey, just 'cause he's big doesn't mean he's stupid."

"No, that's true. He just happens to be big and stupid."

"Well, I love him. He's the fastest horse around and he can find his way home from anywhere. Besides, he's saved my life a time or two from fast waters and crumbling slopes."

"I do know that, Fen. I love that horse, too. But taking him into the ring to perform a drill team routine with a hundred other horses might not be the best way to show him off. He might end up looking like the old, blind bull in a china shop. Well, Alex and I are going for a walk. Your mother will be home late tonight because she has a dinner meeting. Your father is around, waiting for the new horse to arrive."

"New horse? What new horse?" Fen stopped at the kitchen door and turned around.

"Apparently, someone is sending Mack a crazy horse, telling him he can have the thing if Buck can gentle it. Otherwise, they're going to have to put it down. It sounds like some kind of gentlemen's bet to me. The owner tried to use the traditional methods to break the horse and the horse wouldn't give in. So your father wants to prove what the natural horsemanship methods can do. It's kind of like an advertisement for his ranch, although Lord knows he doesn't need any more work." Rosie sighed and shrugged. "Maybe it's more like promoting the natural horsemanship methods. You know how important that is to your father, Buck and Pete."

"Then I'd better get stuff done so I can watch the show. Do you know what kind of horse it is?"

"No. Just that he's a dark bay stallion, about sixteen and a half hands high. How's that for a load of horse?" Rosie raised her eyebrows.

"Yahoo! Dad rocks!" Fen yelled as she slammed the back door.

Boss jumped around Fen as she headed for the chicken coop to grain them and collect their eggs. Boss loved to chase the chickens around the coop and out the gate, so Fen always ended up herding them back in with a broom. The dog enjoyed chasing chickens, goats, horses, vehicles and just about any random object that moved. He even chased his own shadow and a flashlight beam, giving Alex hours of enjoyment running the beam around a dark room, watching Boss jump and dodge for the light.

Fen fed the pigs and cleaned out their water trough. The pigs were the only objects in motion on the ranch that Boss avoided. Soon after the McCulloughs had brought the pigs home and put them in their pen, Boss dashed under their fencing and the chase was on. Boss quickly found out, however, that pigs do not run away. They stand, stare and then herd their would-be chaser into a corner and try to determine if the thing they trapped is edible. Boss was saved by Pete, who had loaded the pigs in the pen and had come back around their shed to see how they were doing. He snatched Boss up with one hand and took him to Alex. The poor dog trembled in the boy's lap for the next hour and never went near the pig pen again.

The chores done, Fen went to find Hack. He trotted to the fence and happily walked into the barn to be groomed and tacked up. His saddle weighed about as much as Fen and she needed a stool to get his bridle on. Fen walked Hack out to the big rock she used as a mounting block. Into the ring they went, with the sheet of paper that illustrated the drill team routine stuffed in Fen's pocket.

The partners warmed up with some walking, jogging and loping, Fen loving the feel of the powerful horse under her body. His jog was big and smooth and his lope felt like a well-oiled rocking chair. It was a warm day and a light breeze blew across the fields and Hack was feeling frisky. Fen stopped him at the gate and took the paper out of her pocket to go over the routine in her head.

"Hack," she moaned. "This is impossible. Why did I sign up for this event? I should have stuck with barrel racing and let you stick with trail riding and flat racing with the big boys. We don't need to do all this fancy rodeo stuff. Oh, well. Buck always says it's good to try new things with your horse. It's supposed to strengthen the bond between us. Not that we need any more bonding exercises. You'd eat at the dinner table and share my shower with me if you could." Fen patted her big, black horse. "Let's make a vow, right now, not to get frustrated with each other. We're new at this and it will take time. Of course, we only have six weeks to learn it and be able to do it, perfectly, with a gazillion other horses in the ring, all of us going in different directions with music blaring in our ears. Nothin' to it, right bud?" Hack bounced his head in agreement or maybe just impatience. He was not a horse that liked to stand still.

Horse and rider practiced for about two hours until they were both ready to send each other to auction. Hack started tugging on the reins with his huge head and Fen answered by yanking back. Hack did complete circles on the forehand just for fun, scraped Fen along fence rails, crow-hopped halfway across the arena and ended with a buck that pitched Fen over his head. He galloped off with a final toss of his head, leaving his rider cussing in the dust.

"I get it, Hack," Fen said irritably, brushing off her shirt and pants. "It's time to stop." As she was leading him out of the arena, Fen tried to encourage them both. "You know, we actually didn't do that badly for the first time. We can do all the maneuvers, just not at the right time or in the right spot or at the right speed. But it's a start."

Hack stuck his nostril over Fen's ear and sighed. Fen gently pushed him away and walked to the barn. The horse followed her listlessly with the lead rope tossed over his neck, occasionally yanking at tufts of grass. Fen was too tired and irritated to take his rope and pull him up, even though she knew Hack didn't deserve the tasty treat.

"So, you finished your bull riding session with old 'Bodacious' here?" Fen's father had come out of the house. "You know all this time I thought this animal was a horse. He looks like a horse, he smells like a horse, he wears tack made for a horse but . . . ."

"Oh, ha, ha. Everyone's a comedian when it comes to Hack," Fen retorted. But you'll see. He'll be fine on rodeo day."

"Okay. You know best, my dear."

"Hey, Buck was the one who suggested I try it."

"Really?" Mack looked skeptical. "Maybe he was kidding, Fen."

Fen thought for a moment as she and Mack walked Hack into the barn and started untacking him. Hack leaned into her and gave a big sigh. His sighs were like yawns. They made everybody else sigh, too. Mack and Fen sighed together as they looked at the black beast. Fen gave him a hug.

"You think so?" Fen asked. "Do you think Buck was kidding? He sounded so serious. Of course, Buck always sounds serious. You think he's playing me for a fool?"

Fen had to laugh at her own gullible nature. She did take on more dares than any other girl she knew. Clancy was always challenging her to do one thing or another that he thought up, then telling her to "lighten up" when she landed upside down and yelled at him. Although, more often than not, she came out of the challenge on her feet, surprising them both.

"I think you should do it just to catch him in his own joke." Mack chuckled. "Hack actually looked pretty good out there for the first practice. It's you I'm not sure about."

"Thanks, Dad. Well, I'm going to do it because I said I would. I'm going to beat Buck at his own game and we'll see who has the last laugh."

Just as Fen was letting Hack out to pasture, a truck and trailer pulled up the driveway. Father and daughter walked out to greet the new horse that Rosie had mentioned that morning. Alex and Rosie had come back from their walk and were standing in the front yard. Buck came out of the tack room, took off his gloves and shoved them in his back pocket. Pete had just finished hammering the last of the fence boards for the paddock next to the driveway where the horse would stay. He put his hammer and nails in his tool belt and stood with Buck.

The truck pulled up and a large man stepped out. The trailer was rocking back and forth and the animal inside was squealing and snorting. Everyone backed up as the sound of hooves banging on the sides of the trailer made it hard to hear introductions. Rosie stood behind Pete but where she could still see what was going on. She was not a woman to be caught unaware or unprepared. She instinctively pulled Alex in front of her and wrapped herself around his body, sheltering him in the cradle of her arms. Whatever was in that trailer, Rosie wanted it to go back where it had come from. Her gut told her that this horse could take a life or at least change one, forever.

Chapter Eight

"Name's Dickson. Joe Dickson." The big man stuck his hand out to Mack.

Mack shook the man's hand and introduced himself and his family. He had to talk loudly to be heard over the kicking and squealing coming from inside the trailer. Everyone did their best to ignore the din. Fen couldn't help walking around the back of the truck to try to get a look at the source of the commotion.

"Like I said on the phone," Joe started. "The horse is yours if you can keep him from killing someone. We tried what we could but he's no good around people or other horses. The guy who gave him to me said he's a Thoroughbred and won a bunch of money a few years back. Course, he didn't come with any papers so you couldn't race him in the big time. But around here," he swept a long, beefy arm towards the horizon, "you might be able to win some wagers."

"What happened to him to make him so mean?" Fen asked.

The man looked at Fen. "Mean people make mean horses, sweetheart."

"Well," Buck looked at Mack and shrugged. "We might as well get him out of the trailer 'cause he's none too happy in there."

"He ain't happy anywhere," Joe mumbled.

"Let's put him in the paddock out front here where we can keep an eye on him," Buck suggested, looking at the height of the fence Pete had just fixed. "How high can he jump, Mr. Dickson?"

"I don't know." Joe looked at Buck and shrugged. "But I wouldn't give him too much space to get a running start."

They all chuckled but nerves were running tight and Joe was obviously anxious to leave. Buck opened the gate to the paddock. Joe backed the trailer in and Buck hopped over the fence and waited for the banging from inside the trailer to stop. He opened the trailer door and the horse spun around and leaped out, tearing across the pen in huge strides. The stallion galloped back towards the trailer, tossed his head and flashed the whites of his eyes showing fear and panic. He reared up and kicked his hooves out, letting out a loud squeal. He galloped around the pen, over and over again, kicking up huge clouds of dirt so that he was almost hidden in the swirls of dust he left behind.

"It's a good thing I like a challenge," Buck exclaimed, watching the stallion make continuous circles around the enclosure.

"Good luck, my friend," Joe said. "Let me know what happens, will ya? We have kind of a bet going on at my place, you know, between the 'horse whispering' thing you do and the way we train 'em. We know we failed so we'll be right impressed if you can work some magic and turn him into a horse, instead of what we call him."

"What do you call him?" Mack asked, tentatively, afraid to hear the answer.

"The devil."

Joe climbed into his truck and drove slowly down the driveway, taking one last look at the horse. He was a beautiful animal. He was a tall, dark bay Thoroughbred, gleaming with sweat. His dark mane and tail were long, thick and glossy. Under his forelock was a white marking in the shape of a perfect crescent moon.

"We forgot to ask what his real name is," Fen said.

"We'll think of one when we find out if we can keep him," Mack replied.

"What are you going to call him until then, Buck?" Fen asked, knowing that Buck always named his horses as part of the training process.

Buck watched the horse for a few minutes, noting his high stepping feet, the easy bend of his neck and the quick lead changes that created a smooth gait at any speed.

"Well, Wild Thing is the first thing to come to mind but perhaps we should give him the benefit of the doubt and call him something more respectful."

The horse stopped in the middle of the pen and stared at the people gathered around. A breeze blew his mane, tail and forelock to one side revealing the crescent moon between his radiant eyes.

"How about Crescent?" Buck said. "It makes it sound like he's part way to becoming something big and bright and awesome. I mean really awesome, like the Grand Canyon is awesome. Not awesome like the way people use the word these days for the best bagel they've eaten."

Everyone stared at Buck. He was a man of few words, often not even bothering to complete his own sentences. It was difficult to engage him in a real conversation, but this was as profound a thought as any of them could come up with at the moment.

"Crescent it is," Pete said, quietly.

He turned around and smiled at Rosie, still standing behind him. He put his arm around Rosie's shoulder and pulled her up to his side. He wanted Alex to get a good look at the beautiful horse now standing proudly in the ring. Pete quickly let his arm drop and kneeled down to look at Alex. The boy's eyes were alight watching the horse's every movement.

At that moment, Boss came running around the side of the house to see what all the excitement was about. The Thoroughbred saw the dog coming and started galloping around the ring again. Despite the horse's kicking and bucking, Boss's herding instincts got the best of him.

"No!" they all shouted as Boss darted under the fence and chased the horse around the pen. Pete instinctively put his hand on Phoenix's neck to keep her back, even though he knew she was smart enough not to tangle with a wild animal who felt trapped.

The horse stopped in his tracks, put his head down and stared at the little dog, jumping and yipping in the dirt. Boss must have had a moment of recollection. Perhaps some vague memory of pigs came to mind. This didn't look like a pig but Boss was taking no chances. He knew that if the thing you chase doesn't turn and run away, it's time to skedaddle in the other direction. Boss turned tail and ran towards the fence, sliding under it just as the horse slammed on his brakes, crashing into the freshly nailed boards.

"Oh well," Pete said, moaning at the thought of replacing the new boards. "I guess now there are two things that dog won't herd on this ranch, pigs and one crazy Thoroughbred." Pete sighed and headed for the tool shed.

They all laughed and went their separate ways, allowing the horse time alone to get accustomed to his new home. Rosie was more than ready to lead Alex in the opposite direction, although he and Fen would have happily watched the stallion all day.

"Ladies!" Mack called to Rosie and Fen as they walked away with Alex at their side. Mack's tone was serious and his face stern.

"Yessir," they both replied, walking towards him.

"I don't want any of you to get close to that animal," he demanded, jabbing his finger at the horse blowing and trotting in the pen. "He's dangerous and I want no accidents to happen because we've been curious or careless. Understood?"

"Yessir," Rosie and Fen said, together.

"You promise me?" Mack said, looking at each of them in turn.

"Yessir," they echoed again.

Fen knew she meant to keep her promise. She knew how dangerous a horse could be. Rosie would certainly not let Alex get in harm's way. But Fen's heart had pounded when the horse had come leaping out of the trailer. She had trembled watching him pound around the ring. How could she stay away from such a beautiful animal? He was a Thoroughbred who had raced and won! Fen vowed to watch Buck every chance she could and wait for the day she could get into the ring with the wild stallion.

It wouldn't be long, though, before Fen would have a different plan for this horse. It would be a plan which would have nothing to do with her, but everything to do with Frank and getting him off her ranch. What Fen didn't know was that someone besides Buck would get in the ring with the stallion, but it wouldn't be her.

Fen couldn't have known that someone else had plans of their own. She wasn't the only one who was drawn to the power, beauty and mystery of the stallion. The horse would, ultimately, decide for himself, as all wild creatures should do, what his fate would be. Was he capable of trusting a human? And if he was, would the person he chose be able to trust him in return? Could they take the perilous journey of love together or would they choose to stay in the comfortable and safe but lonely place of solitude?

Chapter Nine

It was late afternoon when Clancy rode down the hillside on Bo, his favorite trail horse. Clancy was a John Wayne fan and the only boy Fen knew who admitted that he cried while watching the movie, *True Grit*, when the actor's horse, Bo, died in a shoot-out. Fen and Clancy had watched the movie at least twenty times. They could recite most of the lines and sing the theme song, although Clancy couldn't carry a tune to save his life, so it didn't have the same heart-warming effect it had in the movie. In fact, Fen would get halfway through the song and end up rolling on the floor in laughter. She also got stomachaches from extended giggling, watching Clancy do his imitation of John Wayne's gritty drawl and swaggering walk.

Clancy and Rosie lived just over the ridge from the McCulloughs' ranch. After his father was killed, Clancy often rode Bandit or Bo along the path that led to the McCulloughs' home, earning money doing whatever odd jobs Mack and his ranch hands didn't have time to get done. Rosie had been waitressing and working at the library, but couldn't make enough money to pay the bills that piled up. When Renee started working more hours at the law office, she hired Rosie to be home with Fen and Alex at the end of the day and cook dinner for the family.

Clancy had always been one of Fen's childhood friends, but with all the time he and Rosie spent at the McCullough's home, they quickly became part of the family. It never bothered Fen or Clancy that he was older and a boy. Clancy quickly learned that Fen had enough stamina and courage to keep up with him. He also realized she was a smart kid who could get him out of trouble when his schemes didn't go as planned. And Fen liked Clancy's adventuresome spirit and willingness to put up with her stubborn nature. They both knew they made a good team.

The sun was sinking towards the mountain tops when Clancy loped up to the McCulloughs' barn. Fen had already tacked up Hack and was ready to go. She thought about taking Scoot, but she had given him a work-out with the barrels after lunch and he looked so happy, snoring in the sun between snacks of sweet meadow grass. Besides, Fen could tell that Hack was restless after their tedious and frustrating drill team practice in the ring that morning. A ride out on the range and through the woods would do them both a lot of good.

"Hey! You think it's too late to ride to Riverbend?" Clancy asked.

"No. Mom won't be home for dinner again, so everybody is getting their own dinner. Pete said he would feed Alex."

"Great! I remembered a headlamp so we don't have to worry about getting caught out too late." Clancy pulled it out of his pack, along with a package of cookies and a canteen of water. "I brought all the essentials!"

"You always do," Fen laughed. "And I brought my camera and binoculars in case we find the cougar and the herd."

"Fen, I gotta tell ya. Carrying a camera is a little on the nerdy side, but the binoculars are just plain geeky."

Fen loved the binoculars that Pete had given her. She had seen so much wildlife since she had learned to use them and had identified a lot of birds she had never been able to name before.

"I don't care if I look like a nerd. People already avoid me. What difference does it make?"

"People don't avoid you, Fen. You're just, um, different from other girls and so it's hard for them to get to know you."

"Well, I'm not interested in what they like and they don't care about what I like. I get bored with their conversation. They talk about the mall where I don't go, celebrities who I don't know, television shows I don't watch and clothes and make-up that I don't wear. And they talk about boys. Ugh."

"Yeah, I agree. We're a pretty dull topic of conversation," Clancy said, nodding with a serious look on his face. He turned his horse and headed down the path towards Riverbend, Fen following close behind.

The two friends rode for awhile in silence which was always comfortable between them. The sun was gleaming off the snow-covered mountains and the rolling hills were a lush green with the spring leaves and grass. Wildflowers were growing like a tapestry, blanketing the meadows with splashes of yellow, red, pink and blue. Fen and Clancy could hear the river in the distance, but knew it would take about half an hour to get to its banks where it snaked through the valley, deep and cold in some places and shallow and rocky in others.

The horses picked up a jog on the smooth path. They knew the terrain well and moved with ease around bushes and groves of tall trees. There was a light breeze and the horses shook their heads catching every scent of spring. As the sun slowly slid behind the mountain peaks, Clancy started looking at the ground for tracks. Fen wanted to see the animals so she kept her eyes on the horizon and the far fields and hills. They both kept their ears alert for sounds of the wild herd.

"Hey, check it out." Clancy hopped off Bo and pointed to the ground. "That's a cat track. Here," he said, handing Bo's reins to Fen. "Pony Bo while I walk."

Fen took Bo's reins and walked ahead on Hack, leading Clancy's horse behind her. They walked for awhile until Clancy lost the cougar tracks in the leaves of the woods.

"I guess we should have brought Boss," Clancy muttered. "He could have followed the scent."

"Yeah and we would be tracking Boss for three days. You can track a lot of animals, Clance, but Boss would take you in circles till Christmas."

Clancy laughed. He mounted Bo and they started off again, anxious to get to Riverbend. After a short while, Fen dug in her pack and took the binoculars out to get a good look at a distant field.

"Clancy, wait. I think I see something." Fen squinted into the binoculars and told Hack to halt. He stopped moving, having heard the word, halt, nearly a hundred times in the arena that morning. He sighed and leaned against the tree next to him.

"It's a horse and foal! Look!" Fen whispered with excitement.

Clancy took the binoculars and looked out into the field. Not having much experience using binoculars, he fiddled with the focusing dial a lot and kept looking over the top of them to where he was supposed to be seeing something.

"I see them!" he said, finally. He watched them for awhile and then scanned the field for the rest of the herd. "They're alone."

"Yeah. That's odd," Fen replied. She took the binoculars and looked at the woods and shrubs surrounding the clearing where the two horses were grazing.

"Let's cross the river and see if we can get closer," Clancy said.

They quietly forded the river and walked slowly along the edge of field and forest, trying to stay hidden for as long as possible. As they moved in, Fen stopped briefly to scan with her binoculars again.

"Clancy," she whispered. "You aren't going to believe this. There's a cougar hiding in the grass at the edge of the field, on the right, under that big cedar tree."

"No. Are you serious? Let me see!" He took the binoculars but couldn't find the cat in all the undergrowth. "How do you see anything with these darn things, anyway?" He gave them back to Fen with a sigh.

"Practice, Clancy, nerdy practice. Trust me. There's a cougar in those bushes over there with his eyes on that foal."

"You think I'm close enough to get a bead on him?" Clancy slowly pulled out the shotgun from its harness on his pack.

"Yeah, but you can't shoot him, Clancy!"

"You want the foal and maybe the mare to die, too?" He looked at Fen with a scowl.

"No, but, but . . . . I don't know. I don't want a cougar dead, either."

"Well, you can't always have everything you want. Stay here, Fen."

Clancy walked Bo slowly along the edge of the woods, avoiding branches and rocks that might snap or clunk on Bo's feet. Finally, he was close enough to see the cat in the grass. Clancy quietly halted Bo by sitting back and slowly exhaling. He put his rifle to his shoulder and took aim. The mare suddenly looked up from grazing. She had sensed motion or scent or something else that humans have long lost the ability to feel. She whinnied to her foal and started to move out of the clearing.

Just as the foal began to follow her mother, the cougar sprang forward running at top speed towards the horses. The mare squealed and turned to face her attacker as the filly dodged and weaved through the grass. The cougar ignored the mare and sped towards the easy prey, knowing he could deal with the bigger horse after the kill.

With his rifle cocked and his eye on the lens Clancy followed the rapid movement of the cat. Running inches behind the fleeing filly the cougar slowed for a split second to make the killing leap. Clancy pulled the trigger, the shot reverberating off the hills and echoing through the canyons. The cougar jumped in the air and with Clancy's second shot, went down.

Fen gasped. The cat had fallen into the undergrowth of the field. But within seconds the cat popped up again. He spun around and fled to the woods, vanishing in a heartbeat. The wild horses stopped dead for a moment and looked at Clancy. He put his shotgun down and watched them bolt through the field and into the woods, running for the river ahead.

"I'm glad you aren't a better shot than that, Clancy." Fen was trembling as Clancy jogged back to where he had left her. You nearly killed that cougar."

"Oh, it was a perfect shot, dead on, two inches above his ear tips." Clancy smiled and turned to face the open field. Suddenly, they heard a loud, gusty whinny coming from a distance. "That didn't sound like the mare we just saw," Clancy said.

Fen and Clancy looked at each other and took off at a full gallop across the field. Fen's heart was racing. No Thoroughbred could have outrun Hack. That call could have only come from a strong lead stallion looking for his lost mare and with him must be the wild herd of Riverbend.

Chapter Ten

Clancy and Fen slowed to a lope at the edge of the field and headed down the path, the river on their left and the woods on their right. They didn't want to spook the herd if it was in the next clearing. They slowed to a walk around the next bend and, sure enough, the wild horses were milling about in a small opening in the forest by the river, waiting for the stallion's cue to flee. The horses had heard the familiar whinny of the missing alpha mare and the gunshots. The dun stallion was standing tall, his nostrils flaring, snorting out puffs of vapor like a dragon in a story book. He returned the mare's call with his own deep whinny.

Out of the woods emerged the mare and her foal, jogging across the field. The stallion loped to meet her. His mate was tired and winded and stood for a long time, leaning into him. They breathed through each other's muzzles, rubbed their necks and withers together and nickered softly, communicating without words.

The stallion poked his nose down to sniff the filly who was hiding behind her mother. The stallion snorted and the baby jumped back, startled by her father's big nose and strong exhale. The mare nudged her baby back to the big horse. He nuzzled the foal and rubbed her withers. The baby shivered in delight. She started hopping about like a young lamb and the other mares and yearlings came around to get a look at the new addition to the herd. As the sky darkened, the horses soon went back to grazing and dozing, while the mare and her foal lay down for a long needed sleep, safe now in the protection of the stallion and the herd.

"The baby is so adorable!" Fen exclaimed in a quiet voice, watching the mare and foal through her binoculars.

"Have you met a newborn who wasn't?" Clancy teased. "But I have to agree. It's a good-looking foal."

The filly was long-legged and slender. Her chestnut coat gleamed in the last golden rays of the sun and they could just barely see the small teardrop star between her large, bright eyes.

"I think we should call her, Little Rain, because of the shape of her star."

"That's a good name," Clancy replied, watching the movement of the herd. "So, Fen. You can tell it's a 'her' from here?" he asked, skeptically.

"Binoculars are kind of handy that way, Clancy," Fen said, sarcastically.

"Gimme those things, smart aleck," Clancy grinned and grabbed for the binoculars. "Wow. Cool." He watched the mare and foal for a few minutes. "So, you know how Christmas is right around the corner. I could really use a pair of these things."

"Around the corner? It's April, pal. Besides, we don't exchange presents and I can't afford these things. Sweet talk somebody else." Fen snatched the binoculars back.

Clancy just smiled and went back to watching the herd from a distance. The yearlings tussled with each other while the older mares grazed. The adults stood in small groups, flicking flies away from each other's bodies, their long tails swishing back and forth in constant motion. Clancy enjoyed every chance he had to observe the wild horses, undisturbed by people who halter and bridle them and keep them in corrals, taking all the wild nature out of them. But he also appreciated the gift of having horses to train and ride. He would never understand why these animals were usually so willing to be tamed, saddled and ridden. He knew if he was given the choice, he would fight to his own death to maintain his freedom.

In the fading light, Fen pulled out her camera and took a few pictures of the herd. They weren't the best pictures she had taken, but she could still make out each horse and their markings. As the two friends watched the reunion of the mare and her stallion and the peaceful nature of the horses at the end of the day, Fen glanced at Clancy. He looked like he was in a trance, far away from where they were, yet drinking in the scene like a thirsty man, taking long gulps of water from a cold river.

"Clancy?" Fen asked, hesitantly. "Do you think about your dad a lot?"

"Every day, Fen. He's my first thought in the morning and my last thought at night."

"I'm sorry. I'm sorry you had to go through all of the hard times during that first year and now the constant heartache you must feel. I hate death." Fen gazed at the herd and wished that sadness and grief existed only in books.

"Thanks, Fen. I thought that, too, for awhile. But after thinking about it a lot and feeling angry and sad and hurt, I began to realize that death is really just part of life. Think about it from a horse's point of view. They grieve the death of a herd member and then move on to another field or a different valley. They continue to live their lives, watch foals being born and other herd members die. It's the way it works. Like with horses and all living creatures, we can't change what nature has in store for us. So, I think about my dad and hope he's out there somewhere, watching my back and helping me move forward."

Clancy looked at Fen with an expression she had never seen before. It was like he was in physical pain, as if his heart was going to burst open and all the love inside was going to pour out, only to be swallowed by the earth beneath them. Fen met her friend's gaze with tears streaming down her face.

"I know this won't help," Fen choked back a sob. "But I remember writing a poem in sixth grade, comparing our emotions to a river. It was stupid. It was such a typically nerdy Fen thing to do, trying to please my Science teacher and English teacher in one assignment." Fen rolled her eyes, trying to gain control of her emotions.

Clancy smiled at her. He was glad they were on horseback because, otherwise, it would have been difficult not to take her in his arms, just to hug his best friend, just to let her know that everything was going to be alright as long as they kept talking.

"Anyway," Fen continued. "I wrote this poem about how feelings of sadness, anger and guilt are always flowing through us, like a river of blood through our bodies. But our heart is like the headwaters of the river. It's where we hold all our family members, friends and animals who we love, to replenish the strength we need to keep us going in bad times. It's like they create a well spring of love that never goes dry. The power from all their love is what makes the hurt flow downstream to the sea, where it swirls and blends with all human emotion to create new life."

"Wow," Clancy grinned. "I bet you got a couple of "A"s on that one!"

"Actually, the Science teacher gave me a "C", saying that blood doesn't really create new life and the English teacher gave me a "B", saying it was a bit too morbid for a sixth grade poem." Fen rolled her eyes and shrugged. "Teachers have no imagination. Anyway, that's not the point, blockhead."

"I got the point." Clancy smiled and shifted in his saddle. He suddenly looked away and winced as though the point had become an arrow that struck a tender spot. His jaw and brow became tense and his eyes hard. "What I don't understand, what I will never understand is why he went back to professional bull riding when he had retired two years before. He knew he couldn't keep up. He knew he couldn't stay on for eight seconds. He didn't have the reflexes, the strength or the stamina. And he knew Mom and I needed him. The last year of his life he was travelling more than he was home. But he did it anyway."

"Maybe he just loved it so much he missed it."

"He loved it more than Mom and me? He missed it more than us?" Clancy scowled.

"I didn't mean it that way, Clancy." Fen felt awful. She had obviously said the wrong thing, which she seemed to do quite often. "I'm sorry for bringing it up."

"No. I'm glad you did. Nobody talks about him anymore, not even his best friends and all the guys he rode with, not even Mom. It's like he never existed. I don't want to stop thinking about him. He will always be part of me and I want to share his stories with other people. I want people to remember him. It helps me to talk about it, to keep him part of my life even though he isn't here."

It was dark and they knew they had to get home. Clancy turned on his headlamp and they loped and jogged as much as possible to make good time. They finally reached the McCulloughs' ranch as a breeze began to stir and a large cloud covered the moon, just rising over the treetops.

"Well, we had quite an afternoon," Clancy said, smiling at Fen.

"We always do!" Fen grinned back. "Can you make it back home alright in the dark?" She noticed the stiff breeze and looked up at the ominous sky, clouds rolling in from every side of the valley.

"Oh, sure. Bo knows the way blindfolded." He waved good-bye and quickly disappeared into the night.

Fen shivered, sensing a big storm whirling in on the wind. Dark clouds were billowing overhead, quickly covering the twinkling lights that lay somewhere far beyond. Fen much preferred seeing the big, open sky, clear and teeming with stars. She liked being able to see what was ahead and be certain of the path that lay before her.

The wild stallion let out a lusty neigh from the front paddock. Fen watched his shadow and stared at his eyes, glowing in the dark. For the first time since Buck's arrival she doubted he could tame an animal. That man had called him dangerous and her father had warned them to keep away. For the first time in her life, Fen was scared of a horse.

She looked at the shadow again. He was standing still, looking at her, the breeze flowing through his mane, forelock and tail. The stallion was like Alex, Fen thought. He was afraid and alone, not knowing what lay ahead. It was no wonder they both had tantrums. It was their only way to proclaim their fear and demand their freedom from people who didn't understand them.

No, Fen decided. She would not be afraid of this horse. She would learn to love him as she had always loved Alex. They were both full of fear and confusion. They both deserved patience, respect and love from the people who cared for them. Fen knew that it would only be through the love of others that the horse and her brother could learn to love in return.

Fen went to bed that night with a deep sense of uncertainty and sadness. Life could be so complicated and it seemed that things often didn't turn out the way she hoped they would. There was too much to think about and too many things she had no control over.

Fen worried about Hack and making him look foolish in the rodeo, but she couldn't pull out now without making it look worse. She thought about the beautiful, wild foal they had seen with a cougar stalking the herd. Frank and his suspicious manner and foul nature were a constant source of stress for Fen. And what would the future hold for Alex and Crescent? Fen missed her mother, with her spending so much time at work. And she dreaded going back to school, confused and ashamed about not having friends.

Fen rolled over and cried into her pillow. She was worried that even with all her efforts, everything would turn out badly. Most of all, Fen was sad about Clancy having to live his life without a father. But there was another feeling, one she couldn't put her finger on, an emotion she couldn't put a word to, something outside of her own understanding that tugged at her subconscious. She fell into a restless sleep, wondering why life just couldn't be as simple as Geometry class. You drew lines from points to points, you measured the distances and got the right answer every time, as long as you remembered to check your work.

Chapter Eleven

Clancy woke up the next morning in a twisted pile of sheets and blankets. He had tossed and turned all night and had too many nightmares. He sat up in bed and ran his strong hands and long fingers through his rumpled hair. He could hear the rain pelting on the roof.

"Great. Rain. Aren't chores going to be fun today?" he moaned, sarcastically.

He flopped back down on the pillow and tried to organize his befuddled brain. It felt like his head was spinning with feelings and thoughts he couldn't sort out. First, he thought about his conversation with Fen last night. He had never resolved the issue about his dad's death and had never broached the subject with his mom. He knew it had been too painful for her at the time and then the months and years went by and it felt odd to bring it up.

He thought about his mom dating this guy, Tom. She had been out with him twice before and Clancy didn't like it. He knew his mom must be lonely and she deserved to be happy. But he didn't like Tom and didn't really think his mom was that crazy about him either. Renee had told him that Rosie just needed company and someone to make her feel like a woman again. That was just too much information for Clancy. He remembered blushing and walking away, saying something about having chores to do.

Then there was this thing with Clara Perkins. Her father had hired him to teach her how to barrel race. She was an eastern rider with a lot of dressage experience under her belt, but she wanted to be a western cowgirl to fit in with the other girls in the area. There was nothing wrong with that, but Clancy knew Fen would be furious if she found out that Clancy was her instructor. Besides, it was obvious, even to Clancy, that Clara was interested in him in more ways than a barrel racing teacher. He wasn't sure he was ready for a girlfriend and if he was, it wasn't Miss Fancy Pants Perkins. She was pretty alright, but definitely not his type.

Besides that, Clancy had been to the Perkins' ranch enough times to get an uneasy feeling about the place. There were too many ranch hands and too few horses. The McCulloughs' ranch was brimming with horses. Mack and his three ranch hands, along with Clancy's frequent help, couldn't keep up with all the work of doing the chores and maintaining the property, as well as buying, training, selling and shipping horses. But the Perkins' place had ranch hands hanging around, watching Clancy teach Clara and drinking coffee at eleven o'clock in the morning. Something was amiss, but he couldn't figure out what.

Clancy's last thought before deciding to get out of bed to face a wet, muddy day of fixing fences, mucking stalls and cleaning out troughs, was of Fen. They had been friends forever. He had always thought of her as a cute, sassy, adventuresome kid with freckles and a messy ponytail. She had always been someone he could pal around with when his buddies weren't available.

But the day before spring vacation he was at his locker working on his combination. He had this locker and the same combination for almost three years. He could unlock it with his eyes closed, balancing a pile of books and his lunch sack in one hand. He was doing just that when he turned and saw Fen walking down the hall towards him. Her blond hair, brushed and glossy, was flowing down her shoulders. Her face had a rosy glow and she was smiling, probably because a boy had just passed her, having taken a second look as she walked by, a slight sway in her hips. She was wearing a light spring skirt that flowed around her thighs. Clancy noticed that Fen's body had curves. How come he hadn't seen them until now?

He had looked at her for a moment and then went back to working on his locker combination. He couldn't remember what number he was on and dropped his lunch bag and books, trying to start the process all over again. Then Clara Perkins walked by and Clancy forgot his combination altogether. He picked up his books and lunch, realizing he didn't have time to get into his locker. It would have to wait until after math class.

Clancy had sighed as he walked into class, remembering that his math homework was in his locker. He had forgotten or lost his homework so many times there was no way Mr. Leonard would believe it was in his locker and that a ninth grader couldn't remember his own combination. He didn't even want to try to explain. What Clancy didn't realize was that Mr. Leonard would have understood why the boy had momentarily forgotten three numbers after watching two pretty girls walk by. At the age of forty, the math teacher seemed ancient to Clancy, but Mr. Leonard still remembered the feelings he had as a teenager. It was one of the reasons he was such a good teacher.

Clancy thought about last night as he groped around his bedroom searching for a pair of pants and shirt. He had led the way home, watching for dangerous spots on the trail. He kept turning around to make sure Fen was okay, when he really just wanted to see her smile. She had been so excited about seeing the cougar and the herd. It made him content to see Fen happy, her face glowing in the beam of his headlamp. For all of her glamorous good looks, fancy hair and clothes, Clara Perkins was not the girl Clancy preferred looking at or spending time with.

For being almost fifteen, Fen was a girl with too many worries on her mind. Clancy had seen it on her face many times in the past year, although they hadn't talked much about her feelings. Now he wished that he felt more comfortable around girls, the way some of his friends acted. Maybe then he would be able to get closer to Fen and help her through whatever problems she was having.

"Ugh!" Clancy exclaimed, falling back onto his bed and smashing his pillow into his face. "You avoid girls! Remember? They're too confusing and distracting! They're too complicated! You don't understand them and you never know what to say! Well, except with Fen." He had to admit that, until now, he never had trouble talking to Fen. But he had never really thought of her as a girl, as in capital letters. "Boy, I'd better never tell her that. She'd sock me." Clancy pulled the pillow off his face and sighed.

"I'll just get dressed and muck stalls and fix fences and clean troughs, IN the pouring rain and that will take my mind off everything. Then I can come in and make a huge breakfast of waffles and eggs and bacon and hash browns and watch John Wayne flicks the rest of the day." Just as Clancy was starting to feel better and thought he could get out of bed, he remembered one more thing he had to do. "Oh, no!" The pillow went back over his face. "I have to give Clara her lesson this afternoon! AAAAAGH!"

"Clancy! What the heck is going on up there!" Rosie called from downstairs. "The day is moving on without you! Come down for some cereal before chores!"

"So much for a man-sized breakfast. I'll be like Alex and eat one piece of cereal at a time just to postpone going out in the rain. Well, from this day forward I vow I will not get involved with girls. I'll be like Pete. I'll be free and easy, independent and alone. I'll get a dog so I won't be lonely." Clancy thought for a moment. He didn't really know if Pete was lonely or not. "Oh, heck. How am I supposed to know what someone else is feeling when I don't even understand my own feelings?"

During the past couple of years, Clancy had seen Pete watching his mother sometimes, when she was playing with Alex, spending time with the McCullough family or riding her horse, a lovely red roan named Allegro. His mother had a beautiful voice and sang at all the church performances on the holidays. Clancy noticed that Pete religiously avoided church, except on the holidays. But Pete had never asked Rosie out on a date, so Clancy hadn't thought much about it, until now. Pete and Clancy's dad had been friends when Hal had died.

Clancy wondered if maybe that was why Pete was hesitant to show any feelings toward Rosie.

"This is ridiculous," Clancy muttered. "I have no clue about all this lovey dovey stuff. All I know is I've gotta get on a horse fast before my brains turn into scrambled eggs."

Clancy got into the dirty jeans, t-shirt and sweatshirt he had worn the previous night. He put on a blue sock from the floor then searched his room looking for the other one, as if he had ever cared if his socks matched before. After trashing the place, he finally found the matching sock in the underwear drawer of his bureau. Clancy slumped down the stairs and plopped himself on a kitchen chair, looking out the window as if gloom and doom would follow him the rest of his days.

"Well, you're in fine spirits today," Rosie remarked, looking at Clancy's rumpled hair and dirty clothes.

"I hate rain."

"Well, you don't mind taking trail rides in the rain."

"That's different."

"Oh. Well, eat your cereal and let's start on the chores."

"Yahoo," he responded with a scowl.

Rosie sat down beside Clancy and put her hand on his. She had never seen him this down. Not since the year after his dad's death when they had muddled through together, scared, sad, bitter and always worried about money.

"What's up, buddy?"

"Everything." Clancy put his head in his hands. "I can't make sense of anything these days."

"Can you tell me one thing? Maybe I can help."

Clancy looked at his mom. She was still strong and pretty, even though her big, blue eyes had taken on a look of sadness and tension he hadn't noticed before. When Rosie was happy her face glowed, just like his own. That's what people had always said about them. But the glow was gone and it made him sad.

"Mom, why did Dad go back to bull riding when he knew he couldn't keep up with the professional circuit riders? He should have known something bad was going to happen. He always told me how dangerous it was and wished that I hadn't started doing it."

Rosie sighed and put her hands on her cheeks. She looked out the window and watched the pouring rain quickly melt into a light shower. The sun was peering out between dispersing clouds and Rosie quietly wished for a rainbow.

"Clancy, your dad didn't die from bull riding. Not really." She looked hard at her son, breathed in and slowly exhaled. "He had cancer. The doctors tried different treatments but it had gone too far. He knew he had less than a year to live. He didn't want to spend the year lying in bed, knowing you were going to watch him die slowly, taking pain killers that made his brain numb to the outside world. He wanted us to remember him as a bull rider and a man who was trying to do his best with all he had left." Rosie wiped a tear from her cheek, realizing that for all the tears she had cried there were always more waiting, like a well that never runs dry.

Clancy stared at his mother in disbelief, his dark eyes like coals scorched with fire. He clenched his fists and swore. His breath came in shallow puffs as he tried to gain control of the ball of anger and hurt rolling up from his belly.

"Why didn't you tell me?" he burst out, slamming his fists on the table.

"I was going to Clancy." Rosie sobbed. "I just, well, time went on and I didn't know what to do. I didn't know how to tell you. I didn't know if it would make you feel better or worse."

"Mom. Dad's dead. Nothing could make me feel better or worse."

Clancy stood up and started pacing the kitchen like a caged animal. He walked around the table, over and over again, bumping into chairs and punching cabinets. Rosie sat quietly looking out the window, her hands clasped in silent prayer. Clancy knocked the phone off the wall and it clattered to the floor. He and Rosie stared at the dangling wire and listened to the dial tone. Clancy sighed, picked up the phone and put it back on the wall. He sat down next to his mother.

"I'm so sorry, Clancy." Rosie was crying, her head in her hands. "I was so sad and angry. I was scared about how we were going to make it and I just couldn't think clearly about anything."

"Well, I know how that feels." Clancy took his mother's hands in his, tears rolling down his face. "We've done okay, Mom, and we're going to keep moving on and doing what we have to do to be happy, whatever that is."

Rosie looked up at Clancy and wiped her eyes on a napkin. She took a deep breath, trying to regain control of her thoughts and feelings. As difficult as it was to watch Clancy's anger and hurt, she was relieved that she had finally told him the truth.

"You don't like Tom, do you?" Rosie suddenly asked.

"No, not really. But if he makes you happy, then I'll get used to it."

"He's really not the right guy for me." Rosie wiped her eyes again and blew her nose on the napkin. "But, it's slim pickins' around here and I'm not getting any younger and well, I get lonely sometimes, Clance." Rosie sighed. "He does like to talk about himself. He talks more than any man I know." She rolled her eyes and they laughed together.

"Well, that's certainly unusual for men around here," Clancy replied.

"That's because the women do all the yappin' and the men don't have a chance to get a word in edge-wise!"

"It's probably just as well that way," Clancy sighed. "We guys don't have much to say anyway." They both laughed again and started clearing the morning dishes.

The rain had stopped and Rosie's rainbow came out, gently floating over the foothills and mountains, a misty mirage that glowed and faded with the movement of clouds and shadows. Rosie always took the time to watch rainbows because they reminded her of all the thoughts and emotions, experiences and memories, activities and people that came and went in her life. They always seemed to move through her life too fast and yet carry so much meaning. She couldn't hold onto any of them, so she paid careful attention to each one as they quickly passed her in their own moment.

Chapter Twelve

Clancy spent the morning doing chores and then practicing his roping in the ring. Roping events were the only ones he did in the rodeo, but he always ended up in the champion ring for his age group at the end of the day, as part of any team, as well as in the solo events. He used Bandit and Bo, having trained them both in case one went lame. As a young boy, Clancy had been learning to bull ride, like most of his friends. But after his father was killed, Rosie forbade him to ride. She was afraid she would lose him, too.

Clancy was bitter at first but he knew his mother was right. Rosie needed him around to keep the farm maintained and bring in money as he got older. He also knew that the fear of losing a father and a son was too much for his mother to bear. It was difficult for Clancy to watch the other boys bull riding, especially in the big rodeos, but he knew he was doing the right thing.

On the McCulloughs' ranch, Fen was grooming Scoot, getting ready to practice her barrel racing. Scooter loved to be groomed and Fen spent quite a bit of time at it, knowing how much he enjoyed the attention. Besides, he always tried to eat all the grooming tools which slowed down the process. Fen curried his golden coat, massaging certain areas that made him twitch his lip, stretch his neck out and nibble on her shirt buttons for the sheer pleasure of being scratched. She brushed every snarl out of his silky, white mane and tail. Scoot's forelock was long and Fen always braided it so that he could see clearly. Besides, she thought he looked cute that way.

Buck always said that every horse had at least one bad habit. Scooter's only vice was that he liked to eat. He would eat anything whether it was horse food or not. Over time, Scooter had eaten popcorn, fruit tarts, donuts, popsicles, hot dogs and pizza with pepperoni. He had even guzzled orange soda right out of the bottle when someone was nice enough to hold it up so he could suck it down. A long, orange stain down his neck was left as evidence of the snack. Scoot's favorite food was peanut butter on crackers, which took him forever to chew. Fen and Clancy would laugh till their bellies ached, watching him suck the peanut butter off the roof of his mouth.

Scoot was forever sticking his nose into people's pockets for a treat. One time, Scoot stuffed his nose into the pocketbook of a visiting relative and ate her lipstick before anyone noticed. If Fen came to get him without washing her hands from breakfast or lunch, he would lick them until they were gooey and sticky from his saliva. Fen's father chided her for letting him continue such a disgusting and annoying habit, but Buck said that as long as the vice wasn't dangerous or it didn't bother the owner, it was alright to let it be. She liked Buck's advice, taking pleasure in Scooter's appetite.

Hack had two peculiar habits. One was sighing. His barrel would give a big heave and then he would let out a long, soft sigh. Hack would sigh while eating, sigh while being groomed, sigh when he was put in for the night, sigh when he was let out for the day and sigh when Fen came in with a treat. He sighed when another horse pushed him away from the water trough and sighed when he was rolling in the grass. It was quite startling when he sighed with a rider on his back, making them feel as if a large wave was rolling under them. Buck told Fen horses sigh for the same reasons that people do. They're either happy, sad, bored, annoyed or in deep thought. They both agreed that all of those reasons could apply to Hack, except for the one about being in deep thought.

Fen noticed that Hack's sighing had the same effect as yawning, being somewhat contagious. She got a big kick out of watching people catch the disease. When people spent too much time around Hack, they started sighing, too. Sometimes, when Pete came in for dinner, he would sit down, take a deep breath and let out a long sigh. Fen would smile, knowing that Pete had probably just given her horse a nice face rub, massaging behind his ears, under his chin and down his chest, which produced the biggest sighs.

Hack's other odd habit was leaning. Buck had tried to train Hack not to lean because he was so big it was potentially hazardous to people. Pete also complained that Hack's leaning caused the literal downfall of numerous fences, gates, posts and loosely built sheds around the ranch. During his time at the McCulloughs' ranch, Pete had replaced almost every piece of wood in Hack's paddock and roaming range, at one time or another. The minute the horse leaned, his fifteen hundred pounds would pop the nails off that particular leaning spot and Pete would find himself down in the dirt, quickly scrounging around for the loose nails that were dangerous to people, dogs and horses.

If Hack was left on cross ties too long, he often took a nap, leaning his heavy head on the ropes. The wall hooks would suddenly pop out and the horse would crumple to the ground with a resounding, "THUD". Up he'd come, legs splayed out and eyes wide open. He would let out a snort and look around as if to see if anyone had noticed.

"Buck, I've had it with that horse!" Pete complained one day after spending an hour rebuilding a small shed Hack had leaned into and knocked over. "You can train a stallion to dance to country music and bow on command. Can't you please train that darn block of a horse to stand straight on his own four feet? Most horses sleep standing up, for heavens sake! Lord knows those hooves are big enough to hold up the small buildings he takes down! I'm tired of it!"

Fen secretly believed that Buck hadn't tried too hard with the training process. Both she and Buck got a kick out of Pete's frequent trips to the tool shed and, in Fen's mind, she thought Hack even thought it was a bit amusing. Hack would slowly chew and sigh, happy for the company as he listened to Pete groan and sputter, fixing the mangled pieces of the horse's destruction.

But sometimes Hack's habit caused problems for his owner, too. If Fen stopped to talk to someone too long, she would find herself leaning back on him which made Hack lean harder on her. It usually ended up with Fen on the ground and Hack looking down at her as if to say: That's what happens when you only got two feet, cowgirl.

Hack's cowgirl spent most of the day practicing with her equine partners and when she was finished her whole body was exhausted. She had to admit, though, that this practice with Hack went much better than their previous attempts. Fen could almost imagine that she and Hack could at least stay in the arena and not seriously injure anybody during the drill team performance. She sighed as she left the barn at the end of the day, knowing school started tomorrow and her prison sentence would continue for another six weeks. She knew they would fly by with so much to do, but summer vacation couldn't come soon enough.

While Fen's family was eating dinner, Clancy knocked on the door to see if Mack needed anything at the grain or hardware stores. When Clancy was planning a big shopping trip for the next day, he was in the habit of stopping at the McCulloughs' house to see if they needed anything from town. Fen thought it was funny that Clancy often stopped in during dinner hour but, as always, she invited him in to eat.

"Where's your mom?" Clancy asked, taking his boots off at the door as everybody did at Renee's house.

"She's coming home late again," Fen sighed.

"Now that's the price you pay for being smart," Clancy said. "See, I figured it all out a long time ago. I act ignorant to keep people's expectations low. It takes less work."

"Well, Clancy," Pete said. "If that's what you're aimin' for, ya hit the target!"

They all laughed knowing that, although Clancy wasn't a great student at school, he was smarter than any boy his age when it came to what was meaningful in his life. He was a respected hunter and fisherman. He was more knowledgeable about the native plants and animals than any trained biologist and he knew how to survive in the woods with just an ax. He could build a barn, fix a fence, repair a tractor and handle the business of a ranch. He knew how to get along with people and how to earn respect. That's all he ever wanted, anyway.

As Clancy joined them at the table, Mack, Pete and Frank went back to talking about the price of hay. Fen started petting Boss who was sitting by her chair. She happened to look down at Clancy's feet.

"How come you have matching socks on, Clancy?"

The men stopped talking and shifted to look at the boy's feet. Clancy looked down at his two blue socks and wiggled his toes.

"Uh, I don't know. I guess I just got lucky."

Mack and Pete grinned at each other. Mack thought only a woman would notice what color socks a person was wearing, but Pete had to admit he was impressed that Clancy had the same color on. At Renee's house people did get the chance to check it out. Pete had noticed that Rosie's socks always matched but Clancy had some issues with that. He was glad that Rosie didn't care enough to make her son change his own socks.

Fen and Clancy told the men about seeing the cougar and the wild horses the night before. The men agreed the kids should keep the sighting to themselves, just in case there were ranchers around looking for horses.

"But there are too many domestic horses around that need training," Fen said. "Our paddocks are chockfull. Why would someone want to take the wild ones?"

"It's just the kind of thing that's best kept to yourself. That's all," Mack said, sternly, glancing at Pete who looked equally concerned.

"So, how's your mom, Clancy?" Mack asked, obviously trying to change the subject.

"She's okay, I guess." Clancy sighed. "She's out with that guy, Tom, again."

"Really?" Pete asked, a bit too loudly.

Mack glanced at Pete and took a drink of milk. Mack looked at Fen who rolled her eyes, frowned and glared at Pete. Pete stabbed at a piece of meat on his plate like it was a moving target and the only thing on his plate worth eating.

"Do you like him, Clancy?" Pete asked.

"Not much. He talks too much. And he brings her dumb presents she doesn't want. I think she's just lonely, ya know?"

Fen looked at Pete and he returned her look. She fluttered her eyelashes at him. Pete chewed the piece of meat slowly and wiped his mouth with a napkin.

"She probably is lonely," Pete said, ignoring Fen's look. "I wouldn't know about that. I like being alone, as long as I got my buddy, Phoenix, here." Pete reached down and gave the big, fluffy dog a scratch behind the ears. "Well, I've had enough," Pete said, getting up with his plate still half full.

He trudged to the kitchen and bumped the swinging door open with his foot, forgetting that Renee asked everyone to use their hip to avoid marking up the old, but finely finished wood. Mack winked at Fen and she smiled back. They both noticed that Pete had suddenly lost his appetite after the news about Rosie being out with Tom.

Pete came out of the kitchen. "I think I'll take a short trail ride before hittin' the sack." He went to the front door and put his boots on, one over a grey sock and one over a green one.

"I'd better be getting home, too," Clancy said. "I still have homework to do."

"I thought that was due the day after vacation started?" Fen asked.

"Yeah, well, I charmed Ms. Cavenaugh into an extension." Clancy winked and headed to the kitchen with his plate. Frank followed Clancy and they both left the house out the kitchen door. Fen and her father laughed as soon as they were alone.

"I think Pete wants something more than a shaggy wolf dog to keep him company. What do you think, my dear?" Mack asked, grinning and wiggling his eyebrows up and down, making Fen giggle again.

"I think he needs a swift kick in the pants and an invitation from one Rosie Clark 'cause it ain't gonna happen any other way!" Fen responded in a mock huff.

They both laughed and went to the kitchen to share a box of cookies. When Renee wasn't home they could get away with such gluttony, at least until she found the empty box that had been purchased just two days before.

Chapter Thirteen

School reopened the last week of April and the month of May seemed to fly by. The new stallion continued to stay in the paddock out front, still not able to socialize with the other horses. Buck worked with him every day and seemed to be making some progress. Between doing her homework and chores and practicing with Hack and Scoot, Fen took every minute she could to watch Buck work with the wild horse.

Fen noticed that Frank spent quite a bit of time watching Buck and Crescent, too. She wondered if maybe he was becoming interested in learning natural horsemanship. She wanted it to be true, but Fen had strong suspicions that Frank's intentions were not good. When Fen was with Frank, she always had a creepy crawly feeling down her spine and a flippy floppy feeling in her belly. It made her suspicious of what might be on his mind and made her wary of his actions.

On the one hand, Renee had told her daughter how important it was not to judge people too quickly or too harshly. "A good judge always gets the facts before passing sentence on someone. You need the facts to know if the person is guilty or innocent. Without real evidence against someone, it's not fair to assume something that might not be true, come to wrong conclusions or be critical." Fen knew that she, herself, was guilty of passing judgment on people too soon.

On the other hand, Fen recalled what Rosie had told her about intuition. "When you get a flip flop feeling in your stomach and the creepy crawlies down your spine, you better pay attention. It's your intuition telling you that something or someone isn't right." Fen decided that if an opportunity arose, she would take the chance to test her gut feelings about Frank's intentions. That opportunity came about one evening, just as Buck was getting ready to go home. Fen heard him talking with her father about Crescent.

"I'm making progress with that stallion, Mack, but I just don't have enough time to spend with him. I've got all the other horses to work with and chores to do. It's hard to keep his ground manners maintained and find the time to teach him the next skills he needs to be ridden. I haven't even tried putting a saddle on him yet."

"Maybe Frank could work with him some," Fen suggested. "He's been watching you quite a bit. Maybe you could give him some training tips to practice with Crescent on days when you're too busy or can't be here."

Mack and Buck looked at Fen in surprise. They both knew how much she hated Frank. Buck was immediately suspicious of Fen's suggestion, but wasn't about to question her in front of Mack.

"What do you think, Buck?" Mack asked.

"Well, we've been talking about it some and he has watched me work with the horses. We could ask him and see what he thinks."

"Will do," said Mack. "I'll try to keep an eye on the situation for awhile to see that it goes alright."

"See you all on Monday then," Buck said.

Mack talked to Frank that night. Frank agreed to add training sessions with Crescent into his schedule on the weekends, as long as he was paid the same wages that Buck was getting. Mack reluctantly agreed, knowing that he wasn't getting the same quality of horsemanship. He was having a hard time convincing himself that it would be good for the horse to be left to Frank's training, even if it was only for the two days each week when Buck was gone. It was even more difficult justifying the arrangement to Renee. But they both knew that the horse would have to be put down if he didn't become trainable or at least more manageable and soon.

Their daughter had her own reservations about Frank working with Crescent, even though it had been her idea. Fen watched the ranch hand and the horse work together the next Saturday and realized that Frank really hadn't learned much from Buck. He was having a hard time controlling the horse and Fen could tell that Crescent definitely didn't trust the man at the end of the longe line. Frank wasn't Buck and Fen could tell that the horse wasn't happy about the change of hands.

After that first session, Fen noticed that Frank took Crescent to the indoor arena for training, rather than keeping him in the front paddock. With all of her homework and chores to do, as well as practicing with Scoot and Hack for the rodeo, Fen didn't have time to watch Frank work with the horse. She worried about Crescent and the time spent alone with Frank. All she could do was check on the horse every morning, leave a carrot in his feeding trough each afternoon and hope he would learn to trust someone.

Sometimes, Fen just stood and watched Crescent move in his paddock, alone with his own thoughts. He was such a beautiful animal. His dark, gleaming coat was sleek, yet rippling with muscles. The long, silky, black locks of his mane and tail floated as he loped in a steady rhythm, as if moving to music only he could hear. The stallion looked like he came from another country far away, an exotic island where wild horses had never seen a human.

It was early evening. Fen had finished her chores and was leaning against the fence watching the stallion. Usually when she stopped to watch the horse, he would prance around, pace the fence at a fast trot, paw at the ground with his head down or stand at the far corner of the paddock with his back to Fen, his tail swishing in a steady rhythm. But this time, Crescent stood in the middle of the pen facing Fen. He was still and quiet. His body was calm but his eyes were bright. He was watching her watch him. Fen realized she had pulled a carrot from her pocket and had been absentmindedly tapping it on the fence post. The horse's eyes were moving from the girl's face to the carrot. Fen smiled and held the carrot out, hoping the horse would give in to temptation and approach.

Suddenly, the front door of the house slammed, startling Fen. She looked around to see her mother walking across the driveway. Fen waved to Renee, then quickly looked back at Crescent, only to watch the horse walk away to the far corner of the paddock and stare out across the field. Fen hated to have the private moment with Crescent end, but she was glad to see her mother had come home early from work.

Renee was dressed in her farm clothes, obviously ready to help with the evening chores, which was unusual because she usually worked late on Friday nights. Fen was excited to think she might have her mother home for the whole weekend. Maybe she would have time to give Fen tips on the drill team routine. She needed every piece of advice she could get and her mother was a good rider.

"Mom!" Fen called. "What are you doing home so early and wearing those clothes? I haven't seen you in jeans for months, maybe years!"

"Hey! I've mucked some stalls in the past couple of years, just not enough. I'll explain at dinner. Right now we have work to do, girl!"

Fen drove the tractor while her mother and Pete mucked out the stalls. What a luxury, Fen thought! The job got done in half the time it usually took and it was a lot more fun for all of them. It reminded Fen of the old adage Rosie often repeated: "Many hands make light work".

While the family was eating dinner, Renee announced that she was going to cut back on her hours at the law firm. They all applauded and let out cries of delight. The unexpected burst of excitement upset Alex, so everyone got quiet while Fen quietly explained to him that their mom was going to be home more. That was enough to help Alex return to eating and listening.

"I'm tired of putting my job before my family," Renee said. "I can help get chores done around the ranch and spend more time with my two lovely children! Besides, I haven't ridden my beautiful horse in two months. I'm going to lose my touch and she's going to get fat!" Renee winked at Fen.

Renee had come from the east. She hadn't been around horses before visiting relatives in Montana and meeting Mack at a rodeo. After they were married, Mack took Renee to the race track to watch a horse race as part of their honeymoon. She had watched races on television, but was thrilled to be able to see one in the stands. Just for fun, she bet money on a beautiful bay named Sir Prize. The horse had come in dead last.

After the final race, Renee and Mack went down to the track to get a closer look at the horses and riders. As they were watching, a short, fat man loaded some of the horses onto a big cattle car. One of them was Sir Prize.

"She's so beautiful," Renee said, watching the horse walk up the ramp, her tall, glossy body moving smoothly and lightly as if she weighed no more than a feather.

"Well, lady, she ain't gonna be so beautiful when she hits the meat line," the man said.

"What? What meat line?" Renee asked in horror.

"If they don't come close enough to winning in this sport, they end up going to auction and if they don't get sold, well then," he paused, suddenly realizing that he didn't want to upset the pretty, young lady.

"No!" Renee exclaimed. "Why? Why can't they keep her for some other purpose, like pleasure riding?"

"These guys are in the racing business, not the pleasure business. A horse loses too many races, sometimes they end up being put down."

"That's horrible!"

"Lady, horses are too expensive to just keep around. The hay, the grain, the vet bills, hiring someone to exercise them, boarding them . . ." his voice trailed off. "It all costs too much. It's just the way it is for these animals."

"Well, not for this animal. I want her! I'll take her! I'll pay you," Renee exclaimed, opening her purse.

"Uh, huh. And I suppose you got a truck and trailer to get her home?" The guy looked at Renee with cocked eyebrows and a small smile.

Mack looked at his new wife and the horse. "We'll find one. Bring that horse back down off the trailer. How much you want for her?"

"Nothin'." The man chuckled. "You better save your money to haul this loser home."

Mack and Renee purchased a truck and a trailer that day and brought Sir Prize home. She turned out to fit her name, being a winner in Renee's eyes. She was fast, smooth, steady and the sweetest animal ever to walk the Earth. At least that's what Renee always said about her and no one could or would disagree with her. Of course people weren't in the habit of disagreeing with Renee about much of anything.

Sir Prize was the beginning of the McCullough Ranch which had grown and prospered over the years. The horse was getting older, but was still a winner in Fen's eyes. She loved watching her mother ride Sir Prize through the fields of tall grasses and wildflowers that surrounded their home. They were both elegant, graceful, strong and full of spirit. Fen always loved hearing the story of Sir Prize and she was proud of her mother for seeing all that was good in the horse that had come in last.

When Renee came home from work, she often took a quick ride on Sir Prize before starting chores. Fen loved Renee's new schedule. She was so glad to leave school knowing that her mother would already be home, gardening, playing with Alex, baking or just puttering around the ranch doing whatever needed to get done. When Fen saw Clancy in the hallway at school she told him about her mother's shorter work days.

"That's great, Fen. You guys can do more trail riding together. She's a good rider. Maybe she would even get back into the rodeo scene."

"Oh, I doubt that. She enjoys watching all of us without worrying about preparing for competition herself. By the way, can you come over this weekend and help me with Hack? He's having a little trouble getting this drill team routine through his thick skull."

"I'd like to, Fen, but I'm really busy. Mom needs me all day Saturday and, well, I have to be at the Hidden Valley Ranch on Sunday." Clancy looked away to avoid Fen's reaction.

"Hidden Valley? Isn't that Clara Perkins' place?" Fen asked, her voice tentative.

"Yeah. Mr. Perkins is giving me big money to teach his daughter to barrel race. She wants to be ready for the rodeo in June."

"What?" Fen exclaimed, indignantly. "You're teaching Miss Priss to ride the barrels? Clancy, how could you?"

"Mom and I need the money, Fen, and it's a good way to get a reference so maybe I can get other instructing jobs."

"But, but, it's not fair! I've worked so hard to get the blue in this rodeo. I don't need more competition!"

"Actually, Fen, the competition will be good for you. It'll give you the chance to really hone your skills. You know you're the best barrel racer around, as well as the youngest. Besides, she can't get that good in two months. Although, I have to say, she's a good rider and pretty persistent."

"Really?" Fen said, sarcastically. "And her looks have nothing to do with your sudden interest in barrel racing instruction?"

"Hey, I can't help it if she's kind of pretty. Besides, she's not my type with all that hair gel and make-up. How's a guy supposed to kiss a girl when she's got lipstick on without getting it all over? Not to mention tasting the stuff." Clancy grimaced. "Yuck."

"You are such a traitor, Clancy!" Fen turned her back and stalked off. Her ponytail tossed from side to side as her long strides increased into a jog.

"Oh, boy. I knew she'd be mad, but calling me a traitor is fightin' words." Clancy sighed as he watched Fen disappear around the corner to the next hallway. "This is why men became cowboys. It was much easier than staying home with their woman. And I always thought it was the kids that drove them out to wander the range."

After school Clancy sat in his truck waiting for Fen. He knew he was lucky to be able to drive before reaching the legal driving age. After his father died Clancy had convinced the Department of Motor Vehicles that he needed the independence to be able to get to school and work. Besides, he had been driving every kind of vehicle, from dirt bikes to trucks, since he was six years old. Being tall gave him an advantage, too, especially when it came to reaching pedals and seeing over steering wheels.

Clancy turned on the radio and hummed to the country western tune. He knew the words but he thought it sounded dorky to sing along. Fen finally emerged from the school building but, without looking towards Clancy's usual parking space, she hopped on the bus.

"Holy cow. She is mad. She hates taking the bus."

His relationship with Fen had always been simple, like with his male friends. He reminded himself that he had made a vow to avoid girls, just for this reason. They were confusing and complicated and he had no one to talk to about their mysterious behavior.

"Well, I guess I'll have to talk to Mom about this one. She knows Fen better than anyone, besides me."

Clancy started up the truck and slowly pulled out onto the main road. He opened the window, letting the breeze blow in and ruffle his hair. He turned the volume on the radio way up and started singing at the top of his voice, hoping to drown out his own thoughts.

Chapter Fourteen

Fen got off the bus and dragged her backpack into the kitchen. She was so angry she could spit. Alex was still at school and the house was quiet. She made herself a peanut butter, cheese, tuna and potato chip sandwich and sat on the porch swing.

"How can he do this to me?" Fen griped for the hundredth time since she had talked to Clancy earlier in the day.

But Fen knew the reason Clancy had taken the job at Hidden Valley Ranch and she felt badly that she had made him say it out loud. Clancy was embarrassed about the financial situation that he and his mom were in and he was the only one who could pull them out of debt. Rosie was always working, besides getting paid for taking care of Alex, but she never seemed to earn enough money to pay all the bills. She hadn't finished high school, getting married and staying home with Clancy as he was growing up, so it was difficult to find a good paying job in their small town.

Even though Fen understood Clancy's situation, she still resented his time with Clara. She worried that he would be too busy with "Miss Priss" that he wouldn't have time to spend with Fen, particularly if word got out about his good instructing skills. But Fen knew her feelings were selfish ones and she wasn't being fair to Clancy. In fact, she was proud of his skills and knew it would make life much better for him and Rosie if he could get jobs training horses and their riders. Fen had to admit that there was more to it than all of that. She carried a small feeling of jealousy about Clancy spending time with Clara. After all, he had admitted Clara was pretty.

"Oh, heck!" she exclaimed. "This is exactly why I don't like boys. They are distracting and frustrating."

But it had never seemed that way with Clancy before. Fen suddenly realized that she had never really thought of him as a boy. He was just her friend and a lot more fun than the girls she knew. His comment about kissing had surprised her. She had never imagined Clancy kissing anyone. Fen didn't like to think that Clancy might have a life separate from her own that he didn't share with her. She sighed, realizing that there were some things she didn't know about her best friend.

Renee pulled into the driveway with Alex in the backseat, having picked him up from Creative Learning School on her way home from work. Fen was happy to see her mom and Alex. Sometimes a little distraction from her own problems was a good thing. When Fen was younger, she always went to her mother for help and advice. But since Renee had started working more hours, Fen felt badly about taking up her mother's time when she was at home.

Whenever Fen had a problem too big to solve by herself and her mother seemed too busy to listen, she often went to Rosie for advice. Rosie would listen, they would talk about the issue and sometimes come up with a solution to the problem. At the very least, Fen would feel better about the situation, just having talked about it and listened to Rosie's ideas.

Rosie was full of what she called her "life lessons" and Fen could recite most of them. When an argument couldn't be resolved or a problem fixed, Rosie would usually end the conversation with a plate of cookies, a glass of cold milk and two of her favorite sayings rolled into one: "It sounds like it's time to agree to disagree and let sleeping dogs alone." Fen knew it really meant that sometimes it was better to just let things go.

During one of their conversations, Rosie had told Fen a life lesson the girl would never forget. "Honey, whatever you do, never go to bed angry at someone, including yourself. It makes you toss and turn all night and wake up grumpy at the world. You can't see anything straight and clear if you're mad at the world. So do what you gotta do to make things right before you put your head on that pillow."

After dinner, Fen finished her homework, took a shower and got into pajamas. She sat on her bed and picked up the phone. Not really sure what she was going to say, she punched in Clancy's number and chewed on her fingernails.

"Good evening!" Rosie's chipper voice answered.

"Hi, Rosie. It's me, Fen."

"No kidding. Boy, am I glad you called."

Fen smiled. "Is Clancy there?"

"Yes. As a matter of fact, he's right here hanging his head over a huge pile of cookies with a gallon of milk at the ready. I hope you're going to talk to the boy."

"Yes, ma'am," Fen replied, almost seeing the smile on Rosie's face.

Fen waited until she could hear Clancy breathing into the phone. "Clancy, I'm sorry about today. I shouldn't have said what I did. I understand what you need to do. I was just being selfish."

"It's okay, Fen. I get where you're coming from. I'm sorry it has to be this way."

"Me, too. Well, as long as we're still friends."

"Hey, we've been madder at each other than this before and gotten over it. We'll always be friends, Fen. Besides, this job I have at the

Perkins' ranch might turn into an interesting situation for both of us, if my instincts are right."

"What do you mean?"

"Well, I'm hearing some pretty strange conversations around that place and Miss Priss Clara likes to talk." Clancy rolled his eyes at his mother who smiled and left the room.

"Really? What about?"

"We'll talk tomorrow. It's just gonna make you madder and you know what my mom says about going to bed mad."

"Oh, boy. I can't wait to hear," Fen said, sarcastically, as if her life needed to get more complicated.

"So, am I picking you up or do you want to take the bus again?" Clancy couldn't help teasing Fen to lighten up the conversation.

"Yes, Mister Smart Aleck. I would love a ride."

"See ya tomorrow, then. And Fen, thanks for calling. Now I don't have to eat all these cookies and end up on the floor, moaning about a stomachache and getting no sympathy from Mom, not to mention getting a bad case of pimples."

"No problem. Although, maybe Miss Priss wouldn't like you so much if you suddenly sprouted a pizza face."

"I don't know. She's pretty hot on my tail." Clancy smiled into the phone. "Why, just the other day . . . ."

"Alright, alright," Fen interrupted. "I don't want to hear it! But I do want to hear about what's going on at the Perkins' place. See ya tomorrow, lover boy."

The two friends hung up knowing they were going to get a good night's sleep, their argument over and their friendship strong. What they didn't know was that problems grow like pea plants and it would take more than their friendship to solve the ones already sprouting, destined to grow into vines stronger and thicker than the two friends could weed out together.

Chapter fifteen

It was the last week of May and the weather had turned warm, the sun shining everyday across the huge Montana sky. Mack had left on Wednesday for a week on the road. He had taken a trailer full of horses that were well trained and ready to sell to their new owners, who had been waiting months for their horses to arrive. They knew it would be well worth the wait. They had paid good money for the animals, but none were better trained and easier to get along with than the ones from Mack McCullough's ranch. The horses would do anything their rider asked and always showed professional character in the arena and a calm temperament on the trail.

Friday afternoon, Renee asked Fen and Alex if they'd like to go to town to get an early dinner at Bob's Grill, a take-out diner where customers could sit and eat their meal by a swiftly running river and watch kayakers challenge the current. By going to eat early, they would miss the dinner crowd which Alex didn't like. Renee promised Alex he would still have time to watch a movie at home before going to bed, a ritual he couldn't miss. The three of them piled into the jeep and headed for town. As they sat at a picnic table by the river, eating their bison burgers and thick, greasy French fries, they saw Clancy coming across the street.

"Hey, you guys!" Clancy called. "Fancy meeting you here."

"Dad's away for the week selling horses, so Mom suggested we go out for a treat," Fen replied, her mouth stuffed with fries and ketchup.

"Maybe I'll get an ice cream. I've got to be home for dinner soon, but one little three-scooper won't ruin my appetite." Clancy went to the take-out window and ordered a cone with "peanut butter bang", "peach blast" and maple walnut ice cream all piled onto a waffle cone.

"Clancy," Renee said, looking at his snack. "That is disgusting."

"No," he said. "It's original, creative and adventuresome, just like me!" He proudly took a big lick, sampling each flavor in one mouthful. "Besides, I always order this 'cause I know I'll like it."

Fen and Renee just looked at each other and stuck their tongues out. Alex mimicked them and then started breaking his French fries into pieces. Putting a piece into his mouth he looked at the river and watched a leaf being carried by the current.

"What's wrong with my choice of ice cream?" Clancy exclaimed. "Like my mom says: 'Don't yuck somebody's yum'." He looked away as though he were insulted. "Hey. Isn't that Frank, your ranch hand, talking with one of Mr. Perkins' hands?"

Renee and Fen followed Clancy's gaze. Across the street, the two men were talking, their heads together in a conspiratorial way. One laughed and took a long drag from his cigarette. Frank spat on the street then wiped the back of his hand across his mouth.

"I've seen Frank in town quite often, talking with Perkins' ranch hands," Renee said with a frown. "I'm in town everyday. I know a lot of people, see some things I shouldn't and hear too much gossip. But something is definitely up with Frank. I just haven't figured out what." She took a sip of her iced tea and sighed.

"It's funny you should mention that, Mrs. McCullough, because I've seen Frank at the Perkins' ranch, too." Clancy didn't look at Fen, knowing she was scowling at him.

"What are you thinking?" Fen asked, giving Alex a French fry. She hoped he would eat it whole this time, without breaking it into three even pieces as he always did.

"I don't know. But I do know the place is odd. They have too many ranch hands and not enough horses. They can't seem to sell the ones they have, probably because they aren't trained well. I wouldn't get on some of those horses, they're so wound up. And you know me. I'd ride a bull if I could."

Clancy stopped licking his cone and they all sat in silence, waiting for the awkward moment to pass. Fen quickly looked down after catching Clancy's expression, embarrassment and a bit of resentment passing quickly across his face. But Renee's thoughts had already moved on to solving the puzzle. She drummed her fingers on the table, brow furrowed and jaw twitching, mannerisms that Fen had come to recognize as her mother in deep thought.

"When I am looking at a case that comes across my desk in the law office, I do the same thing each time. I put the events of the crime in chronological order to see if anything fits. Sometimes a series of events proves to be just a set of coincidences, but sometimes it leads me to the right conclusion. So let's start with Frank, since he is the most recent addition to our happy family. Besides, none of us like him so he makes a great suspect." She smiled at the kids and wiggled her eyebrows.

"Frank came looking for a job about, um, four months ago," Fen said.

"Actually, it was five months ago," Renee replied, being particular about details. "It was just when your father, Buck and Pete were exhausted and needed another ranch hand. Mack had mentioned it to several people in town as well as the local ranchers, in case they had too many men on their payroll. So," Renee continued, putting her finger in the air, "we have point of supposition number one. Frank showed up when he probably knew Mack was desperate for workers and wouldn't ask for references."

"Point of suppa what?" Clancy asked, scratching his head.

"Point of supposition," Fen responded. "It's just an observation or thought that might lead you to a fact. When you make a supposition, it helps you to ask questions and get information to prove or disprove your observations or ideas. Then the supposition turns into a relevant fact or just a dead end and you have to start over again."

Clancy had been looking at Fen with his mouth open, a rainbow of ice cream melting down his fingers and onto the table. "No wonder you get "A"s in school all the time." He wiped his hand on his jeans and continued slurping on the cone. "Well, I've seen Frank and Perkins' ranch hands talking and so have you, Mrs. McCullough," Clancy added.

"Point of supposition number two." Renee put up a second finger. "Frank works at a successful ranch, meaning ours. He is frequently seen talking with ranch hands who work at a business that is going under fast, meaning Perkins' place." Renee glanced at Clancy's face to make sure he was following her line of thinking. She knew Fen would already be two steps ahead.

"I get it!" Fen finished Renee's chain of thought. "Maybe Frank's being paid by Perkins to get information from our place! It's like when one company sends a spy to work at a competing company to find out how to improve their business and get more customers." Fen looked at her mother and then at Clancy. "We know they need horses and they need to get the ones they have better trained," Fen continued, taking another bite of her burger. "The hands that Perkins hires only know the old ways of 'breaking' a horse which most people don't like anymore."

"Point of supposition number three is more complicated because we have more possibilities," Renee said. "Is Perkins paying Frank to work at our place to learn how to run a successful ranching operation? Is Frank trying to learn where Mack gets his horses? Did Frank get hired on with us to learn the natural horsemanship techniques so he can start training Perkins' horses? Or did he come for some other reason?"

"I don't think he has ever asked Buck to teach him," Fen said. "He does watch Buck sometimes, but after watching Frank with Crescent it's obvious he hasn't learned much." Fen shook her head, remembering the beautiful stallion that wasn't learning as fast as he should.

"So what could Frank be getting out of his job at our ranch?" Renee queried.

"Well, if he's watching Buck to learn about natural horsemanship, Perkins hasn't gotten his money's worth. The ranch is still failing," Clancy muttered between bites of his cone.

"Yikes. You sure ate that fast," Fen said, watching Clancy pop the last piece of cone into his mouth.

"Hey. I'm a working man," Clancy said, proudly. "I need my protein. By the way, do you think Alex is going to eat all those fries?"

"No," Renee laughed. "Go ahead and help yourself. It would take Alex till breakfast to consume all of those fries, the way he eats them."

"So if it's not about training techniques, what information would Frank or Perkins want?" Fen asked. Suddenly, she stopped chewing and looked at Clancy and then her mother. Renee returned her stare, knowing what Fen was thinking.

"What?" Clancy asked, looking at the two females sitting across from him. "What am I missing here that you two brilliant minds have obviously figured out?"

"It is about getting horses!" Fen exclaimed. "What do my father, Buck and Pete know that other ranchers don't even pay attention to?" Fen asked, her voice raised and tense. "What did we tell Dad and Pete about and they made a point of telling us to keep the information to ourselves?" Fen stared at Clancy and he stopped eating.

"Holy horses," Clancy said. "And Frank was there when we were talking about it!" Clancy smacked his sticky hand on his forehead.

"Frank is trying to find out where the wild herds are so they can corral them and sell them. But who's going to buy a wild horse that isn't trained? Perkins needs a trainer."

"There are other natural horsemanship trainers around, Clancy," Renee replied. "In fact, I just did the legal work for a young couple that recently moved to town and bought a house. The husband mentioned that he was a trainer and looking for work. Or Perkins could try to get Buck to work for him by offering more money than Mack is paying. Perkins must have a wad of cash somewhere to be paying ranch hands who aren't working. I heard he made a bunch of money in Kentucky with his dressage business."

"Well," Fen remarked stiffly. "Clara seems to have all the newest clothes and accessories any girl would want, except me, of course." She glanced at Clancy who smiled and gave her a wink.

"I can keep my eyes and ears open at the Perkins' place and see if I can get more information. If Frank can do it, so can I. A spy for a spy!" Clancy laughed at his own pun.

Fen and Renee stared at Clancy then looked at each other. They rolled their eyes and smirked. They were both surprised that Clancy had come up with the pun so quickly and they thought it was pretty amusing, but, just for fun, they weren't going to let Clancy know that.

"What?" Clancy looked miffed. "You know, like 'an eye for an eye', only I made it, a spy for a spy! Pretty clever, huh?"

Fen and Renee looked at Clancy with straight faces. "We got it, Ace," Fen said, sarcastically, throwing a fry at her friend.

"Hey, I thought it was pretty good for, ya know, something that just popped up off the top of my head." Clancy sighed. "No one appreciates my humor. Anyway, Fen and I should take a trail ride soon and make sure the wild herd is still there. Perkins has the perfect place to hide those horses if he's nabbed them already. It's not called Hidden Valley Ranch for nothin'."

"The mare and her foal and the stallion," Fen groaned. "All those beautiful horses could already be corralled."

"Let's think positively, Fen," Renee said. "I'll alert Mack, Pete and Buck to what Frank might be up to. Unfortunately, as they say in my business, it's all speculation and we have no evidence to prove anything."

"Clancy and I are pretty good at sniffing things out," Fen said, staring hard at Clancy.

He knew that look. He had seen it too many times before. Not only was a trail ride in their near future to find the wild herd, but a trip to Perkins' ranch, unseen, was the next obvious move. He wasn't even going to think about the trouble he could get into with his mom or the law. But Renee was a lawyer and they were only kids, after all. She should be able to bail them out of any legal trouble.

More intimidating than his mom or jail, was the distinct possibility that they might end up looking down the barrel of a shotgun at Perkins' ranch. But for Clancy, life wasn't life without adventure and all the more fun with Fen riding shotgun. He smiled and thought about sharing his second pun of the day with Fen, but since she hadn't appreciated his first attempt at humor he wasn't going to take the chance of getting shot down again.

"Man, I'm getting pretty good at this word play thing. Too bad nobody else appreciates it," he muttered to himself as he walked away from Bob's Grill.

Clancy stuffed his sticky hands into jean pockets, gritty with hay. A pocketknife fell neatly into his palm. He was reminded of his father's frequently made comment: "A real man always carries a pocketknife." Clancy wondered what it would really take to become a man in his father's eyes. He would never get the chance to ask him, but Clancy knew it must take more than what somebody carried in his pocket.

Chapter Sixteen

On Saturday morning Fen told her mother that she would watch Alex so Renee could do something on her own. Fen knew that it had been a long time since her mother had a day to herself without having to think about work, the ranch and her children.

"Between your office, housework and us, you haven't done so many things you like to do, like go for a trail ride, take a swim in the pond, bake bread, whatever. So today is your day to do what you'd like!" Fen smiled at her mother and took a spoonful of cereal.

"Well, it would be nice to take a dip in the pond, take Sir Prize for a hack and bake some of my famous oatmeal bread, which I haven't been able to do in a long time," Renee said, smiling at her daughter. "Thank you! And you will both be rewarded with freshly baked bread smothered in butter and honey." Renee abruptly crossed her arms and frowned at Fen. "I am suddenly suspicious that giving me the opportunity to do something on my own was really a ploy to get me to bake bread. But I will ignore your selfish intentions and enjoy the time I am being given by my sneaky daughter." Renee smiled, putting her hands on her hips. "You should consider becoming a lawyer someday, having learned the art of getting what you want while making the other person feel as if you are doing them a favor!"

"I deny any selfish motivations or intentions!" Fen declared, closing her eyes and sticking her nose up. "And I am insulted by your unfair accusations of being sneaky or manipulative!" Fen glared at her mother and huffed in pretend annoyance. She finished her breakfast by putting the bowl to her lips and slurping down the remnants of milk and cereal. "Besides, I am going to be a horse trainer and not have to sit in an office and solve other people's problems when I have enough of my own."

"Apparently, that last statement is true," Renee said, under her breath. "Besides, my dear, lawyers don't suck on cereal bowls and put their dirty socks on the kitchen table, like cowboys do." She handed Fen a pair of mismatched, but equally dirty socks.

"They're not dirty! I've only worn them for a week!" Fen grabbed the socks. "Come on, Alex, things can only get worse around here if we stay much longer. Next thing, she'll ask me to do the laundry."

Fen took Alex to collect eggs, clean the chicken coop, feed the goats and pigs and watch the horses in the pasture. Alex liked to walk through the fields and pet each horse, saying their names, colors and breeds. Before he and Fen had left the kitchen, he had taken two apples out of the basket on the table. He had cut one green apple and one red apple into small pieces and put them in a bag to carry.

As they walked through the field, Alex had to stuff the bag inside his shirt so that the horses wouldn't get the apples. Unfortunately, the horses' sense of smell was too good not to detect the freshly cut fruit. Fen laughed as the herd followed them around the pasture. Brother and sister had to dodge and weave to avoid the eager animals. Periodically, Fen would turn around and throw her arms up, gently shooing the horses away.

Renee laughed, too, looking out the kitchen window as she watched the line of eager horses, jostling for better position for the apples. It looked like a sloppy parade, led by children who did not like this game of follow the leader. This is what she had missed, she thought to herself, these two years of being the smart lawyer lady. She was still that lady, part-time, but she was happier spending time at home with her family. Fen and Alex seemed more relaxed and cheerful, too.

After they had made their rounds, Fen headed to the house thinking that Alex might want a snack. She thought Alex had brought the apples for himself or the horses, so she was a little surprised to see that he was still carrying the bag. But instead of heading for the house, Alex was taking a detour to the back paddock where Crescent had been moved. There were three horses in the adjacent paddock because Buck wanted to get the stallion used to being with other horses. This was a safe and easy way to start the process of having Crescent join a herd.

Fen followed Alex around the big barn towards Crescent's paddock. She became concerned and trotted to catch up with him. She remembered her father's words that under no circumstances were they to approach the horse. But Alex walked calmly and steadily to the paddock fence and waited for Fen to catch up. The stallion, who had been standing on the far side of the paddock looking out over the fields, turned and walked towards the boy. Fen reached the fence and pulled Alex back.

"No, Alex. That horse is beautiful, but he's still dangerous. You can't get too close."

Alex put his arms up, his sign to be lifted. Fen wasn't sure what to do. Alex was so dependent upon following a routine and this seemed to be part of some ritual he had. Fen picked up her brother so he was at chin level with the top board of the fence. He opened his bag, pulled out a piece of apple and placed it on the board. He pulled out another piece of apple and placed it farther along the board. Alex repeated the process until all the apple chunks were on the fence, carefully placed in a pattern of red, green, red, green, all the way down the line.

The stallion waited for Alex to be finished then walked over and began eating each chunk of apple. He chewed slowly, swallowing each piece before he passed on to the next one. Fen had to laugh. Crescent ate just the way Alex did! She wondered how much he and Alex had in common, besides their eating habits and their instinct to fear what they didn't know.

When the horse had eaten each piece, Alex held out his hand. Fen knew she shouldn't let him do it, but she couldn't help herself. Somehow she felt that Alex had created some kind of bond with the horse and he would be safe. She walked Alex up to the fence and Crescent put his head over the board and nickered. Alex stroked the horse's face and ears and long neck. He brushed his fingers through the stallion's forelock and mane and then smelled his hand, closing his eyes and smiling. Fen had done that many times herself, loving the touch and smell of a horse. Finally, Fen put Alex down and pulled him away from the paddock. The horse stayed where he was and watched the girl and her brother walk around the barn and out of sight.

Fen was amazed at what she had just seen. This was a different horse than Buck, Frank and her father knew. It was clear that Alex had done this many times before, probably every day of the work week when her mother was at work and Rosie and Alex were alone. Fen wasn't usually good at keeping secrets. She was really being tested this week, not being able to talk about the wild herd and now, vowing to keep Rosie's secret, too. It would have to be up to Rosie to admit that she had gone against Mack's rules to let Alex near the horse. It occurred to Fen that this secret could be used to defend the horse's character, if and when it came down to deciding whether Buck could train him or not.

Fen knew that her father would only keep a horse so long before letting it go, saying it was not trainable. He couldn't afford Buck's time to be spent on just one horse. Alex's relationship with the horse proved that Crescent was not only trainable, but could become a good-natured stallion. Fen prayed Buck could bring the horse around soon so that Rosie wouldn't be compelled to tell Mack what she and Alex had been doing, against his orders.

Fen and Alex walked to the house for some lunch. The kitchen smelled delicious with freshly baked bread, butter and honey on the table. Sister and brother gorged themselves and then lay down on the living room floor, groaning, Fen blaming her mother for her own gluttony.

"My fault?" Renee laughed. "Oh, no. I am the innocent baker of the bread. You are the guilty parties for being little piglets! Now, lazy ones, let's work off our over-eating with a short trail ride. Yes?"

"Yes!" Fen jumped up and went outside to tack up the two horses, while Renee got Alex ready. He always had to wear a helmet when sitting on a horse. Renee wished Fen would do the same, but the western tradition of a cowboy hat would not be broken by her stubborn daughter.

Fen mounted Hack and Renee lifted Alex up to sit in front of his sister. Hack's saddle was big enough to hold the slender girl and her little brother. Renee mounted Sir Prize and they took off on a familiar trail that wound through the woods by a stream, Boss bounding after them. The spring flowers were all in bloom. The ferns were unfurling with sweet fury and the trees were dressed in green. The scent of the rich earth wafted up from the horses' hooves as they walked. Alex hummed and swayed with the horse's motion. He seemed to have a knack for sitting on a horse and moving with the animal's rhythm, a skill that took some people years to learn.

"I love having you home more, Mom," Fen said to Renee who was following close behind.

"I love being home more!" Renee laughed. "I should have done this a long time ago."

"I agree. I thought of it a long time ago," Fen said and then felt a little guilty about her impulsive remark.

"Why didn't you say something, Fen?"

"I don't know. I guess I figured that moms make all the decisions. Besides, it was important for you to be at work a lot to get your practice going. I didn't really understand that until recently."

"Well, I want you to know that you can tell me anything, although it's not as if I told my mother anything!" She smirked, knowing she had hidden many adventures from her parents. She was not foolish enough to think that Fen wouldn't do the same with her.

They picked up the pace to a slow jog and Alex flapped his hands in delight. He put his head back, letting the sun splash off his freckled cheeks. His sun-dappled face was calm and his clear, blue eyes darted from treetop to treetop. It always made Fen happy to see her little brother at peace and engaged with the world. They came to a small clearing on a hill that gave them a view of their home.

"So, how are things going?" Renee asked, tentatively.

"Okay. Sometimes things get a bit confusing, but generally it's fine."

Renee was quiet, offering space to let Fen tell her more. Boss was busy digging a hole by a tree where he had seen a chipmunk disappear. The dog was halfway down the hole already, only his bottom and wagging tail peeking out. Fen and Renee laughed at his antics, knowing the chipmunk was half a mile away by now.

"Are you nervous about the rodeo?" Renee asked.

"A little. Hack is not doing as well as I would like. It's really not his thing and maybe I'm pushing him too hard."

"Well, it's good to try new things with your horse. It builds new skills for both of you and it increases the trust and confidence you have in yourself, as well as in each other. That's why I never became a really good rider. I stayed with what was easy and in my horse's comfort zone. You can't do that if you want to get better and have more fun."

"Yes, but what if we fail? Hack might lose confidence in himself and his trust in me."

"I think you and Hack have a strong enough relationship to go through a few challenges together and still keep the trust. Besides, if you don't try, you can't succeed. I've watched you and Hack and so has Buck. We both think you two are doing a great job."

"But will it be good enough?"

"Good enough for whom?" Renee asked, looking at her daughter.

"Well, for me, I guess. And I suppose I want to prove that we can do it so other people will know it, too. People love to make fun of Hack and me because he's so big and I'm small for my age. I guess I do look a little funny riding him, but we've always been a great team. Sure, people know Hack's fast, sure-footed and reliable, but they think he's stupid and it's just not true."

"I agree with you. But you know what Buck would say about competition. You compete against yourself because you want to develop your skills and strengthen your bond with your horse. You are working as a team to get better as a team. It's not about what other people think."

"I know. But I still can't help feeling a little bit of the I-told-you-so disease."

Renee laughed. "Well, you're human, Fen, and it's certainly acceptable to have human emotions. I know that Buck would agree, as well as admit that he has a little bit of that 'disease' himself! Just don't let it get the best of you and Hack." Renee looked at the sky. "We should head back, honey. The days are getting longer, but the schedule stays the same on the ranch."

They turned and headed back down the trail, retracing their hoof prints. Boss scrambled down through the woods, way out in front of the horses, hearing his dinner bowl calling to him.

"Mom?" Fen asked. "How come Pete and Rosie don't, you know, well . . . ."

"Have a romantic relationship?"

"Yeah. I mean, they're both alone and Rosie could use a man around the house. And Pete and Clancy are so much alike, it's almost scary. For Rosie, it would just feel like having another really big Clancy around! Hmmm." Fen laughed. "Maybe I just answered my own question!"

"Well, I'll tell you what happened, but you have to promise to keep it a secret." Renee looked back at Fen and smiled.

"Oh, no! Not another secret!" Fen rolled her eyes.

"How many secrets are you keeping, young lady?" Renee asked with a grin on her face.

"One too many so one more shouldn't hurt."

"Well, Pete was in love with Rosie before she met Hal, you remember, Clancy's dad. But Pete was too shy to tell her and probably wasn't sure he was ready to give up his precious independence," Renee said, rolling her eyes. "Anyway, Hal proposed to Rosie after they had been dating for only a few months. It took Pete by surprise, but he wasn't about to create a ruckus by telling Rosie he wanted to be with her, too. So, Rosie and Hal got married. Pete missed the wedding, by the way, saying he had business out of town."

"Why doesn't he tell her now before she marries that hairball, Tom?"

"Hairball?"

"Yeah. Have you checked out his hair, Mom? It's like a black mop. It can't be real. He's probably bald underneath," Fen said in disgust.

"What's the matter with being bald? Anyway, have you looked at Pete's hair lately? The man hasn't had a decent haircut in years."

"Yeah, but that's different. That's just Pete. And that's another thing. Rosie could clean him up a bit."

"Maybe Pete doesn't want to get cleaned up. See, he likes who he is and doesn't want anyone trying to change him."

"Oh, this is too confusing. Adults are so complicated. I thought teenagers were bad, but we've got it easy compared to grown-ups. I just wish he would take the chance and see what happens. Adults are always telling kids that you won't succeed if you don't try. Sometimes you have to take risks to make good things happen. But adults don't follow their own advice!"

"I know, honey. Pete's never been much of a risk-taker when it comes to expressing his feelings and developing new relationships. But who knows? Maybe he will if he finds out old 'hairball' is moving in." Renee and Fen laughed together. "Whatever the case, Pete has his reasons." Renee stopped Sir Prize and turned around to look at her daughter. "Fen. I believe there's a reason for everything, even if we don't understand what it is. Sometimes we learn the reason and sometimes we don't."

"You mean there are reasons for death and horse brutality and people not being with the one they love and for Alex having to live with his disability? What are the reasons for all of that?"

"I wish I knew, honey, but I'm not that smart. Besides, if you look at all of those things, there was something good that came from each one."

"From Hal's death, Mom?"

"We have Clancy, Fen. And he wouldn't be the same person if his father hadn't died. We might not even know Clancy because Rosie and Hal were planning to move to Arkansas before Clancy was born."

"Arkansas? Who would be crazy enough to move there?"

"See what I mean? There's a reason for everything."

Fen pondered her life without Clancy and realized things would be a lot different and not in a good way. But she couldn't find a good reason for her brother's disability. What good could ever come of that?

Chapter Seventeen

The horses were hungry and knew it was graining time. Fen and Alex went to the barn to untack Sir and Hack and bring the rest of the herd in for their food. Renee went in the house to get cleaned up and start dinner. She was always glad when Pete stayed for dinner, especially with Mack away from home. She clicked on the answering machine to hear his voice, reassuring her that all was going well and he missed them.

Fen found Pete in the machine shed working on an old tractor. It was his special project and when he had a spare moment he would tinker with it, hoping to get it running for the antique barn exhibit at the mid-summer festival.

"Hey, Pete!" Fen called as she and Alex headed out to get the horses.

"Hey to you, munchkin!" he called back, looking up as she trotted by.

Pete suddenly realized that Fen was no longer a "munchkin", but a young lady with things to do, worries on her mind and challenges to face. She was growing up in a complex world with lots of questions to answer. Fen was already facing the stress of serious competition that required dedicated practice. He knew she must have difficulty getting along with other girls because she never brought friends home or was invited to other people's houses. On top of it all, Fen would have an ever increasing work load at school. Pete chuckled, realizing that her worst worry would be the boys she would have to contend with. He had heard her mention it all.

"Well, she's sensitive but tough. She'll get through it all right," he muttered to himself. "Besides, she has Clancy to watch her back." Pete smiled, knowing that Clancy could well be on the way to becoming one of the boys Fen was going to have to contend with. "Good thing he's a good kid."

Pete finished tinkering and went to help Fen and Alex turn the horses in and give them their grain. He knew they could do it alone but he enjoyed their company. Alex had learned what kind of grain each horse ate and how much to give them. And he was the only one who liked making the sloppy beet pulp mixture for the older horses. Alex added ingredients and stirred the goop, humming as he worked. When the chores were done Pete, Alex and Fen walked to the house together. The sun was on the horizon and it cast a golden light on their valley, lighting up Pete's cabin by the stream. A fox trotted by, stopping to get a drink of the cold, clear water. Boss and Phoenix were too busy playing to notice the fox, but Pete and the kids took a moment to enjoy the beautiful view.

They dropped their shoes by the door and took turns washing their hands in the kitchen. As Fen set the table, Pete took the photo of Mack down from the piano and put it at Mack's place at the head of the table.

"Pre-emptive strike," Pete said to Renee.

"Thanks, Pete," Renee smiled.

"What's a pre-emptive strike?" Fen asked.

"Well," Pete thought for a moment. "It's kind of like when you take the offense. You take action before someone or something takes action against you. You've thought ahead and have a plan that gives you the advantage and improves your chances that things will go your way. I guess that's one explanation."

"Huh," Fen mumbled, putting the utensils at each place as she ran this new information through her mind.

"I noticed Frank's truck is still here," Renee remarked.

"Yeah," Pete replied. "I think I heard him in the indoor arena working with Crescent."

"Well, I'm glad he's making an effort," Renee sighed, only half-believing her own words.

"I don't trust him, Mom," Fen muttered. "Crescent doesn't seem to be getting better. He almost looks more anxious since Frank started working with him."

"I know, honey. It's been frustrating for everybody, including your father. Alex?"

Alex came around the corner into the dining room with a stuffed horse in his hand. He hovered around the long dinner table, making his horse fly through the air in wide, loopy circles.

"You need to get cleaned up. Wash your hands and face, please," Renee said as she pulled glasses out of a large oak cabinet and started putting them on the table.

Alex slowly headed to the bathroom, softly whispering to his equine friend. Sometimes Fen was envious of her brother's condition, living in a world where no one could enter at will, expect too much or demand a response. He was free to be himself.

"I should go out and feed the older horses their beet pulp," Fen said. "I'll be back soon." She turned to Pete who was putting out napkins. "By the way, you might want to try a pre-emptive strike with a certain Rosie person we all know and love." Fen spun on her heels and walked out the door.

Pete stood there with his hands on his hips, staring at the door with his mouth open. Renee just smiled and walked through the kitchen door, letting it swing closed behind her. She chuckled as she stirred the spaghetti sauce, proud of her daughter's no nonsense way of getting things done or at least started.

Fen trotted to the barn, proud of herself for putting the cards on the table with Pete. Boss trailed behind, tired from his trail ride. Fen figured he covered about twice as many miles as the horses did, dashing around the woods madly chasing woodland creatures he could never catch. Fen stopped at the grain room, grabbed the tubs of gunky pulp and went to each of the senior horse stalls, putting their ration in the feed buckets. Each horse got strokes and hugs from Fen. In return, they nickered softly and blinked at her with their soft eyes and long lashes.

As Fen was returning the tubs to the grain room, she heard Crescent's whinny from the indoor arena. Fen walked to the arena door and peered through the door which had been left ajar. The overhead lights were off and it took Fen a minute to get her eyes adjusted to the shadowy, dim light. She watched Frank for a minute as he struggled to longe Crescent, using the techniques and commands that Buck had showed him. The horse was doing a pretty good job, but looked nervous. The stress showed in the taught muscles in his neck and back and the stiff way in which he moved, his tail whipping back and forth. The whites of his eyes glowed in the dark arena. Fen knew that when she could see the whites of a horse's eyes, the animal was afraid.

Frank started cracking his long, leather whip. Buck had told him never to use the brutal piece of equipment that was dangerous to both the horse and the trainer. Fen could see that Frank was getting frustrated, wanting more out of the horse than could be expected with this person at the longe line. Finally, Frank started yelling at the stallion, cracking the whip harder and faster. Whether the first lash was intentional or not, Fen would never really know, but the next crack came too close. The whip landed on the horse's back with a terrible snap. The stallion squealed and reared.

Fen watched in horror, waiting for what would come next. Frank paused for one moment, his hand raised, his mouth open, as if time had stopped. Fen would always remember it like a photograph, Crescent rearing in the background with teeth bared and nostrils flared and Frank's arms raised with the whip high in the air, his mouth open, eyes flashing. Then the moment was over and Frank was whipping the horse, over and over again, yelling and swearing at the terrified animal. Crescent bucked, galloped and careened around in a circle, tearing at the longe line, an unearthly scream rising from his throat and erupting into the dark, dense air, like a ghost crying from its dark realms.

Fen couldn't stand it. She ran out to stop Frank from beating the horse. Frank brought the whip up again. Its long arc reached back over his head, catching Fen across the chest and whipping around her arms and waist, like a cobra squeezing its prey. Fen fell to her knees in blinding pain. She cried out and went into instant shock, her body dropping to the ground in a curled heap. As Frank swung around to see what happened, the angry horse tore lose from the man's hands, galloping around the arena in crazed circles.

Boss had been prowling around the barns and outbuildings in his nightly wanderings, but made a bee-line for the arena when he heard Fen scream. The dog dashed through the door and immediately started barking and nipping at Frank's legs.

"Shut up, you stupid animal!" Frank yelled, kicking at Boss.

The dog headed for the open door and took off at a dead run. Crescent continued to gallop around the arena, bucking and kicking, wildly tossing his head in the air. Boss streaked around the barn and headed for the house, barking the whole way. Renee had heard the noise from the kitchen. She recalled seeing Frank's truck still outside and knew that Fen had gone out to the barn. Her maternal instinct told her something was wrong. Renee pulled the pistol from the wall and headed out the door.

"What are you doing, Renee?" Pete exclaimed.

"You stay here with Alex, Pete. Boss sounds hysterical."

Just as Renee was heading for the barn, Clancy pulled up in his truck hoping for dinner. His mom was out with Tom again and he was sick of boxed macaroni and cheese. But as he watched Renee run around the barn with a pistol in her hand, all thoughts of food flew from his mind. He jumped out of the truck and ran after her, Boss barking at his heels.

"What's going on?" Clancy yelled.

"I don't know!" Renee called back as she ran for the arena.

They slid the huge door open together and jumped back as the stallion galloped towards the opening, longe line whipping out like the tail of a kite in a strong breeze. There was no stopping him and they didn't try. He tore passed them, leaving whirls of dust, sweat and froth. Once the horse saw an escape route from the evil man and the darkness, he wasted no time racing for freedom.

"Fen!" Renee cried, seeing her daughter lying in the dust of the arena floor. She started running to her but heard Clancy's voice in time.

"I'll get Fen. You've got the pistol!" Clancy yelled.

"Stop, Frank Mercer or I'll shoot you down!" Renee shouted, pointing the pistol at the man who had been heading for the back exit of the arena.

"It was an accident!" Frank stopped and turned around with his hands outstretched. "She shouldn't have been here!" he yelled. "She's always gettin' in the way. I keep tellin' Mack that." Frank put his hands on his hips and stared at Renee.

"Don't say another word," Renee glared back as she walked towards Frank.

Clancy bent over Fen. She was conscious but not moving. Her face told him that his best friend was in serious pain. Blood was oozing through her t-shirt and down her bare arms. Clancy took off his shirt and wrapped it tightly around Fen's body, hoping to slow the blood flow. He picked her up gently and cradled her in his arms. Careful not to jostle her limp body, Clancy quickly walked towards the door.

"I'm heading for the hospital, Renee!" he called over his shoulder. "Take Frank with you and call the police."

"Hey! That animal's a menace," Frank yelled in a surly voice. "I was just tryin' to help and she got in the way," he shouted, gesturing in Clancy's direction."

"Don't you dare blame my daughter or that horse!" Renee cried. "We should have fired you months ago, but now I'm calling the police to arrest you for abusing an animal and assaulting a child!"

"Wait a minute now, lady. Mack wouldn't like you firin' me with all the work that needs to get done 'round here. Besides, you didn't see me do nothin'. I didn't hurt no animal or assault nobody," Frank said smugly. "You just wait till the boss gets back and see what he has to say 'bout all this."

"You must have forgotten the fundamentals of herd rules, Frank," Renee said, sarcastically. She was standing tall, legs apart, the gun pointed at Frank. "I'm the alpha mare around here. And when the stallion's away, the alpha mare can play. And this mare's game has always been to get you the heck off my ranch. And when my stallion gets home and sees his filly in the hospital, you'll want to be as far away from here as you can get. Besides, I know what you're up to with Dale Perkins. Now put your hands up and start walking."

Frank sneered and swaggered by Renee, slowly heading for the house but thinking about his next move. He had been caught and the game was up for him. He knew he had better make a run for his truck, hoping the lady didn't really know how to fire a gun. He was smart enough to notice she hadn't cocked the thing, so if he was fast enough he might have a chance to get away. Once he had escaped, he would figure out what to do next.

Clancy had wrapped Fen in a blanket and laid her down on the back seat of Renee's truck. Boss stayed in the house with Alex, while Pete came out with the keys, Phoenix growling at his heels. Renee walked around the barn with Frank in front of her. As she turned to take the keys from Pete, Frank saw his chance and dashed for his truck. He quickly revved it up and blew down the driveway, Renee shooting at his tires. But it was too dark and she was out of practice. They watched Frank disappear into the night.

"Better get Fen to the hospital," Pete said. "I'll call the cops."

Pete made the phone call, telling the police that Frank Mercer had assaulted Fen McCullough. He assumed Frank was headed out of town but couldn't say for sure. Pete intentionally omitted the issue of suspecting that Frank was involved in horse stealing with Dale Perkins because he wasn't sure what was up with that. Besides, if Perkins was out capturing wild horses without a license, Pete, Mack and Buck would want to take care of that on their own.

Clancy was sitting in the truck with Fen's head on his lap. Renee was speeding towards the hospital half an hour away. She had turned right out of their driveway and onto the main road, knowing that Frank had turned left. She knew he was heading for the Perkins' ranch before getting out of town. Renee vowed to take care of Frank, as well as the problem with Perkins, but she needed Mack, Pete and Clancy to stop Perkins at his game.

What Renee didn't know was that as her daughter lay quietly in Clancy's arms, Fen was already planning to make a pre-emptive strike on her own terms. Despite the pain of the lash marks and her anguish for the stallion's abuse, she knew there must be a way to make Frank Mercer pay for his evil ways. Fen also knew they had to find Crescent, the horse who had to become not only big and bright and awesome, as Buck had predicted, but the key to opening her brother's locked heart.

Chapter Eighteen

"**I**'m not quitting!" Fen yelled at her father who was sitting across from her at the dining room table. Despite the pain from the stitches, the layers of bandages and one arm in a sling, Fen was set on riding in the first rodeo of the summer.

"Fen, I can't let you participate in that rodeo with one good arm. It's ridiculous! You'll fall off and get more hurt or possibly killed. I am not taking that risk!"

Mack was sitting over a large mug of coffee, his eighth cup in twenty-four hours. He had driven straight home after a call from Renee, arriving at sunrise. He was exhausted, wired from too much coffee and his daughter was pushing his stress buttons. His head felt like one of those pinball games in the arcades they had at the mall. And it wasn't even seven o'clock.

"I can do it, Dad! I have worked so hard and so have Scoot and Hack. It's not fair to them or me."

"They'll get over it, but you might not get over what happens if you try!" Mack looked at Buck who had been sitting quietly at the table over his own cup of steaming coffee. "Buck? What do you think about all of this?"

Buck had been up all night, too, looking for a crazed stallion towing a longe line. He had driven his truck and ridden his horse everywhere he could go. He had kicked himself for letting Fen talk them into getting Frank involved in Crescent's training. He suspected Fen thought it would eventually get Frank fired. Well, it had worked, but her irresponsible plan could have had serious consequences for himself, Frank, the horse or her. They were lucky no one had been permanently injured or killed. He couldn't put all the blame on Fen, though. She was almost fifteen and her will and heart made most of her decisions, rather than reason and forethought. It had been Buck's job to make her see the foolishness of her plan and he hadn't.

"Well," Buck took a sip of his coffee and carefully set the mug down. "I think it's not my decision."

"Buck!" Fen cried. "You know how hard the horses and I have worked. You've seen how good Scoot is at the barrels! And even Hack is doing so much better! Why is it Dad's decision?"

"I didn't say it was," Buck said, looking at Fen. "I think it's up to you." He leaned back in his chair and crossed his arms over his chest, avoiding Mack's glare. Buck had never gone up against Mack and he wasn't sure what he was getting himself into.

Mack put his elbows on the table and bent his head into his hands. They all sat listening to the large grandfather clock in the hallway, ticking away the minutes. Fen and Buck looked at each other. Buck took another sip of his coffee then gave Fen a small nod. Mack finally looked up at Buck.

"You really think she can do this?"

"Well, she has the skills." Buck looked at Fen. "All she needs is the will and the courage."

"Yeah, well," Mack sighed. "We can check those off the list." He leaned back in his chair, his daughter staring at him with pleading eyes.

"I can do it, Dad."

Mack sighed again, leaned forward and pointed his finger at his daughter. "Here's the deal, young lady. You can practice for the next three weeks, which is all you got left. But, Buck has to agree to help you practice. AND, if I see one mishap or one fall or one close call, you're done. You got that?"

"Yes, Dad! Thank you, thank you, thank you! I love you!" Fen jumped up and went to her father.

` "You have to understand, my dear," Mack said, gently taking Fen in his arms, being careful not to hurt her wounds. "A father's job is to protect his daughter from harm. I have already failed you in that regard and I won't have it happen again."

"But Dad," Fen replied, pulling away from her father. "You can't protect me all my life and you certainly can't protect me from myself!"

Buck sipped his coffee and smiled. Fen knows herself pretty well, he thought. He just hoped he had done the right thing in supporting her decision to participate in the rodeo. It was Fen's natural inclination to take on risks that were beyond her abilities. Like Clancy, Buck sometimes encouraged Fen to bite off more than she could chew. But she always seemed to cope with the challenges and learn from them. Buck had lived his life that way and never regretted both the struggles and rewards it left at his doorstep. He knew Fen shared this natural temperament and hoped her life would be as rewarding as his. Only time would tell them both the answer to that.

"Can we start today after school?" Fen asked Buck. "I get home at three o'clock. Clancy is coming over at four for a quick trail ride, but we could get a lot done in an hour."

"Fine," Buck replied. He picked up his hat and went to the kitchen to put his cup in the sink. He looked out the window and sighed. Now he needed to turn his attention to the other matter at hand. What to do about that stallion?

Buck went out the kitchen door and stared at the far paddock. All those hours he had spent the previous night looking for the horse had been a waste of time. He had pulled into the McCulloughs' driveway just before daybreak, despondent and exhausted. He put his head in his hands on the steering wheel, trying to pull himself together. He took a deep breath and looked up. He stared at the front yard and his mouth dropped open.

"I'll be darned."

The stallion was standing in front of the porch grazing on the lawn, the longe line still hanging off his halter. He picked his head up, looked at Buck's truck and went back to munching, turning his attention to Renee's flowerbeds.

"Well, at least he knows where home is," Buck muttered, getting out of the truck slowly to avoid spooking the horse. He had led Crescent back to his enclosure and the horses in the adjacent paddock came over to greet him. The stallion returned their greeting with a nicker and Buck smiled. This was a good sign.

Buck walked out to the paddock to work with the horse for an hour. He was optimistic at the beginning of their session, but quickly realized that Frank's treatment had turned the horse sour again. It seemed that all of Buck's work had been for nothing. The stallion was wild and freaky, not performing any of the skills that Buck thought they had mastered. After the session, Buck put Crescent back in his paddock with a heavy heart and went to work with the other horses he was training. He knew that time had run out on this horse. Buck had only said that once in his long career of training. That horse had killed a man.

After school, Fen jumped on Scoot and warmed him up in the front ring. It felt a little awkward, only because she was over-thinking her new condition. After all, she was used to riding with one hand and Scoot didn't seem to notice the difference. Buck came out of the house with a glass of lemonade for both of them.

"Now, Ms. Fen," he looked at her, sternly. "Tell me the most important thing you are going to have to practice to make this scheme of yours work."

"Um, guts?" Fen asked, tentatively.

"Well, yeah, but I think you got that covered already." Buck smiled.

"How about skills?"

"Yeah, and?"

Fen sat on her horse and frowned. Scoot looked around at Buck as if to say: All you people do is talk. Can't we just get on with this?

"Patience, Fen! Patience, patience and more patience!"

"Oh, no. I'm doomed." Fen scowled.

"No, you're not. You learn new things in school everyday. Just think of it as one new thing to learn."

Scoot snorted and shook his head, shooing the flies away and splashing lemonade all over Fen's shirt. He pawed the ground and looked around for something to nibble on. He gave up and started dreaming of the green, tasty pasture that was waiting for him.

Buck took Fen's empty glass and put the two glasses on the ground. He crossed his arms and looked at Scooter who was starting to drop his head and close his eyes.

"Scoot!" Buck barked.

The horse popped his head up and looked around. His eyes were the size of golf balls, his ears stuck straight up and his nostrils flared. He looked like a picture in a comic book. Buck and Fen laughed at the startled horse. Scoot responded by closing his eyes and looking away.

"If a horse can look embarrassed, I'd say Scoot's got the look," Buck chuckled. "So, Scoot, when four-year-old Fen was sitting on your back, oh so many years ago, what was the one word I said was the most important thing about riding?"

Scoot looked at Buck. He was getting really bored of just standing around and somehow knew he was supposed to participate in some way. He turned, looked at Fen and snorted as if to say: I'm sure I know the answer to whatever the heck it is he's askin', but you gotta tell him so we can get on with this procedure.

"Balance!" Fen laughed.

"Yes!" Buck applauded. "Nice job giving her the answer, Scoot. Now, western riders ride one-handed most of the time, but it doesn't mean they aren't using their other hand. You use it for balance. You need it for barrel racing and you're also gonna need it when you're trying to get Hack to do ballet with a hundred other horses in tight quarters. So there is your lesson for today for both Scoot and Hack: balance, balance, balance."

"That's it?" Fen demanded.

"Yup. I can talk all day, but you and Scoot are the ones who have to practice it and it ain't gonna get done if I talk and you sit and Scoot naps. So move it on out you two!" Buck picked up the glasses and walked away.

"Great." Fen glared at Buck. "Some trainer he is. I wonder how much Dad pays him for this kind of nonsense."

Fen spent an hour working with Scoot and their balance. It was harder than she thought it would be and she wasn't sure they were up for the challenge. But Fen knew she had to try. Like it or not, patience and balance would be her mantra for the next three weeks. Neither of these attributes came naturally to Fen, but quitting didn't either. She had too much pride and persistence to give up.

Close to five o'clock, Fen headed to the barn to put Scooter away and get Hack ready for the trail ride with Clancy. She gazed across the meadow hoping to see Clancy coming along on one of his horses. Fen was relieved to see Clancy and Bandit loping down the path out of the woods. The horse was in high spirits. His proud head was held high and his mouth was pulling at the reins, wanting to race across the wide open field in full gallop.

Fen had always admired Bandit's handsome body and spirited ways, believing he could have been one of the wild ones in a previous lifetime. When Clancy allowed it and Bandit was in a lazy enough mood to stand still, Fen enjoyed decorating his naturally painted body with her own hand prints, lightning bolts, stars and ancient Native American symbols to honor Bandit's ancestors.

Fen came out of the barn with Hack ready to go. Clancy hopped off Bandit and let him take a drink from the trough. Both the horse and the boy were coated with a light sheen of sweat. Fen knew Clancy must have let Bandit fly across the meadow. Fen wished she had stayed to watch the scene. Buck had once clocked Bandit at forty miles an hour and since then had referred to the horse as Pure Speed.

"I thought you weren't going to make it," Fen said.

"Are you kidding? And let you go alone? No way. I just had to get by Mom. I have a lot of homework to do and she wouldn't be too pleased if she knew I was taking a ride."

"Don't you think she'll figure it out when Bandit is gone and you aren't home?" Fen asked, her hands on her hips.

"Yeah, but by then it will be too late. It's okay. I'll do my homework later, like at midnight when I usually do it."

Fen was a good student and could get away with doing her homework quickly, but Clancy wasn't as studious as Fen and he didn't really care. He was going to be a cowboy and all the cowboys in movies and books didn't go to school.

"So, what's the plan 'Butch'?" Clancy asked, referring to a character in an old western they had watched countless times. The movie was called *Butch Cassidy and the Sundance Kid*. 'Butch' was the smart outlaw who thought up all the plans for robbing banks and trains. 'Sundance Kid' followed along as the accomplice to do most of the dirty work. It was Clancy's second favorite movie, behind *True Grit*.

"'Butch'? Me?" Fen asked in alarm.

"Yeah. You just keep on thinkin', Butch. That's what you're good at," Clancy said, recalling a line from the movie. He looked away, his face taking on a tough, distant expression. "I'm just 'The Kid'!" Clancy exclaimed in the passionate voice of a heroic actor. "My fearless horse and I will gallop across windswept canyons, over rugged mountains, through narrow, rocky passes, leap off cliffs and otherwise engage in desperate acts to escape the bounty hunters!" Clancy's face quickly slipped back into its typical, calm expression as he looked at Fen. "And generally do whatever you tell me, following whatever foolish plan you've cooked up." Clancy grinned, enjoying the image in his mind of being an outlaw cowboy, careening through the wilderness on his big paint horse.

"Great," Fen sighed. "Why is it that the men in my life are suddenly giving me the reins, when what I need is a tall, rugged hero to pony me to safety?" Fen walked Hack to the fence, mounted and turned her horse towards the trail. "Okay. Let's go, 'KID', and find those wild horses."

"I'm right behind ya!" Clancy winked and spit, riding high in his saddle, enjoying his new found role in their relationship.

"That is so disgusting, Clancy!" Fen looked down where Clancy had spit. "Don't ever let me see you do that again. Ugh."

Clancy slumped in his saddle and wiped his mouth. He had never been good at spitting, anyway. Fen started jogging down the trail, knowing they had to make good time to be back before dark. They loped most of the way and got to Riverbend before long. The clearing where they had seen the herd only weeks ago was empty. They rode further, passing through a narrow opening in the hills into a large meadow. They stopped to look around the beautiful field, which was surrounded on three sides by tall cliffs. Fen sighed, wishing she was watching the wild herd peacefully grazing in this quiet place.

The two friends wandered around the field. There were hoof prints everywhere. Clancy got off Bandit and walked around. His face took on an ominous expression. He knew what had happened in this place and didn't want to tell Fen. He knew her heart would break and that was not how he wanted this movie to end. Westerns weren't supposed to end with the bad guys winning.

"There was a stampede right out through the opening." He pointed at the place the two of them had wandered through. "It was their only escape route." Clancy looked at Fen, his heart sinking as tears began to well up around her eyes.

"We know who did this!" Fen exclaimed, anger rolling up and out of her body. She yelled and pounded a fist on her knee. "We're too late!" she cried.

"No, we're not!" Clancy replied forcefully, jumping back up on Bandit. "We know where they are and your mom can help us get them released, as long as Perkins doesn't have a license to take them."

"And what if he does?"

"You'll think of something, 'Butch'. You always do!" Clancy clucked and Bandit took off at a gallop.

"You know, Hack, you're the only male I can depend on anymore." Fen slapped the horse on his rump. Hack responded with a loud whinny and shot after Bandit. Fen grabbed onto the pommel with her one good hand so she wouldn't be left behind, hanging in mid-air. She was starting to get used to the feeling but she didn't like it one bit.

Chapter Nineteen

The night he fled the McCulloughs' ranch, Frank had made a bee-line for Perkins' place, just as Renee had suspected. Dale Perkins was gone for the week, trying to round up horses to bring home and train. Frank spun into the Perkins' driveway and saw that Mrs. Perkin's car was there. He could see the daughter through the living room window. He drove his truck back to the ranch hands' cabin and banged on the door, then opened it unannounced. All the men looked up at the sudden interruption.

"Hey Frank," one of the men smiled. "You look a bit shaken. What's the matter with ya?"

Frank shook his head and sat down at the table where they were all having coffee. He knew he had to play it cool until he could tell them the whereabouts of the wild herd. If the ranch hands knew the police were after him, he'd be shoved out the door and they would leave him out of the plan for taking the wild herd. Frank figured the McCulloughs wouldn't have a case against him in court because no one witnessed what had happened in the arena. Who'd believe a kid's story? Anyway, if he could help them get the herd, Perkins would owe him a huge favor. Frank knew Perkins had a good reputation in town and could keep him out of jail.

"I've just been fired from the McCulloughs' place, just for trying to train that wild horse they got."

"But I thought McCullough was gone for the week," one of the hands said.

"Yeah, well, the wife did it. She's as crazy as that horse."

"The woman fired ya? Ha! I wouldn't be repeatin' that story. That's humiliating!" said Allen, the head ranch hand for Dale Perkins.

"She had a pistol pointed at my head!" Frank exclaimed. "Would you be askin' for a second chance under those conditions?" Frank scowled at Allen who just smiled back. "Besides, we got to do somethin' fast about those wild horses. The McCullough lady knows what we're up to and those two kids and McCullough's ranch hands will head us off and spook the herd if we don't do it now."

The other hands all looked at each other. That was a problem. Catching those horses was the only way they were going to keep their jobs. They knew they were all living at the Perkins' ranch on borrowed time. Dale Perkins couldn't keep paying them for doing nothing for much longer.

"Frank, do you know where the herd is?" Allen asked.

"They're somewhere around Riverbend, just catchin' what talk I've heard between McCullough and his hands. Oh, and those kids were yappin' about it at dinner one time."

"We can start out later tonight, catch them dozing and have them corralled by dawn," Allen said. "We'll use the abandoned pen by the cliff. No one will see 'em back there. Then we can take them to Canada to the slaughterhouse before Perkins ever gets back."

"What are we gonna to tell Perkins when we hand him the money?" asked another hand.

"We'll tell him a seller came through with a herd he had to get off his hands, then we sold them right off to a guy heading to Colorado to start his own ranch," Allen said.

"Think he's gonna believe that?" Frank asked.

"Well, he's gonna have to. He needs the money and there's no reason he shouldn't believe it." Allen shrugged. "What choice do we have? We'll leave later tonight and have them in the pen by sunup."

They all looked at each other and nodded. Frank smiled. He had just made himself important to the hands at Perkins' ranch and they would make him part of their gang. Allen would put in a good word for him and Perkins would have to hire him on and deal with whatever legal stuff happened later.

By three o'clock in the morning, the ranch hands were packed and tacked and ready to go. Frank proudly led the group because he knew the way. They rode fast and hard knowing they had limited time. Across the fields and over the rolling hills they galloped, unseen in the early morning darkness. Following the beam of headlamps, they found the hoof prints at Riverbend and continued the pursuit, urged on by the smell of horse and the excitement of a round-up.

The stallion and his herd had enjoyed a peaceful week, grazing with no sign of predators or people. The mare was getting stronger, but still wasn't as fit as she had been before the foal was born. She was getting older, although she still maintained her alpha position with no problem. The foal with the teardrop star was growing fast. Her legs looked like twigs compared to her body, which was slowly beginning to round out with her mother's milk. She was already pulling up the sweet spring grass, munching it slowly, getting used to its taste and texture.

It was still dark and a soft rain had begun to fall. The herd gathered under a stand of trees at the base of the cliffs. Lulled by the peaceful week they had enjoyed, the stallion had made a huge tactical error. He had led his herd through an opening in a bowl-like clearing, surrounded by three cliffs of sheer rock.

Just an hour after leaving the Perkins' ranch, Allen spotted the opening to the stallion's pasture. He slowed the other riders down to a quiet walk, the men yanking on reins if their horse made a sound. At a signal from Allen, the riders galloped into the clearing, fanning out in all directions. The herd was surrounded by riders and cliffs.

In the dim light and through the pouring rain, the stallion heard them before he saw them. He squealed a warning and began gathering his horses. He knew there was only one way out and he galloped for the opening. The riders let him go and followed the herd as they stampeded after their leader. The herd and riders drove fast and hard, retracing hoof prints back to the Perkins' ranch.

The stallion tried to veer off and find detours where the men couldn't follow, but there were too many riders. He found himself continually surrounded, herded where the men on horseback wanted him to go. The rain had turned the hard ground to slippery mud. Gullies and holes were forming on what was usually stable ground, making it difficult for the stallion to find escape routes. Flashes of lightning and thunder made for more chaos as the ranch hands shot their pistols to keep the pack together. Allen had been concerned that surrounding ranchers might hear them, but the sounds of the storm were giving him the edge they needed.

The mare and foal were too slow to keep up with the herd. One of the hands was ordered to stay with them. Allen didn't want to lose any of the horses, even if they weren't worth anything to him. One of McCullough's men or his kid and her friend might find the two lone horses and guess what had happened. He knew Mack and his hands were riding the back hills often, keeping track of the wild herds.

By sunrise, as predicted, the wild herd was no longer wild but penned up in the paddock behind the rancher's house. The stallion reared and bucked and squealed in anger and anguish. He had managed to dodge predators and men on horseback for so long. As leader of his herd, he knew he had failed his horses and he was helpless to change their fate.

When the round-up was over, the ranch hands celebrated in the cabin and planned their trip to Canada the following day. Frank had declined their offer to go with them, saying he had some business to attend to. He knew the police would be looking for him by now and he needed to disappear. He planned to return when things calmed down and Perkins was ready to hire him on and defend his case.

The ranch hands' party was interrupted, however, by the surprising arrival of Dale Perkins. He had found success rounding up some horses from other ranchers and had come home a few days early to get them settled in, before calling on Don Lacy to start the training process. He went to the hands' cabin to get some help taking the horses off the trailer and into the paddocks by the house. While he and his men were leading the horses to the front paddocks, Perkins heard a horse whinny from the back of his property.

Perkins walked around the outbuildings, pens, wood sheds and small barns to the old paddock at the edge of his property. It had been abandoned long enough that the pen was almost surrounded by trees and shrubs. Dale was surprised to find it filled with a herd of rambunctious horses. He watched the herd for a moment, then slowly walked back towards the front paddocks, his hands buried deep in his pockets.

Dale approached Allen, who was leaning on a fence rail pondering the situation he was in. He hadn't planned on Dale's early arrival and hadn't thought through the whole story he would tell the boss.

"So, Allen," Dale paused and stared at his head man. "Where did those horses come from?" He gestured vaguely in the direction of the back pen.

"Well, this guy stopped by from Ohio," Allen replied, looking down at his scuffed boots. "He said he was heading to Colorado to start a beef ranch and needed to get rid of the herd he had acquired." Allen looked up at the sky for a moment. "So we took them. Got a great deal, too, 'cause he didn't want to deal with them anymore." Allen glanced at Dale to see his reaction.

"I see why," Dale replied with a frown. "They look like they'll need a lot of training. It's a pretty wild bunch."

"Yeah. That's why the guy was anxious to get them off his hands. But I figure we can handle them."

"I don't see why. We haven't had much luck training the horses we've had so far, using the traditional methods. I think you showed poor judgment taking on these horses, but this might turn into a good thing after all. I've been thinking about trying the natural horsemanship techniques and your decision to buy these horses has made my decision to do just that." Dale paused and looked out across the valley. "I'm going to hire this guy who just moved into town," Dale continued. "His name's Don Lacey. He's had a lot of success using the new methods of training. I talked to him the other day and he said he was ready to start any time. He's pretty expensive, so to cut costs I've decided to have him train a few of you guys to use the techniques, fire some of the hands and make the whole operation run more efficiently and effectively." Dale looked at Allen long enough to make the ranch hand bow his head and shift his feet around a few times.

"Sounds like a good plan, Boss," Allen said formally, glancing at Dale before looking out across the paddock.

"Good," Perkins answered, still staring at Allen. "Now let's make sure that all the horses are fed, watered and divided into manageable groups."

Dale walked off to get a cup of coffee and some lunch, feeling edgy about his new herd and Allen's reaction. He knew that something was going on behind his back at his own ranch and he didn't like the feeling one bit. It was clear that Allen and the other ranch hands were up to no good. Dale was not the kind of man who would put up with dishonesty, no matter what the cost might be to his ranch, the business that he had poured all his money, energy and time into, not to mention his heart and soul.

Dale Perkins had come west on an adventure, hoping to build a prosperous life for himself and his family. But more importantly, he wanted what was best for his daughter. He believed their life back east had not been good for Clara as she grew from a little girl to a young woman. Dale believed in teaching by example and what Clara was seeing in their old life was not what he wanted her to be learning for the future.

Dale wanted his daughter to understand that satisfaction and joy in life was to be found in living with integrity, simplicity, hard work and generosity, not by dishonesty, competition and the exploitation of others, be they people or other creatures of the Earth. Dale knew he had let others take control of his business and his life for too long. It was time to pick up the reins and break new trail on the adventure he started and the journey he would continue. Dale walked into his house and called for his wife and daughter to tell them the good news. He needed a new perspective and fresh ideas and there was no better place to find them than right in his own home.

Chapter Twenty

"**B**alance, patience, balance, patience," Fen whispered to Scooter. They were out riding at dawn, Fen saying her mantra over and over again.

Scooter seemed to understand Fen's situation. He felt no weight on the pommel and knew she was riding one-handed. The horse maneuvered as smoothly as he could but managed to get close to the barrels anyway. He picked up his pace little by little as he felt Fen becoming more stable in the saddle.

At three o'clock in the afternoon, Fen was back out in the arena with Hack, working on their routine. Hack was less sensitive than Scoot to Fen's situation and had to be reminded about her handicap, as well as being constantly directed about where to go and what to do. The horse was trying his rider's patience but doing the best he could. To be fair that's all Fen could ask for, but it was taking a lot of focus and energy after a long day at school.

During practice, Fen became distracted by her thoughts of what to do about the missing herd. She had decided to talk to her father knowing that, as much as he didn't like wild herds being captured, he also didn't like interfering with how other ranchers managed their business. She had an alternate plan, but knew it was crazy and she needed Clancy to help. He had done some mischievous stuff in the past, but this plan was way out of both of their leagues.

Buck came around to give the team some pointers and make sure they were being safe. Mack had been clear about that and Buck was going to do the best job he could to protect Fen from further injury.

"Fen?" Buck asked. "What the heck are you doing? That beast you call a horse has been walking the perimeter of this ring for five minutes. The poor guy's falling asleep. Are you going to work him or not?"

"Oh, yeah, of course," Fen said, sheepishly. She started at the beginning of the routine and tried to focus, knowing Hack would only stay on task if she did. She shrugged her shoulders and smiled at Buck as she did a turn on the forehand and marched Hack on with a nice leg yield to the right.

"What have I gotten her into?" Buck muttered to himself. He turned and headed for Crescent's paddock passing Mack along the way.

"So how's the beauty and the beast today?" Mack asked with a grin.

"They're actually doing pretty well," Buck replied. "It's funny how much a horse and their owner can be so similar," he chuckled. "Fen and Hack are such a great team when they both keep their heads out of the clouds!"

"Renee tells me it's a problem of age," Mack said. "You've got an almost fifteen-year-old girl playing with a horse that will always act like a four-year-old boy." Mack rolled his eyes and shrugged.

"I see what ya mean. If you look at it that way, this might be as good as it gets." They both groaned and went their separate ways.

At dinner that night, Fen talked to her father about the disappearance of the wild herd. Renee just listened, knowing what had happened and feeling responsible for the situation. Her anger at Frank the night of the whipping had allowed her to get careless, telling Frank that she knew what he was up to. Perkins and his ranch hands had obviously lost no time in rounding up the wild horses. With Fen in the hospital, Renee hadn't taken the time to find out if Perkins had a license or not. She had made one call to the town manager's office but the clerk had been evasive, saying she couldn't locate the paperwork at the moment and to call back later.

"Now Fen," Mack said in a tone that Fen had come to call his, calm-down-and-let's-be-reasonable-about-this voice. "Maybe the herd moved on to a different location. There have been cougars seen in the area. In any case, have you been to Perkins' ranch and seen the herd?"

"Well, no."

"Then how do you know he has it?"

"I'm certain he does," Renee broke in. She explained her reasoning based on the information that Pete, Clancy, Fen and she had shared.

"You know I don't like to interfere with other ranchers and their business, but perhaps we could do a little investigating without him knowing." Mack took a bite of steak and chewed thoughtfully.

Fen looked at her mother with a gleam in her eye. Mack rarely did anything risky and this sounded like something right up Fen's alley. Renee looked at Fen and scowled but winked at the same time.

"The first thing to do is call the town clerk and find out if Dale has a license to take wild herds. If he does, then we're done. If he doesn't, you and I will take a circuitous route around the Perkins' place so we aren't noticed and see if he has corralled that herd."

Fen groaned. In all of the drama of the recent events she had forgotten that ranchers could get licenses for taking wild horses. But she didn't care. It wasn't right no matter what the law said. She was not going to be bullied by some stupid laws that government officials made when they didn't ride the range and see the beautiful horses in their native habitat. They didn't see the auctions where horses were sold for a hundred dollars to people who had no idea how to care for these sensitive, amazing animals. They didn't see the slaughterhouses.

"Okay," said Fen. "Can you call the town clerk tomorrow morning?"

"Yes, my dear. It will be the first thing on my list of fifty things to do." Mack scowled at his persistent, determined daughter. He looked at Renee who was smiling. The two were like peas in a pod and he loved them both.

The next morning, Mack was true to his word and called the town clerk, Gloria Maynard. She was hesitant to answer his question, although the information was part of public record and, by definition, anyone could know who had licenses and who didn't. Mack persisted to the point just before rudeness.

"Well, Mr. McCullough," Gloria began. "Mr. Perkins specifically and, by the way, very nicely asked that I not give out the information unless I was unduly pressured to do so, knowing that some people in the area are against the taking of wild horses." The clerk hesitated hoping Mack would get the idea without her having to actually tell him the information. That way if Dale Perkins did complain she could say that Mr. McCullough must have come to his own conclusions. But when there was a long silence on the other end of the phone line, Gloria continued. "You know, Mr. McCullough, Mr. Perkins is new to the area and doesn't want to make people angry. After all, he has a business to start and a family to feed. Besides, our town needs economic growth to maintain our way of life."

Mack was losing his patience with talk of economic growth and how sweet Mr. Perkins had been, but could tell that the clerk was more easily persuaded by nice chit chat than his more assertive way of getting what he wanted. Besides, it was clear that Gloria needed to be gently reminded about the legal issue.

"Please, Gloria," Mack insisted. "My daughter is very concerned about the wild horses. Furthermore, my wife, Renee McCullough, the lawyer in town, is only trying to make sure that things are done within the stated guidelines as mandated by law. We all care very much about preserving our way of life and welcoming the Perkins family, but we also care about the wild horses and want to rest assured that they are not being exploited illegally."

"Alright, Mr. McCullough," Gloria sighed. "The answer is yes. Mr. Perkins does have a license to collect wild horses, although he is not on record for having done so at this point."

When Mack repeated the conversation to his daughter, Fen was incensed. So Perkins had taken the horses and not reported it. She fussed and fumed and whimpered for an hour before heading off to school. At the end of the day, Fen hopped into Clancy's truck and spat out the window.

"Whoa, little lady, that's kind of disgusting." Clancy smiled but then looked at his friend and saw that she was seriously upset. "What's up?"

Fen looked at Clancy and her expression went from anger to tears in a split second. Clancy started up the truck and pulled out of the parking lot not knowing how to respond. He knew that when Fen had a plan and it wasn't going the way she wanted, she could be in a foul mood for hours. If confusion and chaos were mixed into the mess the mood could last for days. From the intensity of her anger he knew it must have something to do with the wild horses.

"So," he finally said. "What's plan B, 'Butch'?"

"You don't want to know." Fen groaned, then stared at Clancy and bit her lip.

"Uh, oh. Right about now I should probably say: You're right, Fen. I don't want to know. Go home and do your homework and let the whole thing go." Clancy sighed. "But, of course, I'm not going to do that because being 'The Kid' and ready to follow any crazy, half-baked plan you've cooked up, I'm going to say: Shoot, little sister." Clancy realized he was mixing up his movie characters, using an old John Wayne expression when he was supposed to be playing 'The Sundance Kid'. But Fen's tears had him all twisted up inside and he couldn't quite make sense of anything, much less have it all come out of his mouth sounding anywhere close to intelligent.

Fen took a deep breath and told him her plan. Clancy listened quietly and then stopped his truck in the middle of the road, staring at the yellow line that ran down the pavement. He knew of only two ways to respond to his friend. He chose the first and most reasonable one.

"Fen, you're nuts."

"I checked the forecast for tonight," Fen said, pretending to ignore Clancy's comment. "They're calling for hours of heavy rain and a storm with plenty of lightning and thunder. In fact, there's a storm warning from six o'clock till dawn. So I think tonight would be perfect."

"Okay," Clancy replied, settling on his second response and the one he usually chose at the end of any discussion with Fen. He started up the truck and they drove to Fen's house in silence. Clancy parked in the driveway, pulled out a piece of paper and they made a list of the stuff they would need and who would bring what.

"See ya at midnight, 'Butch'." Clancy smiled at Fen as she got out of the truck.

Boss darted from the porch and started jumping around Fen's feet, his whole bottom wagging with joy at her arrival. The two friends waved to each other as Clancy headed down the driveway. He knew they were both foolish for going through with such a crazy plan. Although Clancy rarely worried about things, he couldn't help thinking about the risk they were both taking.

"Good thing her mother's a lawyer 'cause we're gonna need one," Clancy muttered as he headed for home. He drove slowly, knowing he was heading towards a pile of homework, a house full of chores and then a dark, wet, dangerous trip on horseback.

Even more difficult was the knowledge that, eventually, Clancy knew he would have to answer to his mother for his actions. Fortunately for Clancy, Rosie was a woman who knew her son well enough to sense when something was up, but know when to ask questions and when to wait until the doing was done. Rosie had long since learned that Clancy did what he had to do, knowing the consequences, weighing the costs and willing to pay the price if he thought it was worth it.

Like his father, Clancy's actions were always based on helping someone in need, supporting a friend or wanting to see justice done, like the heroes in his favorite movies. Maybe his decisions landed him in trouble and maybe they weren't always well thought out, but Rosie never questioned that his decisions and actions came from a heart that was strong, generous and loving. What mother could punish her son for that?

Chapter Twenty One

Clara had come home from school, changed her clothes and tacked up Majesty, her sixteen hand Thouroughbred. They had spent an hour warming up and then practicing for the barrel racing competition. Clara knew they were getting better. Clancy had said so. He said he was impressed with how quickly she learned. Clara knew she was a good rider and barrel racing seemed to come naturally to her, even though she had started out learning English dressage.

After their work-out, Majesty and Clara walked around the ranch to cool down. They headed around the house and barn and front paddocks, towards the abandoned pen at the back of their property. To her surprise, it was now teeming with horses. Clara stopped Majesty a short distance away so her horse wouldn't spook at the energy whirling around the in pen. The stallion was tense and the mares and yearlings were restless and jumpy. Clara noticed the large mare and foal. The filly was adorable and Clara hoped her father would let the little one and her mother stay. Since their move to Montana, Clara had been looking for a young horse to train to ride western, knowing that Majesty would always prefer to be ridden English.

As she watched the herd, it occurred to Clara that they seemed more rowdy than the other horses that had previously been brought to Hidden Valley Ranch. When her father had acquired his license to capture wild horses, Clara had begged him not to use it. Soon after she had settled into her new home, a boy from a neighboring ranch had asked her on a trail ride. They had come across a wild herd of horses in the distance. Clara had brought binoculars and they spent an

153

hour just watching the beautiful animals interact in their own habitat. Clara cherished that experience and didn't want to see the wild herds disappear into corrals and onto trucks.

While the family was having dinner, Clara asked her father about the herd she had seen in the ramshackle pen. Dale repeated Allen's explanation to Clara and her mother. Maybe it was something she heard in her father's voice, but Clara was not sure she believed the story. After her homework was done, Clara slipped into pajamas, turned off the light and looked out her window into the dark night. A steady rain had been falling since dinnertime and it was now pouring off the roof and flooding over the gutter pipes. Clara could just barely see the white fence of the far paddock over the roof of their house. She detected movement in the pen but couldn't make out individual horses, as if she was watching a watercolor painting in swirling motion. She worried about the penned up herd, hoping they weren't used to roaming free and finding natural shelter from the storm.

Clara got into bed and thought about the upcoming rodeo only two weeks away. She had spent weeks wondering if she could get good enough to beat the McCullough girl at barrel racing. Fen was the local hero and it had seemed important to Clara to beat her out to become more accepted by the local people. But now she questioned her desire. Fen had decided to participate in the rodeo riding with one good arm. Clara had to admit it took guts to do that. It was hard enough doing the drill team routine and barrel race with two arms. Besides, Clara had found her own group of friends and had begun to feel part of the community on her own terms.

A few times, Clara had taunted Clancy about Fen, trying to find out what their relationship was about. But Clancy hadn't taken the bait. He had gently defended Fen without chiding Clara. In fact, he had tried to encourage a friendship between them.

"She's a nice girl, Clara," he had said. "You two might get along if you tried. You're both great riders and you could learn from each other. She could teach you barrel racing and you could teach her dressage. Besides, it would save your dad some money. He wouldn't have to keep paying me as your instructor." Clancy had quickly laughed at his own suggestion. "Oh, wait, no! I need that money! Don't talk to Fen at all. You'd never get along! No. Bad idea. You'd hate each other."

Clancy and Clara had laughed at Clancy's sudden realization that he was talking himself out of a job. Clara knew he was kidding and took to heart what he had said about Fen. But she also knew that once girls take a stance against one another, it's really hard for either of them to back down and start over again. Which girl would be the first to try to repair the relationship? It involved pride and always an awkward confrontation. Clara understood it took humility to apologize and she knew neither she nor Fen had much of that. Clara burrowed under her covers, listening to the pouring rain and thinking about how difficult life could be.

As Clara fell into a restless sleep dreaming of wild horses and raging storms, Hack and Bo plodded down the muddy path in the pouring rain heading towards the Perkins' ranch. Fen and Clancy had decided to take the more difficult trail because it was the shortest route and they would end up at the fence line of Perkins' back paddock where the herd was. It had been raining since early evening and the steep trail was rocky and slippery. Both horses were sure-footed but it was putting them to the test. Halfway down the hill, Hack lost his footing and started to slide.

"Watch out! We're losing control!" Fen called out.

Hack kept sliding, struggling to regain a foothold. Fen lost her stirrups and fell forward onto Hack's big neck, holding onto his thick mane with all the strength her one arm could muster. Hack squealed, shook his massive head and skidded farther off the path, crashing into the trees that clung to the rocky soil. In the darkness and pelting rain, Fen felt like she was falling into a deep, dark chasm. Rocks and mud were flying all around her as they bounced from tree to tree. She clung to Hack's neck with one arm and braced her shins around the front of the saddle, praying just to stay on. For the first time in her life, Fen was afraid she might end up under the deadly hooves of a terrified horse, pounding his way out of panic, bolting down the mountain for solid ground and a path that would take him home. For the first time in her life, Fen was scared she might die.

"Clancy! I can't hold on!"

"Yes, you can! You have to! I'm coming!" Clancy hoped Fen could hear his voice, knowing how faint hers had become in the mayhem and din of rolling thunder, pouring rain, blackness and panic.

Clancy had barely heard Fen's call when he turned to see Hack's huge, dark mass barreling towards him, as if a boulder had suddenly come to life in an avalanche. He quickly moved Bo off the path, but stayed close enough to make a grab for Hack's saddle as he passed. When he saw Hack crashing his way through the trees, Clancy yanked Bo back to the trail and up the slope, hoping Bo's presence would calm Hack down and lead him back to the trail. Fen was bouncing around on her horse, reminding Clancy of the ragdolls they used to tie onto their play horses when they were kids, playing in the paddocks and on the trails around the McCulloughs' ranch. From his days of watching bull riding with his dad, Clancy had developed a cowboy's sixth sense of defeat, the moment when the power of the beast could kill a man in a split second. He wouldn't let this be Fen's moment.

Bo pranced around on the trail, moving with the tug of reins and the slap of boots on his flanks. He didn't want to be there, but training and devotion told him to follow Clancy's lead. Hack found an opening in the trees and careened back onto the trail, almost crashing into Bo. In Hack's mad scramble to stay on his feet, his big head and chest pitched forward and his hind end flipped up, making him almost vertical to the ground. Clancy held onto his own pommel, stood in his saddle and leaned out as far as he could. He made a mad grab and caught Hack's cantle, yanking down with all of his weight. At the same time, Fen pulled on Hack's mane with all the strength she had left. Hack's head suddenly popped up and Fen was pitched back into the cradle of her saddle.

The two horses bumped into each other in the darkness, Hack spooked again and stumbled backwards into a tree. The tree snapped in half, but held the horse's weight long enough for Fen to get reoriented. She slowly guided Hack to a drier spot on the trail where they met Clancy and Bo. Clancy was breathing hard, looking up through the treetops into the black sky. The two friends looked at each other and started to tremble from cold, fear and relief.

Clancy dismounted and quickly moved around both horses, checking tack and making sure neither of them were hurt. As he passed Fen's saddle, he gently rubbed her legs and rotated her ankles to make sure she was not in pain. He couldn't look at her without showing emotion. He remembered his father saying that there were times when the brain needed to take over for the heart, that thinking was necessary and feelings could be dealt with later. Clancy knew this was one of those times.

Hack stood on the trail, breathing hard and snorting, watching Clancy make his rounds between the two horses. Two minutes later, Hack acted as though nothing had happened. He pawed at the ground to say that he was ready to keep moving. Fen turned his nose downhill and they continued their journey to the Perkins' ranch. Hack made his way down the path with confidence, but his rider took a few moments to regain her focus. Fen was shaken up, but it wasn't as if she hadn't had close calls and bad falls before. It was part of being a horse girl.

Clancy was more upset than Fen. He mounted slowly and took a few moments to check his position and Bo's mood. The horse seemed calm but eager to go. He didn't like watching Hack gain too much distance between them. Bo was not used to being left behind. He whinnied and walked on before Clancy gave him the usual nudge to move out. Clancy was not about to reprimand the horse for moving without being told. They needed to finish this trip and fast.

"You know, Fen, we're nuts for doing this," Clancy said, pulling the hood of his black sweatshirt and raincoat over his head. The rain was pouring down like someone was dropping buckets of water from the sky. "Even 'Butch' and 'The Kid' wouldn't do something this crazy."

"Like we haven't done crazy things before?" Fen looked sideways to shoot a snide glance in Clancy's direction. She knew he couldn't see her through the darkness and rain, but she also knew he could imagine her expression without having to see her face.

"I'm just saying," Clancy muttered.

"Besides," Fen added. "Most of the crazy things I've done, you've either been right behind me or leading the parade."

"I don't know about that now," Clancy sputtered.

"Oh, no?" Fen asked, sarcastically.

"Doing this is more in the arena of really stupid than just crazy," Clancy said, trying to redirect the conversation. "I'm just trying to make a point. Besides, I've only done a few little pranks." Clancy instinctively looked away, forgetting that Fen couldn't see his mischievous grin.

"Really? Is that so? Well, perhaps we might want to recall when you were seven and I was five and you said it was okay to pick all of Mrs. Steinbeck's prized tulips and bring them home to our mothers? Or how about when you suggested we eat 'just a few' of Mr. Watkins strawberries and you showed up with two milk buckets to fill, forgetting to tell me that Mr. Watkins was a little bored in his retirement and just happened to keep a shotgun at the window, ready for 'greedy rugrats who steal his berries'? Or maybe we should talk about the time you stole Joe Delaney's dog right from his own yard and sent him home with your cousin visiting from Oregon?"

"Hey, that's not fair bringing that one up!" Clancy retorted. "Joe had that dog chained to a doghouse all the time. That sad, little animal was starving, neglected and abused. Joe hated that dog and kicked him whenever the poor thing barked. I was doing the right thing and you agreed, Miss Goody Two Shoes!"

"Okay, okay. I was just trying to make a point," Fen muttered, repeating her friend's excuse.

"You know, Fen," Clancy said, seriously. "We could get into real trouble doing this. Perkins has a license so, technically, we're stealing his property. We could end up in that place for juvenile delinquents, unless my mom kills me first and then you'd be there all alone."

"Clancy," Fen turned to him. "I'd be alone in any place for delinquents. Don't you think they probably separate boys from girls in those places? Besides, do you really think this is a good time to bring that up? I don't need to get more freaked out than I already am."

"Sorry. I'll stop talking. I've seen you freaked out and it's not pretty."

Fen and Clancy finally made it to the bottom of the trail. They tied Hack and Bo to trees at the edge of the woods. The two thieves walked around the fence line, watching the herd shuffle and stomp. Surprisingly, the stallion stared at them but didn't make a noise. They got to the gate and Fen and Clancy looked at each other. This was no time to second guess their plan. Fen pulled the latch up and slowly opened the gate. At first, nothing happened. The stallion lifted his head and flared his nostrils, standing tall above his herd. He maneuvered to an open spot and looked at Clancy, who was squatting in the mud outside the fence.

Suddenly, a flash of lightning seared across the sky and thunder crashed overhead. The stallion let out a loud whinny and bolted for the open gate. Fen put her head down and prayed. They had forgotten that a stampeding herd of horses might not go unnoticed by Dale Perkins and his ranch hands.

The stallion shot out of the gate and turned quickly to the left, his herd following close behind, funneling through the small opening in a flurry of manes, tails and clashing hooves. Clancy was surprised to see that the canny stallion had not chosen to retrace the herd's hoof prints across the Perkins' property, stampeding around the barn and house. Instead, the horse took a trail around the base of the hill and galloped up a slope through the woods. The stallion was heading for new territory with his herd quickly following in his wake. The horses disappeared into the dark before the kids could count to ten. Fen watched the mare and foal take up the rear and hoped they could make the journey, wherever they were going.

Fen yanked hard on the gate to make sure it stayed open. She felt her wrist catch on the latch as the gate sunk into the mud. She looked at her coat to make sure no material had been torn and left on the property. It would have been stupid to leave any evidence behind. Clancy and Fen took the longer but safer route home, going around the base of the mountain. It was way past midnight when they finally reached the McCulloughs' ranch. Fen untacked Hack and put him into his stall. She gave him a good grooming, giving his head an extra rub down just the way he liked it. Hack got fresh water in his bucket and a treat for all of his hard work.

Clancy headed up the path towards home. He felt in his heart they had done the right thing, but dreaded what he knew could happen to both of them. Clancy realized he could have done the job himself without involving Fen. When he had done something he wasn't supposed to, Clancy was good at talking his way out of trouble. But he was not good at looking ahead to avoid the consequences in the first place.

All the way home, Clancy cussed himself out for not thinking about Fen first. He knew that had been his mistake. In their plans and his visions of this night, he hadn't thought about what might happen to his best friend. She could have been hurt or killed on that trail. She could get in serious legal trouble for their impetuous behavior. He trudged home in the pouring rain, wishing he had thought of Fen first and acted on his own. If they were questioned, Clancy knew he would deny Fen's involvement even if she said they had done it together. He would face the consequences on his own to save their friendship and her future.

Chapter Twenty Two

The morning dawned clear and bright. It was quiet at the Perkins' place and Dale took his cup of coffee out onto the porch to enjoy watching the sun rise over the distant peaks. It was the first day of June and he felt like things finally might be going his way since he had moved his family west and started a new life. He had become tired of the artificial showmanship of the dressage world in the east. He was fed up with the emphasis on the clothes, the rules and the way horses were treated by their wealthy owners.

Dale would always respect and admire the horses in all of their elegance and talent and he loved watching the dances they performed in the dressage arena. He knew these dances had always been performed by the wild horses in their native habitat. The dressage world had only refined them and given each move and position a name. But he had grown weary of the people and the money surrounding dressage, so he headed west where he thought he would find honest people and a good life with horses. He wanted to be with cowboys and ranchers who lived in jeans and worked their horses for a purpose, not just for recreation, using their natural talents on the open range and in the rugged mountains. As Dale was watching the sun and contemplating the day ahead, Allen came trotting up to the porch.

"Mr. Perkins?" Allen said in a tentative voice. "We have a problem."

"What is it, Allen?" Dale put his cup down on the porch rail.

"The herd of w . . . the herd of horses in the back pen are gone. They must have escaped in the storm last night."

"What?" Perkins bellowed. "How the heck?" He walked rapidly around the barns and paddocks to the back pen with Allen following close behind. "What in tarnation?" Dale grabbed at the gate still stuck in the mud.

Hoof prints were everywhere outside the pen. Dale and Allen followed the prints out to the base of the hill where they disappeared into the woods. The herd was gone and so was any trace of the horses that had been his property the day before. Dale stared at the ground and kicked the grass.

"Who was the last person out here to make sure the gate was closed?" Dale looked at Allen. "Whose job was it last night?"

"Mine, Mr. Perkins," Allen said, bending his head. "But I swear. I checked it twice, like I always do."

Dale had no reason not to trust Allen. There had been no problems on the ranch until this one. He seemed to be a conscientious ranch hand. "Well then, we must be looking at foul play," Dale said. "Shoot. I never thought I'd have to deal with stuff like this out here." He looked around his ranch, then out to the hills and mountains beyond and finally up at the big, blue Montana sky. He walked silently back to his house and called the police.

Allen went to the ranch hands' cabin and told the men what had happened. In the discussion that followed one of the hands asked where Frank was. "He started this whole thing, after all. Ain't it kind of weird that he disappeared after we done the thing?"

The men all looked at each other and shrugged. No one had an answer. Allen suspected that Frank hadn't given them the whole story about what had happened at the McCulloughs' ranch, but it wasn't his business to ask and he didn't want to get involved in Frank's problems. Besides, he and his men were in a muddy mess up to their own knees right now. Allen needed to find a way to get them out of the quicksand that could suck them all out of a job and maybe into jail.

Allen quietly left the cabin and went out to the back pen. He stared at the empty, quiet paddock. He looked at the fence and gate, walked around the area and carefully eyed the ground, hoping to find any clue as to how the horses might have escaped. He spotted something shiny poking up from under a mound of mud. He bent over and pulled out a small, gold bracelet. It had horses and horseshoes of all colors and styles connected to the chain.

"Well, I'll be," Allen smiled. "I just wonder who this might belong to."

Five minutes later, Dale Perkins called the police back to postpone their investigation. He would handle this matter himself. He got in his truck and barreled down the driveway, his wife and daughter watching him go. Clara was glad the horses had been set free but she knew she couldn't say a word. She wondered why her father hadn't suspected or at least questioned her about the incident. Clara was glad he hadn't asked about the bracelet because she would have lied, denying any knowledge about it. She had seen it on someone's wrist and assumed who had given it to her. It felt a little peculiar to be protecting someone she had considered her enemy, but somehow Clara felt it was the right thing to do.

Fen and her father were just finishing breakfast when there was a pounding at the front door. Mack looked at Fen with raised eyebrows. He went to the door and opened it slowly.

"Mack McCullough?" Perkins asked in a gruff voice.

"Yessir, that's me. You must be Dale Perkins. I've seen you around. Won't you come in?" He put his hand out to receive a shake, but Dale pushed passed him when he saw Fen at the table.

Fen looked down at her cereal bowl wishing she could be invisible, wishing she was Alex. No one would dare approach Alex with such anger. Her father would protect Alex from Dale Perkins or anyone else who tried to intimidate her brother, knowing it would set off a tantrum fueled by fear. Fen looked up at Perkins who was standing over her with his hands on his hips.

"You're the thief!" Dale barked, pointing his finger at Fen.

"Now, hold on!" Mack exclaimed. "That's my daughter and I don't allow people to speak to her in that tone, except myself of course."

"This belong to you?" Perkins held out the charm bracelet. He glared at Fen who slowly nodded her head.

Renee came into the room from the kitchen, having heard voices raised in her home. She had decided to stay home for the morning to see Fen off to school and do a few household chores.

"What's going on?" she demanded, looking at Perkins.

Perkins looked at Renee and his tense face became a little softer. "One of my ranch hands found your daughter's bracelet in the mud outside the gate where we penned up some horses a few days ago. Somehow they all disappeared last night." He looked at Fen. "What do you know about this, young lady?"

"Well, Fen?" Mack asked, sternly. He and Renee sat down at the table and motioned for Perkins to sit. He pulled out a chair, sat across from Fen and stared at her. Mack looked at Renee. Her eyes silently pleaded with him to try and listen to whatever Fen had to say.

"They are wild horses and they deserve to be free!" Fen suddenly burst out, staring at her father. "I had to do it! It's so unfair! We are losing all the wild herds because ranchers aren't taking the horses that are already waiting in farms and backyards, horses that just need to be trained right. When ranchers do try to train them they use the old, brutal ways, breaking their spirit and making them too afraid to go against a man's command. Then they sell the abused animals to people who give them up or have them put down because they can't handle them!" Fen took a breath but she couldn't stop the sudden flow of tears and words.

"The horses are abandoned, neglected, abused and sent to Canada to the slaughterhouses all because of bad trainers and greedy ranchers!" She stared at Perkins through her tears and slammed her fist on the table. "We did the right thing! I don't care what you think or what happens to us. We did the right thing!" she yelled again. There was silence except for the ever present ticking of the grandfather clock in the hallway.

"We?" Mack asked, quietly.

Fen paused and furrowed her brow. Had she said "we"? She couldn't remember. "I meant me. I did it and I don't care." She looked down at her bowl of cereal, the last of the flakes now white and pasty.

"Wait a minute," Perkins said. "You said those horses are wild. They aren't wild. Someone from out of state left them. They were moving on to cattle ranching and didn't want to carry the load."

"That's a lie!" Fen exclaimed.

"Fen," Mack said, sternly.

"Mack," Renee said, softly. "Maybe we should hear her out."

"Hold on," Fen said. She hopped out of her seat and headed for the stairs.

The three adults just looked at each other in silence until Fen returned to the table. She handed Perkins the photos she had taken of the wild herd. The pictures weren't very clear but there was no doubt in Dale's mind that they were the same horses he had seen in his pen. The mare, the foal and the big, dun stallion were unmistakable. Perkins swore under his breath.

"My ranch hands lied to me. While I was gone they must have rounded them up and thought they could get rid of them before I got back. My guess is they were planning to go to Canada but I surprised them by coming home early. By God, what do they take me for?" He sighed. "Well, they take me for what I am, the fool from the east who doesn't know the western man's way."

"Stealing and lying are not the western man's way," Mack said, gently. "Men like that live everywhere."

The two men looked at each other and nodded. Dale turned to Fen and looked at her for a long moment. Fen held his gaze even though her knees were trembling under the table.

"I do have a license to have those horses, Fen, but like you, my daughter has begged me not to use it. I promised her I wouldn't use it unless we were all starving."

"She cares about the wild horses, too?" Fen was startled by this piece of information.

"As much as you do, I would guess," Perkins replied. "Well, I owe you all a huge apology, especially Fen. I guess I better get home and do some firing and call the police again, this time for a different reason."

"Mr. Perkins?" Renee asked.

"Please, call me Dale, if you'll allow me to call you Renee."

"Of course," she smiled. "After you finish sorting things out with your ranch hands, I think you and your family should come over for dinner. I believe there might be a way that all of us can work together to solve some of our problems." Renee glanced at Mack who was looking at her with a puzzled expression.

"Well, that is a very nice offer, Renee, which I will take you up on," Dale responded, tipping his hat before putting it back on his head. "You have my curiosity piqued, that's for sure."

"Mine, too!" Mack exclaimed.

"Good! Why don't I call your wife after the rodeo is over and we'll arrange something," Renee replied.

The three adults stood up and shook hands. Suddenly, they heard Clancy's truck horn go off in the driveway. Fen grabbed her backpack and headed for the front door.

"Just a minute, young lady," Mack said, sternly.

Fen turned with her head down. "I know what I did was wrong, Dad."

"I know you understand that stealing is wrong, Fen. But I also know how strongly you feel about the wild horses. You have the courage of your convictions as my grandmother used to say. That's something to be proud of. I was also going to say that I respect you for not revealing the other part of the 'we' that was involved in your scheme, whoever that might be." Mack raised his eyebrows and looked at the ceiling.

Fen looked up at her parents and grinned, then ran and gave them a hug. "I love you guys!" she exclaimed.

"We love you too, honey," Renee said. "Now get to school before you're marked tardy. After all, we don't want people to think you're naughty!"

Renee, Mack and Dale laughed as they watched Fen hit the screen door, dart across the porch and leap over the front steps, running full tilt to Clancy's truck. She threw her backpack into the bed and jumped into the cab.

"Hey! Slow down there, cowgirl," Clancy drawled. "Please don't tell me that's Dale Perkins' truck sitting in your driveway?"

"Yeah, I'll tell you all about it!" Fen squealed in delight. She started banging on the dashboard with her one good fist, then let out a long, loud coyote howl for the sheer joy of having a huge burden lifted from her shoulders.

Clancy covered his ears with both hands and started driving the truck down the driveway. Using his knees on the steering wheel to keep the truck on the road, he could still protect his ear drums from exploding. He was grateful for having the long legs to make it all work. Having Fen as a friend he needed to be able to improvise at a moments notice. It was one of the things he liked most about himself and about his friend.

Chapter Twenty Three

"**Y**ahoo!" Fen yelled, flying off the porch and running for Clancy's truck for the second time in a week.

"You're not too excited, are you?" Clancy smiled and rolled his eyes. He turned the truck around and headed down the driveway.

"Are you kidding?" Fen shouted. "It's the last day of school! At the end of the long, dark tunnel of my prison sentence, I finally see the beacon of light beckoning me on to the freedom of summer!"

"Are you aware," Clancy grimaced, "that my ear is two feet away from your mouth when we're in this rig?"

"Sorry," Fen said. "I'm just happy!"

"I couldn't tell," Clancy said, sarcastically, then looked at Fen with concern on his face. "Has school really been that bad, Fen? I mean, I know you haven't really found a group of kids that you're comfortable with, but you did well in your school work. And next year will be easier."

"I hope so. It's just no fun, going to school with no one to hang out with."

"Well, my friends at lunch like you."

"They tolerate me, Clancy, because I'm your friend. They never even speak to me."

"Well, you don't speak to them either. Why do you expect other people to make the first move? Sometimes you have to be the one to step up first. You don't mind raising your hand whenever a teacher asks a question. Why don't you raise your voice with kids your own age? How come you'll jump on any horse, but won't jump into a relationship or even a conversation?"

Fen scowled and looked out the window. She always said that she was a horse person, not a people person and that it wasn't right to pretend to be someone you really weren't. She knew, though, that Clancy was right. She hadn't made much of an effort. The two friends were quiet the rest of the way to school. Clancy parked his truck in the parking lot and they both got out and headed for the big, brick building.

"See ya at lunch," Clancy said over his shoulder as he joined a group of friends hanging around the front steps.

Fen sprinted into school, grabbed what she needed from her locker and hopped into her seat for the first class of the day. She was counting the minutes. Classes seemed to drag on all morning but lunch finally came. Fen sat down next to Clancy at their usual table in the lunchroom and opened her bag. She was starving.

Clancy's group of friends consisted of eighth and ninth graders and a mix of girls and boys, most of whom had gone through elementary and middle school together. The ninth graders were all talking at once, telling jokes and teasing each other, excited about their upcoming graduation. Fen was quiet, as usual. She was sad that Clancy was graduating. Next year, she would have to make it on her own in this big place with only a few people she could talk to.

"Uh, oh," Clancy muttered under his breath to Fen. "Watch for incoming."

"Huh? What does that mean?" Fen asked.

"Incoming," Clancy whispered in a monotone voice as if he were narrating a historical documentary. "A term typically used in war time to refer to bombs, mortar, fatal artillery and/or heavily armed troops." Clancy sighed. "In our case, it refers to you-know-who."

Sure enough, trouble with a capital C was coming their way. She was swinging a purple and pink lunch pack, her hair smoothly plaited into a French braid, with a glittery, western, button-down shirt neatly tucked into skin tight jeans. None of Clancy's friends had really acknowledged Clara this year. She had her own set of friends that didn't really mingle with Clancy's group. They all watched her as she sauntered up, some of the boys more interested than the girls were.

"So," Clara said, gesturing at Fen's arm hanging in a sling. "It looks like you ran into a little trouble." She waited for a response but Fen just kept munching on her peanut butter and jelly sandwich. "But it seems being all bandaged up didn't stop you from helping things vanish into the night." Clara sat down across from Fen. "Do you mind if I join you?" she asked, sweetly.

"Do I have a choice?" Fen retorted. She was quietly fuming but was not going to make a fool of herself in front of Clancy's friends.

Clancy had ignored the interchange, pretending to be engaged in a serious conversation with the boy next to him. He felt like he should support Fen, but he was not about to get into the middle of a snippy verbal exchange between two girls, especially when he had been hired by one of their fathers and was best friends with the other one.

"I'm really sorry to see you can't ride in the rodeo," Clara continued in a sweet voice. "I'm sure you had a good chance of doing pretty well before your accident. How did it happen, anyway?" Clara looked at Fen with a sympathetic expression on her face, but her voice was dripping with sarcasm.

"My dad whipped me for breaking one of the Ten Commandments. You can probably guess which one. But if you think I'm not riding in the rodeo, you're not thinking." Fen took a sip of milk from her pint container, her eyes on Clara. "I have a good chance of winning with one arm. I ride western, remember? Western riders don't need two hands to stay on a horse the way English riders do."

"Well, fortunately for me, Clancy here has been giving me a lot of wonderful instruction and I am loving the western ways." Clara smiled at Clancy from across the table and put her hand on his.

Clancy was mortified. He gently pulled his hand away and picked up a potato chip. His whole mind and body screamed at him to dash for the door and drive away into the sunset, never to return for the sequel. What was it about girls? No. What was it about this girl? Why did she have to do this kind of thing? He should never have gotten involved with her. But how could you tell ahead of time which ones to avoid? He had learned one thing. Whatever money he had made from teaching Miss Clara, it was not enough.

"I'm glad Clancy has been so helpful to you," Clancy heard Fen say in a sweet voice he didn't recognize. "So we'll see you at the rodeo, then. Have a good rest of the day and congratulations on graduating and getting out of here." Fen hoped her voice was dismissive enough to send Clara away, just as Clara had dismissed her when they had first met last summer, when Fen had tried to be nice.

"You must have forgotten," Clara responded. "I'm in eighth grade."

"Oh, that's too bad," Fen said in a condescending voice.

The other kids at the table smirked and turned away. Fen had clearly won this verbal joust. But Fen quietly choked on her sandwich, realizing that she had to put up with Clara for one more year. Would her prison sentence never end?

Clara stood up and smiled at Clancy. "See ya this afternoon, Clance. I can't wait for our lesson."

"Oh, I forgot to tell you, Clara. I have to do some chores for Mrs. Bixby." He looked at Fen and smiled. "She's still making me do penance for killing her fence." He turned back to Clara. "So I won't be over to help out. But you don't need me anymore. You have two weeks to practice what we've talked about."

Clara's sweet smile disappeared but she was not going to make a scene and look foolish. "Great! I'm glad you think I'm that good. Thanks for all your help, Clance." She smiled again, turned and sauntered out the lunchroom door.

"Ugh," Fen said. "I must have done something wrong in my previous life to deserve what happens to me."

"Actually, Fen," Clancy replied. "I think most of the time you and I both deserve what happens to us because we pick up shovels and start digging our own holes. It just seems that sometimes the holes get deeper without our help."

"I guess you're right. But I'm ready to climb out of this one and I wish someone would throw me a line," Fen sighed.

Clancy laughed. "I'd be happy to throw you a line, if I wasn't sitting in my own hole. Hey, I forgot. I owe Mr. Jackson ten minutes of lunch hour to catch up on my writing journal." Clancy pitched his garbage into the trash can behind him, hopped up and headed for the door. "See ya after school!"

Fen picked at the rest of her lunch in silence, pondering her situation. She was trying to take her mother's advice and see the glass half full, rather than half empty, so she focused on the fact that it was the last day of school. She was also grateful that the 'incoming' had become the outgoing and she wouldn't have to face Clara again until rodeo day. Suddenly, she noticed a girl from Clancy's group had sat down across from her.

"Do you mind if I join you?" the girl asked in a sweet voice, imitating Clara's greeting.

"Sure," Fen laughed. "As long as you don't accuse me of being a criminal or a cripple." She rolled her eyes and smiled.

"Don't worry. I'm really impressed that you're still riding in the rodeo. I've watched you before and you'd have the barrel race in the bag with two hands. I'd still put my money on you even with the arm in the sling."

"Thanks!" Fen said. "I don't know. You sound more confident than I feel."

"Don't we all?" she laughed. "My name's Emily, by the way. I'm in eighth grade and feeling really envious of these ninth graders."

"Not such a good year?" Fen asked, drinking the last of her milk.

"Well, I'm new this year and it's been hard breaking into a group of kids that have known each other for so long. I don't feel comfortable with, well, the Clara types, you know. But Clancy and his friends have been really nice to let me hang out with them."

"Clancy's a great guy," Fen said. "We've been friends all our lives. I've just never really had a group of girls in my class that I felt comfortable with, so I stick with Clancy and horses."

"Not a bad combination!" Emily laughed.

"So, are you going to compete in the rodeo?" Fen asked.

"Yeah, but I'm really not in the same league as everybody else. My family moved here from Maryland and I learned to ride English. I love the western style but I need a lot more practice. Riding in the rodeo for me is just for fun and practice," Emily shrugged. "I know I can't really compete."

"I don't know," Fen replied. "A lot of the contestants aren't as good as they sound. It's a western thing to bark loud before the competition and then bark louder when you lose, blaming it on your tack or your horse or the barometric pressure, whatever the heck that is. When the old farts lose they like to blame it on an old injury," Fen drawled in a croaky voice, "'that's kicked up again and givin' me some trouble'". Emily laughed. "Are you on the drill team?" Fen asked, hoping to see a familiar face during the practices.

"Yeah! I'm really not good enough but I thought it would be fun to try. I did some drill team work riding English, so I'm hoping I won't make a fool out of myself and Rhumba, my mare with an identity problem. She thinks she's thirteen hands and wants to be pampered like a little fairy princess, when she's really half draft, half Hanoverian and behaves more like a stallion than the ninth grade boys do!"

Fen laughed. "Sounds like you and I should have signed up for a dancing disco duet, rather than a military drill team with a hundred crackerjack riders and their well-trained equine partners!" The girls giggled together.

"Well, my grandfather has an expression that he's said at least a hundred times since I've known him." Emily's face took on a serious expression and her voice became deep and gruff. "'Sometimes just showing up is good enough.'"

"Sounds like a good way to look at things, as my mother would say!" Fen replied. "I hope your grandfather is at the rodeo to remind everybody else of that thought when we get out there in the ring!" The bell rang for the end of lunch and the girls stood up to leave. "It was great to meet you, Emily," Fen said.

"You too, Fen. I hope your arm keeps getting better."

"Thanks! See ya at drill team practice!" Fen smiled as she headed for her next class.

Lying in bed that night, Fen watched her curtains gently blowing in the warm June breeze. It had been so easy talking with Emily that afternoon. Why couldn't she just start a conversation like that? What was so hard about it? She tried talking with Clara last summer, but it had fallen flat and she hadn't made the effort again. Fen didn't consider herself a quitter. She didn't usually give up so easily when faced with challenges, but with people it was hard to get over her pride. She wasn't sure why.

Fen also wondered what had turned her off to Clara so quickly when she might have become a friend. Was it her clothes and hair that she and Clancy had always called, "priss priss"? Was it Fen's resentment of the time Clancy spent with Clara, helping her become a competitor against Fen? Or was it the twinge of jealousy she had felt with Clancy spending time with another girl?

Fen sighed and picked up her stuffed horse, Ringo, who had been with her since she was an infant. He was tattered, patched and stained and Fen thought she was probably getting too old to sleep with a stuffed animal, but she still slept with him every night, anyway. She looked at the worn out horse and he stared back at her with dark, shiny eyes and a stitched up nose, where Alex had taken a bite when he was a toddler.

"Ringo," Fen said solemnly. "Horses are so much easier than people."

Or were they? Fen thought about it. When she was seven and her parents had started looking for a horse to be her own, Mack had said that when you meet the horse that's for you, you will know it right away. He said there would be a spark, a sort of mutual chemistry that you would both feel. Her mother had made a joke about how she had that same feeling when she met Mack. It was the old "Cinderella" story that Fen hated. She had always thought it sounded so stupid to fall in love with someone you didn't even know.

But when Fen met Sundancer that's how it had been. It was the "Cinderella" story but with a horse. The minute she saw him as he came off the trailer with eight other horses, she knew he was the one. She had hopped on and had the greatest ride of her young life. She immediately nicknamed him Scoot because of the way he moved. The owner agreed it suited him perfectly and said that the horse had never looked better.

Fen and Scooter had been a perfect team from the beginning and they still were. It had been that easy.

Ebony had been a whole different story. Fen had trudged into a paddock with mud up to her knees to catch the beast, who avoided her with quicker moves than she thought possible, given the muck and his immense size. When she finally did catch him, she couldn't reach his head to halter him because his nose was stuck way up in the air. Fen finally dragged him by the mane, holding a peppermint at arm's length to get him into the owner's barn. Once on the cross ties, the half-horse, half-wooly mammoth had proceeded to lean on her until Fen fell against a wall and sat down in a pile of horse manure.

Grooming and tacking the horse took half an hour because he kept leaning, stepping sideways and pinning his ears. Fen kept backing away, afraid he was going to kick. Renee had remarked that he was girthy, grumpy, gigantic and, most likely, part grizzly bear. It wasn't perfect alliteration but it was a pretty accurate description of the horse. When Fen finally got him into the ring and mounted, he wouldn't move. She kicked, she whipped, she pleaded, she yelled, she cried. But he was not budging. At some point he began walking with his nose to the ground.

"You'd better do a quick dismount!" the owner yelled to Fen.

Fen didn't catch what he said but soon realized that the beast was about to roll, taking the saddle and her with him. She yelled and yanked hard on the reins. The horse jumped up so fast that Fen popped off the saddle and landed in the dirt. He looked down at the scowling Fen. His expression could only say one thing: What? You don't like a good roll now and then? You're no fun.

The owner finally suggested they try Ebony out of the ring. He pointed to a trail that looped around his property and said that the horse really preferred going on hacks than doing ring work. As soon as Fen pointed Ebony's big nose down the familiar path, he was off like a shot, going from a dead standstill to a full out gallop.

The girl clung to the horse's mane for dear life as they careened around corners, jumped over logs, blew between trees, ducked under low hung branches and splashed through a river, the water pouring into her boots. They galloped back to the front yard and the horse put on the brakes, nearly pitching Fen into the next county. Mack and Renee could only stand there, mouths agape, amazed that Fen was still alive. Alive? She was so happy she almost burst like an overblown balloon.

"This is the horse for me!" Fen beamed, hugging Ebony's neck. Renee and Mack looked at each other and groaned. The horse leaned into Fen and then stuck one big nostril into her ear. If a horse could look happy it was this one. He hadn't known it at first, but this was the girl for him. She had proven herself a worthy partner on that old, boring trail.

But three years later, Hack was a well-trained, sweet horse that Fen could depend on to keep her, if not in the saddle at all times, at least off the ground. She had never fallen off and he had saved her back end many times in tough situations. Pete and Buck had to agree he had become the best trail horse they had ever seen.

Fen lay in bed, enjoying her memories of the day they had brought Hack home. People had given her a hard time about calling him Hack because Ebony was such a beautiful name and it fit his majestic size and color so well. When people asked Fen why she called her horse, Hack, she always said the same thing.

"My father says: 'You can't judge a book by its cover. You can't judge a horse by its color. And your horse's name should reflect who they really are.' Well, hack is what he likes to do and what a horse likes to do is who they really are. Ebony might be what we see on the outside, but Hack is who he really is on the inside."

As the rain started coming down, Fen stood up to close her window. She looked at the few remaining stars and the grey clouds against the dark sky. Maybe people were like that, too. Maybe Emily was more like a Scooter and Clara was more like a Hack. Fen laughed to herself thinking about what Clara would say about that! Fen had been nice to Clara at first but maybe, sometimes, it took more than one shot. As Fen climbed back into bed she vowed that, if the chance arose, she would try being friendly to Clara again. Maybe it would work the second time. After all, anyone who pleaded with her dad not to take horses out of the wild couldn't be all bad!

Chapter Twenty Four

"**O**kay, Scooter," Fen said in a gruff voice. "Stop eating my shirt so I can get on. I know these balance exercises and warm-up drills Buck suggested are boring, but ya gotta help me out here." Scooter looked at Fen with droopy eyes and took one more nip at her button. "Just remember who feeds you!" Fen glared at the grumpy horse.

It was the second day of vacation, less than two weeks till the rodeo, and Fen wanted to take every minute she could to practice. Yesterday, she and Clancy had taken a trail ride in search of the wild herd. They followed the path they thought the horses had taken, up the hill and through the woods behind the Perkins' ranch. It wasn't long before they lost hoof prints or clues of any kind that a herd of horses had recently galloped away where they were now walking. It was as if the herd had disappeared into thin air.

"They didn't even leave piles of poop," Clancy said. "How is it that I can spend an entire afternoon cleaning up horse manure and this herd leaves not one pile after a two hour trek?"

"Maybe it's because Perkins didn't feed them," Fen said in disgust.

"Ah! That's the answer!" Clancy threw up his hands. "We just won't feed our horses then we won't have to clean up after them!"

"I'm glad our mothers didn't think that every time they changed our diapers," Fen retorted.

Clancy sighed looking out towards the distant hills. They had reached a clearing on the ridge, which gave them a view that reached thousands of miles beyond where they sat.

"No wonder he's the lead stallion," Clancy said in frustration as well as admiration. "He can outwit us and Perkins' ranch hands."

"Clancy," Fen replied. "I don't think that's a really good test of I.Q. but I think you're right. He certainly took the smart route."

The two friends gave up the search and turned back, deciding to take their time getting home. They sang their favorite songs, imitated movie actors and pretended to be members of the Lewis and Clark expedition. It was disappointing not to find the herd but they decided it was a good thing. If they couldn't locate them, most likely they were well hidden and protected from Perkins' ranch hands. So they took the long way back to Fen's house and had the most relaxing ride they had experienced in a long time. They both found that just taking a ride could take away all their worries, at least for awhile.

But today, Fen was not thinking about trail riding or wild herds. She was all business as she groomed and tacked up her horse. Scoot took the opportunity to do his favorite thing, which was finding stuff to eat. He chewed on a bucket hanging on a stall, snapped at a butterfly flitting through the open door and grabbed at the reins before Fen could get them over his head. Finally, Fen led Scoot out the barn door, but not fast enough before the horse snatched a lead rope hanging on the fence.

"Drop it, Scoot," Fen said, sternly.

The horse looked at her, dropped the rope and hung his head. It was a trick Fen had taught Scoot when she realized that this vice was not going away. She liked to show newcomers to the ranch how smart Scoot was by performing this trick, although her father said that teaching tricks was for dogs and not in keeping with the pride and elegance of the horse. Fen sometimes thought her father took things too seriously.

But Fen was the serious one today as she led Scooter into the ring. It only took one stern command and a hard squeeze to get her horse focusing on his job. They did the practice drills and exercises Buck had suggested, including walking around the barrels with Fen's left arm held out straight from her side. She felt like a one-winged plane. She knew it looked ridiculous and hoped no one was watching. They had done this exercise too many times and Fen quickly got bored. She started watching the butterflies darting about and the grass blowing around in the light breeze that had stirred.

"I guess this is what it means to spend your time watching the grass grow," Fen said, yawning. Scoot had his head hung so low that his nose was practically making a track in the dirt. "Alright, enough of this nonsense. Let's get going." Fen squeezed Scoot with her legs and they began the course at a jog. After about three times around, Scoot turned around as if to say: Hey girlfriend, isn't the point of this whole game to go FAST?

Fen laughed at Scoot's expression and encouraged him to lope for the next few rounds. He was happier, which meant he increased his speed each time they went around the course. It was hard to slow him down once he got focused on the barrels. Mack had told her to keep the gait to a lope until she was confident she could hang on at a gallop, but Fen was getting tired of pulling Scoot back with only one arm. Maybe she was ready and maybe she wasn't, but Scoot was sure chomping at the bit to go. Fen knew she had to try at some point so, as Rosie sometimes said, there was no time like the present. She led Scoot out the gate and turned him around to face the arena.

"We're going to gallop this time, Scoot, but please stay under me. I've already fallen off twice. We were lucky no one caught us. Dad would put the nix on the rodeo if he'd have found out."

Fen took a few deep breaths and adjusted her helmet. When Mack agreed to let Fen continue to practice for the rodeo, Renee had insisted that she wear a helmet. Fen had vehemently argued with her mother.

"No one wears a helmet around here, Mom! I'll look stupid! Everyone will stare at me!"

"Why would you want to be in a rodeo in the first place, if you don't want people looking at you? And do you think people won't notice a barrel racer with an arm in a sling? You'll probably make the papers," Renee had calmly replied.

"Mom! I'll look ridiculous! Do you want your daughter looking like an idiot in the papers?"

"Fen, I don't like to have to say this, but it won't be the first time you've looked, um, idiosyncratic."

"Idiowhat?" Fen exclaimed. "What is that supposed to mean?"

"It means different, dear." Renee smiled. "Perhaps you can start a new rodeo fashion statement!"

"By wearing a helmet? Right. Me. Fen McCullough is going to start a fashion trend by wearing a helmet. Maybe Clara Perkins should wear the helmet, then. She could get it done up in purple and pink with sparkly blingy stuff all over it!"

"Great idea, honey!" Renee replied. "Why don't you suggest it to her?"

"Right, Mom," Fen said, sarcastically and rolled her eyes. "Anyway, this is Montana. People don't start fashion trends in Montana."

"Well then, you can start a safety trend and maybe it will catch on. Regardless of your strong opposition, the deal is, no helmet, no rodeo. End of discussion."

Fortunately, Fen had been wearing the helmet on her last dive off Scoot. He had rounded the last barrel at a lope, but quickly switched gears to a gallop as he headed for the home stretch. The quick gait change had sent Fen cartwheeling over Scooter's shoulder and onto the left side of her back, hitting her head on the ground. She had a headache for a day but didn't have symptoms of a concussion, which her health teacher, raised in cowboy country, had been wise enough to teach her students. Since then, Fen had made sure to keep Scoot at a lope, holding him back when she felt his energy increase.

But Fen knew that if they were going to be ready for the rodeo, they had to start practicing the real thing. She gave Scoot a swift kick and he took off at a gallop through the gate. They rounded the first barrel smoothly. The second barrel was a little less tight, but Fen knew their time was still good. They headed for the last barrel across the ring. Scoot was excited and Fen had to pull him up a little as they skidded around the sharp corner. They hit the barrel, it rocked from side to side and then settled back into the dirt.

Fen made the mistake of glancing under her left elbow to make sure the barrel was upright. Her weight shifted just a little and she felt it coming as Scoot shot for the straightaway. His head came up too quickly after the wheeling turn, sending Fen off balance. She grabbed onto his mane with her left hand, but slid off Scoot's back and landed hard on her back. The dust billowed around her as she lay there for a minute, assessing any pain or damage. Scoot shuffled over and stared at Fen lying in the dirt, his reins dangling on the ground. Fen could almost hear his thoughts: Watcha doin' down there? The finish line is on the other side.

"I hope it's only you and me here, buddy, or the gig is up," Fen groaned. She stood up and looked around, afraid someone had seen the fall. "It looks like we got away with it again, Scoot, but we have to get this right!"

Fen quickly dusted herself off and got back in the saddle. The next few rounds went well as Scoot seemed to catch on to what was happening around the last barrel. He pulled himself up more smoothly, allowing Fen to be in good seat before he raced for the gate. Overall, she was pleased with the practice. Fen gave her horse a good bath, a treat and led him to his pasture.

As Fen went into the house for lunch, she passed Buck coming out. Her mother was at work, Alex was at summer camp and Pete and Mack were out fixing fences, so the place was quiet.

"So, how's it going, Fen?" Buck asked, putting his hat on.

"Great!" Fen said.

"Uh, huh," Buck said in a tone that made Fen turn around. "You best be changing your clothes before your mother and father get home." He looked out towards the driveway. "You'll want to get rid of the evidence." He started whistling as he walked down the porch stairs, heading for the barn.

Fen ran upstairs and looked in the full length mirror in her mother's bathroom. Her entire back was covered in dust. She started to wipe it off and watched clods of dirt fall to the floor. Fen groaned. She went to her room, changed her clothes and shook the dirty ones out the window before putting them in the laundry basket. She returned to the bathroom to clean up the floor, realizing how lucky she was to have Buck around. He understood her need to do this and trusted her judgment, knowing there would be mishaps but believing that she could handle them.

After lunch, Fen went out and tacked up Hack. He was sleepy from the midday sun and she had woken him from a lovely doze under a shady tree. Through the entire tacking up process, Hack leaned on Fen and periodically let out a long, deep sigh.

"Oh, snap out of it, you big galoot. We have work to do."

Hack looked at her and sighed again. Fen rolled her eyes and dragged him out of the barn. As they started working on the routine, Fen realized that Hack had actually memorized the drill and she was pleased with his performance. But she also realized that he was a huge horse with a long stride doing precise maneuvers in a small place. He was built for moving at top speed across the plains and using big muscles to scramble up and down mountains. This was just not his thing.

Fen knew her efforts to hold Hack in check and make him do curly-cues and spirals were making them look bouncy and out of rhythm. She felt like she was out of her saddle most of the time and her brains were turning into scrambled eggs from all the jouncing around. Buck passed them on his way to Crescent's paddock. He stood at the rail for a few minutes to watch, his cowboy hat pulled down so that his face was in shadow.

"So?" Fen asked, not really wanting to know the answer. "How do we look?"

"Well, a little like you're on one of those mechanical ponies in the mall that people put coins into and . . ."

"Okay, alright, I get the point," Fen huffed. "Do you have any suggestions, Mr. Trainer Extraordinaire?"

"Sure, uh, you could Velcro your hind end to the saddle. Actually, glue might work better. Maybe you could try putting cinder blocks on his rump. Or you could gain about a hundred pounds."

"Thanks, Buck. I knew you'd have all the answers. Who hired you as a trainer, anyhow?"

"I believe you have asked me that question in the past." Buck pushed his hat back and smiled. "Good luck," he said and walked off.

Fen continued to work for awhile, leaning back to keep her bottom in the saddle and letting Hack move with a little more speed to make him less bouncy. Tomorrow was the first day of drill team practice with all the members working as a group in the ring with only eight days to get it right. It would be interesting to see how Hack did with other horses in the arena. Thinking about it gave Fen the feeling that she would be experiencing a disaster in her near future. Just as she was dismounting, Clancy pulled up in his truck. He was fuming and had a black eye.

"Holy cow! What happened to you?" Fen exclaimed.

"That jerk, Willis McCutchins. He's railin' on me for being at the Perkins' place too much. He's got a thing for Clara and he thinks I'm making tracks in his territory, like she's some kind of animal you stalk. I told him I'd been helping her with the barrel racing and we were all done. I wouldn't be back. But he didn't believe me and took a swing."

"Oh, no, Clancy! Is he in the hospital?" Fen knew that when her friend got started, he sometimes got carried away.

"No. But this means I can't go home for awhile . . . . like two years or so. I hope Mom doesn't keep me from participating in the rodeo." He put his hands on his hips and looked away. Fen knew he was close to tears. "Why can't I keep my hands to myself?"

"Probably for the same reason I can't keep my mouth shut, stay out of other people's business and stop doing crazy stuff. My mother calls it impulsivity."

"Is it contagious?" Clancy asked. "Maybe I caught it from you."

"Oh, no. You're not blaming this one on me! Well, the best thing for any problem is . . ."

"A trail ride," they both said together.

Ten minutes later they were on the trail, heading up into the hills with Boss happily bounding after them. Fen was riding her mother's horse and Clancy was riding Mack's horse, Brandy. They hadn't been riding for more than twenty minutes when they came around a bend in the trail and saw Clara Perkins sitting on her horse, crying. Fen and Clancy looked at each other and shrugged. They walked closer and saw that Clara had a leash in one hand. When Clara saw them she stopped crying, quickly wiping her eyes. She started to turn her horse around when Clancy called to her. Clara turned around and waited for them to jog up.

"What's wrong, Clara?" Fen asked.

Clara looked into the woods and then back at Fen. It had always been difficult for Clara to know whom to trust. She was so used to showing the confident, strong side of her personality to others and keeping her true, insecure self private. That way she wasn't vulnerable. If people didn't know her, they couldn't really hurt her. But she needed help now and somewhere, deep down inside, she felt she could trust Clancy and Fen. She just hadn't allowed herself to take the risk.

"Something is wrong," Fen said. "Maybe we can help you."

Clara looked at Fen and then Clancy. It was time to trust someone or she could lose the one thing she loved the most. Maybe people were unpredictable and unreliable, but Clara's dog had always been there for her, trusting, affectionate and loyal. It was worth risking her own pride to return that kind of love and devotion.

Chapter Twenty Five

"It's my dog, Lily." Clara's voice caught. "She's been gone since last night. She has a big pen where she stays when I'm not home. Sometimes she leaps up on the gate and the latch springs open. I keep asking my dad to fix it," Clara sobbed. "I've been looking for her all day. It's not like her to run away. I don't understand it."

"She's a beautiful dog," Clancy turned to Fen. "She's a big pure-bred Bernese Mountain Dog, all black, brown and white with lots of soft hair. She's a sweetheart, too."

"And she's pregnant," Clara sobbed again. "She's due to have her puppies next week." They all stared at each other.

"Do you have something with her smell on it?" Fen asked.

"Yes." Clara pulled out a thin sweater. "She loves to sleep on my clothes."

Fen was surprised. Boss slept on her clothes all the time, but she hadn't expected glamorous Clara to allow that from a dog.

"Well, let's try the old-fashioned way of tracking," Fen said. "Let Boss sniff it and see if he can pick up the scent."

"Do you think it will work?" Clancy asked.

191

"Can't hurt," Fen replied. "I don't like to say it, but if Lily got hurt or is trapped somewhere we could be wandering around these woods for weeks and not find her."

"Fen's right," Clancy said. "If she's hurt her instinct is to stay quiet so predators won't find her. She may not answer to her name. Besides, we're going to lose light in the woods in a few hours. Let's give it a try."

Fen dismounted and called for Boss. He scrambled out of a hole in the base of a large tree where he had been trying to dig out a family of squirrels. Clara tossed her sweater down to Fen. She held Boss's collar and put the sweater to his nose, letting him paw and sniff the fabric.

"Go on, Boss," Fen urged. "You're a good tracker. Do your job. Go on now!"

Boss put his nose to the ground and started to sniff. The three teenagers waited while the horses stood and looked around the woods, alert for any horse-eating branches that were snapping in the breeze. After a few minutes, Boss trotted away. He didn't seem to be going in a specific direction, but just randomly wandering through the woods the way he always did. The horses followed in the general direction that Boss was going, staying on the trail without losing sight of him. Fen started getting discouraged when it was clear that Boss was not on the trail of anything. He was just sniffing up trees and peeing on rocks.

"I don't know," Fen said. "He tracks wild animals, but maybe he isn't smart enough to follow a new scent. It's like he doesn't know what we're asking him to do."

"Let's give it a chance," Clancy said. "He might be doing what we're doing, just trying to get close."

The sun was sinking behind the horizon and the woods were becoming dim, the dappled light fading into shadows. After about half an hour of following Boss, Clancy looked back at Fen. They shrugged, knowing what the other was thinking. When do we give up on this?

Suddenly, Boss started barking. He rarely barked in the woods unless he sensed danger. The three teenagers all reined their horses in.

"He's caught the scent of something nasty," Fen said. "It could be bear or cougar, maybe a wolf pack or something dead." Fen tried to swallow her last words, realizing that it would upset Clara. She looked back at Clara and apologized.

"Don't worry, Fen," Clara said. "I've already imagined the worst."

Boss took off running, his nose to the ground. The three teens kicked their horses into a lope, following the dog along a well worn animal path. Suddenly, Clancy yanked on Brandy's reins and the horse came to a quick halt. Fen was riding so closely behind Clancy that Sir banged into Brandy's rump with her big nose, popping Fen out of her saddle and onto her horse's neck. Sir looked around and glared at Fen.

"Hey, Clancy! What the heck are you doing?" Fen shouted, trying to wiggle back into her saddle.

"Clara, stop!" Clancy ordered.

"What?" Clara had already stopped, trying not to laugh at Fen's awkward position.

"We know this place, Fen," Clancy said. "This is where the poachers leave hidden traps out for bear. We can't go any farther and we can't let Boss go, either. Someone's going to get nailed in there. We can't risk the horses or Boss."

"But Clancy," Fen pleaded. "Lily could be in there caught in a bear trap! Boss seems to be hot on someone's scent and it could be hers. We have to go in there."

"I'll go alone," Clara said. "You call Boss back. I can't let you guys do this. I'll leave Majesty here so she doesn't get hurt. Do you know how to spring a bear trap if I do get caught?" she asked, nervously.

"Oh geez," Clancy muttered. "No way you're going in there alone. We know how to spring traps but you can't do it yourself. It's supposed to hold a really angry half-ton bear, so there's no way you can spring it without help." Clancy looked at Fen and they both dismounted.

"Clara, you stay here and watch the horses," Clancy ordered. "If we don't come out before dark or you hear us call for help, go to Fen's house. It's the closest one around. Fen and I will go in together so that we can help each other if something happens. We could tie Boss to a tree but I think he'll be helpful tracking Lily down, if she's in there." Clancy looked at Fen. He was her dog, after all. She had to make that decision.

"I'd still love a three-legged dog," Fen said with a nervous little smile.

"Give me the leash, Clara." Clancy said.

Fen and Clancy took off into the woods with Boss, leaving Clara worried and feeling terribly guilty. She was endangering them all for her dog, who might not even be there. She watched them walk out of sight, their eyes on the ground, looking for traps in the leaves and undergrowth of the summer forest.

Boss was quiet for awhile and then started barking again. He took off, heading for the base of a tall, rocky cliff. Fen and Clancy carefully followed. Within a ten minute walk they had counted fifteen traps. Suddenly, a sharp clap sounded. Fen shrieked and Clancy wheeled around, afraid he was going to see his friend caught in a trap. But she had just kicked an edge of the metal contraption and it had snapped without her leg inside. Fen had her hand over her mouth, realizing what trouble they might have been in. The two looked at each other, their hearts pounding.

"Who would use these horrible things?" Fen asked, eyeing the forest floor even more suspiciously than before.

"Uh, your father for one, when the beavers start cutting down his trees, changing his fields and trails into ponds." Clancy looked at Fen with raised eyebrows.

"Oh, right," Fen replied, a little sheepishly. She made a note to herself to have a chat with her father about letting nature take its course, at least as far as the beavers were concerned. "How do you suppose Boss misses these things?" Fen asked, as they continued tip-toeing through the undergrowth.

"Maybe he smells them, the metal or the stuff they squirt all over them to tempt the bears."

"Well, obviously Lily's senses aren't that keen," Fen said, looking at the base of a large rock.

Lying in the leaves was one very big, very sad dog. They walked up to her, speaking quietly and calmly, knowing that a hurt dog can be a dangerous dog. Boss had stopped barking and was lying next to Lily, licking her wounded leg. It was caught in a trap and bleeding. Lily was panting and looking up at them with soft eyes that were full of pain. Lily stared at Clancy and started to whine.

"I don't think we have to worry about her biting us," Fen said. "She knows you, Clancy."

"Okay, big girl, we're going to get you out of here." Clancy knelt down next to Lily and stroked her gently, saying her name. "Fen, I'll need your help."

Fen and Clancy used all their strength to pull the trap open and slide Lily's leg out. It was bleeding enough that Clancy took off his shirt and wrapped it around the leg as a tourniquet.

"Clancy? How the heck are we going to get her out of here. She's huge and carrying a litter."

"Didn't you know I moonlight as 'Superman'?" Clancy replied, calmly. "Just keep me away from traps 'cause I won't be able to see a darn thing over this beast of an animal."

Clancy knelt down, took a big breath and grunted as he carefully picked up the scared dog. He carried her like a baby, his arms wrapped around her back with her belly up to protect the pups. Fen led them back through the bear trap area, following what she could remember of their trail. Boss hopped along ahead, easily dodging every one.

When Clara heard Fen's shriek, she had begun to panic. The horses, hearing Fen's outcry and sensing Clara's fear, had started to whinny and stomp, tugging nervously on their lead ropes that were tied around trees. Clara realized she needed to remain calm, no matter what happened. They didn't need three freaked out horses on their hands, as well as whatever problem was happening out in the woods. She took a deep breath and started stroking and talking to each horse, quieting them as much as she could. Finally, Fen appeared with Clancy walking behind, carrying Lily in his arms. Clara started to cry, not knowing if her beloved dog was dead or alive.

"She was caught in a trap," Fen called. "But she seems okay." As they got closer, Fen explained. "She's bleeding some, but Clancy does great tourniquets and she seems calm, considering her situation."

Clara was still upset but trying to regain her composure. She realized that she hadn't ever really been in a crisis and her behavior was not helping anyone. Her dog was alive and safe and they needed to focus on getting out of the woods, not making her feel better.

"Clara, you're going to have to carry Lily on your lap," Clancy said. "Neither of you can lift her onto mine. Let's get a blanket from my pack to lay her in."

Fen pulled a blanket from Clancy's pack as Clara mounted Majesty. Fen put the blanket on Clara's legs and tucked the sides under the saddle. She rolled a log over next to Majesty so that Clancy could step up and gently lay the dog in Clara's lap. They wrapped the dog in the soft folds of the blanket for extra support. Clara would need to ride with no reins so she could hold Lily in place as they rode down the steep terrain to safety.

"Are you going to be okay with this?" Fen asked.

"If you can barrel race with one hand, Fen," Clara shrugged, "I guess I can walk my own horse with no hands."

They all shared a smile, despite their situation. Clancy and Fen mounted their horses and looked back at Clara to make sure everything looked stable. It wouldn't do to have either the girl or the dog slide off as they headed down the steep hill.

"The McCulloughs' ranch is the closest place so I say we head there," Clancy said.

The girls nodded in silent agreement and they started off. After an hour of slow, downhill riding in the fading light they finally caught sight of Fen's home. They all let out a sigh of relief. Lily had been completely still and softly whining for the past half-hour and the teens were concerned it had been too much for her. The weight of her puppies was an extra burden on Lily and their well-being had caused great anxiety for the three riders. They rode up to Fen's house and Renee came out onto the porch with Alex. She understood the situation right away and went back into the house to get her keys.

"I'll get Lily in the truck," Clancy said. "Clara, you call the vet and tell them we're on our way. Fen, help me with this."

Fen opened the door to her mother's truck and Clancy carefully laid the dog on the seat. Clara came out of the house and got in the truck, gently putting Lily's head on her lap. The scene looked all too familiar to Clancy, seeing a loved one in a lap heading for help. Renee got in and reminded them to call the Perkins and tell them to meet her at the vet's office. She peeled out of the driveway, her first responder light flashing on top of the truck. She was thankful she and Mack had both volunteered and been trained to be first responders. It had been a great experience for both of them, had been helpful to the community and it certainly came in handy when you needed to get somewhere fast.

The call to Mrs. Perkins was difficult to make. Fen made it clear to her that Clara was fine, but Lily was in uncertain condition. She quickly described what had happened and that Renee was on her way to the vet with Clara and the dog.

"Oh!" Susan Perkins cried. "That dog is Clara's best friend. They have been through so much together. And now with her one week away from having pups! We have all looked forward to this time so much. I can't imagine how Clara will feel if Lily or her pups don't make it."

"Mrs. Perkins, I understand how you feel. I am so sorry this happened, but Lily seems like a strong, determined dog. We have to hope for the best."

"Thank you so much, Fen and Clancy, too. You were wonderful to help Clara when she was in distress, risking your own safety for them. We are very grateful. But we'll talk later. I need to get to the vet's office now."

"You're welcome, Mrs. Perkins. We're just glad we were in the right spot at the right time. Take care and please let us know how things are going." Fen put the phone down and looked at Clancy. "Dad is away for the day. I need to see Pete and Buck."

"Me, too," Clancy mumbled.

They found the two men in the arena with Crescent. The stallion was up to his old tricks, but seemed to be more calm and obedient than he had days before. It looked to Fen like Buck was making progress again. Clancy told them what happened and Fen ended up in Pete's arms crying an ocean of tears. The men stood in silence for awhile until Fen could pull away, leaving Pete's shirt looking and feeling like a wet rag.

"Life can be tough, Fen," Pete said, gently. "I don't have to tell you that. But we are all here to help each other get through the rough times. Why don't you go to the house, make some of your world famous chocolate chip cookies and wait for a phone call. We'll finish the chores. Can you stay and help out, Clancy?"

"Always," he said, rubbing Fen's back.

Clancy let his own tears slowly roll down his cheeks and watched them quickly melt into the dust of the arena floor. Tears were like that, he thought. They disappear so fast, but the sad feelings remain for so long. Maybe Buck and Pete thought it wasn't manly to cry, but he didn't care. His own dad had cried when they spent their last night together and Clancy knew there wasn't a person on Earth that could match his father for being the kind of man Clancy wanted to be.

Chapter Twenty Six

T he call from Susan Perkins came in at ten o'clock that night. Everybody was at the McCulloughs' house, restless from stress and waiting in the quiet gloom of the house, drinking coffee and eating Fen's chocolate chip cookies. Mack had come home late and been filled in on the day's events.

Fen came into the living room and repeated what Mrs. Perkins had just reported on the phone. "Lily is sleeping comfortably and the vet could hear puppy heartbeats in utero." Everybody cheered and clapped while Clancy gave Fen a big hug. Renee gently pulled Alex close to her body and let him rock and hum. She let out a long sigh of relief.

"It is time for all of us to hit the sack," Mack declared. "I know one young lady who has to get up very early for her first day of drill team practice at the fairgrounds." He looked at his tired daughter and smiled.

"Yessir," Fen saluted and smiled back. She gave hugs all around and went upstairs to get ready for bed with Alex following close behind.

Renee came up later to say goodnight. She sat on Fen's bed and brushed her daughter's hair off her brow. "So you had quite the day, young lady."

"I'm glad it's over," Fen replied, heaving a sigh of relief.

"You sound like Hack!" Renee chuckled. "I want you to be careful tomorrow, Fen." Renee's voice turned serious. "I know this means a lot to you, but if Hack can't hack it, sorry the pun, you may have to pull out. I'm talking about the barrel racing, too, my dear. Don't think I don't know what's been going on around here."

"What do you mean?" Fen asked, trying to sound innocent.

"Perhaps you'd better start doing the laundry, so that smudged jeans and torn shirts don't get seen by a mother's eye." Renee looked at Fen, sternly. "It's a good thing I can keep secrets, too."

"You're the best." Fen gave her mother a hug. "I promise that I'll pull out if I need to. I'll be mad as a hatter if I have to, but I will."

"Well, I can't expect you to be happy about quitting, but we need to be reasonable about the whole thing, although I know the word reasonable is not in your vocabulary at this point." Renee smiled at her daughter, remembering how much she was like Fen when she was young.

"I'll work on it, Mom," Fen giggled. "Goodnight."

"Goodnight, my love." Renee turned off the light and closed the door.

It seemed like Fen had been asleep for five minutes when the sun woke her up, stealing through the open window with a warm breeze behind. She jumped up and got into her riding clothes, ready for a serious work-out. She and Hack were both being tested in front of the whole dream team and its leader. Fen had no idea how it would go, but she had to give it a try.

Renee insisted Fen have some breakfast, so she slammed down eggs and bacon and then rushed out the door as Clancy pulled up in his truck. Neither Mack nor Renee could bear to watch the practice and they realized Fen really didn't want them to. She was nervous enough without them being there, too. It proved to be a good decision for all of them.

Everyone watching would have agreed. It was a disaster from beginning to end. Hack got off the trailer at the fairgrounds and wanted to meet every horse there. Fen was dragged from one member of the team to another so that Hack could sniff and snort his way through the crowd. Finally, Clarence Willy, the director of the program, collected them all in the arena to divide them into groups, go over the routine, give them verbal directions and walk through the pattern. Hack didn't want to be a member of the group he was in, so he kept trotting over to a certain mare he had taken a liking to. She was not interested and took every opportunity to kick him, which Hack seemed to think was a sign of affection. Fen was exhausted after half an hour of tugging, turning, backing and circling.

Fen noticed that Emily was having a little difficulty following the directions but, overall, her horse was doing really well. Clara was in perfect line all the time and pretended not to notice Fen's difficulty. The practice started in full force with the groups walking and then jogging the routine. Hack decided he preferred loping, so he was always in someone else's spot, running into the hind end of another horse or going completely off course, prancing around in happy, little circles. At some point in the whole mess, Hack became impatient with too many horses in a small space. He decided it would be more fun to herd some of the more intimidated ones around.

The more easy-going members of the drill team found the situation amusing and chuckled at Hack's antics. The more serious riders were annoyed and a few were downright angry. At the end of practice, which lasted two hours but seemed like two days to Fen, Clarence Willy approached her. He did not look like a happy man.

"Uh, oh," Fen sighed. "Here comes the cut speech."

"Fen, you and Hack just don't seem to be able to hack this. Sorry for the pun."

Fen rolled her eyes. It was bad news that Mr. Willy knew Hack's name. But she and everybody else had yelled it so many times, it would have been hard to miss.

"I know we didn't do very well, Mr. Willy, but we've practiced so hard and I really want to give Hack a chance. He's doing so much better than he did when we first started."

"Oh my," Mr. Willy said, trying not to imagine their first practice sessions. "Well, I'm sorry, Fen, but we only have one week to practice as a group and it isn't fair to the others."

"I understand," Fen said, hanging her head. She started to walk away when Emily pulled up on Rhumba, her beautiful blue roan.

"Mr. Willy?" Emily caught his attention. "I think Hack was having difficulty because he has never practiced with a group. I bet I could convince some other people to practice with us, if you'd be willing to give Hack a second chance."

"I'd be happy to join you two," Clara said. She heard Emily's suggestion and had walked over on Majesty. "We're each in different groups, so Hack could get a sense of where he's supposed to be in relation to the other horses." She looked at Mr. Willy and shrugged. "We can at least try."

"Okay, okay," Clarence sighed. "I'll give you all a chance, but if he's still not managing in three days we'll have to let him go."

"Thank you, Mr. Willy!" the girls cried.

"Yeah, yeah," he said, waving his hand and walking away. "I'm such a sucker for pretty faces and beautiful horses," he mumbled. Having lost a leg in the war, he had learned to ride again with a prosthetic leg. Clarence Willy knew what it meant to be given a second chance.

"Thanks so much you guys!" Fen was beaming. "You are awesome!"

"It'll be fun," Emily said. "Besides, Rhumba needs the practice, too. And Clara knows the drill so well, she'll be a great teacher."

"Thanks," Clara said. "Majesty's great. She manages to make me look good."

The girls agreed to meet at Fen's after lunch. Fen dragged Hack over to Mack's truck which had just pulled into the fairgrounds. The horse jumped in the trailer and they headed for home.

"Don't even ask," Fen said, looking out the window to avoid her father's questioning look. "But I now have two partners in crime who are willing to help us, so don't worry about a thing."

"Yeah," Mack replied. "I think I've heard the last part of that comment a few times before."

The girls practiced all afternoon, taking snack breaks and letting the horses play in the pasture between their work-outs. It was actually going better than expected and they were in high spirits when Renee and Alex pulled up in the driveway, home from camp and work. Renee was pleasantly surprised to see Clara and a girl she didn't recognize sitting on the fence, chatting and giggling with Fen.

"Hi, Mom!" Fen called. "Hey, Alex!"

Fen hopped off the fence and went to the jeep, followed by her two friends. She suddenly realized that neither of them had ever met Alex and it would be awkward. It always seemed that way when people first met Alex. She wondered if it would turn them off and she would lose her new found companions. Fen was ashamed of herself for thinking that. She loved Alex and was proud of the progress he was making, so similar to her feelings about Hack.

"Alex," Fen said. "This is Emily and Clara."

"Emily and Clara," Alex repeated. "One, two, three girls," he said.

"That's right, buddy!" Fen exclaimed.

Renee caught her breath and smiled at Fen. Alex rarely said anything spontaneous. His teachers had been working on counting, as well as saying people's names, so this was a big step for Alex. Renee knew Fen was just as proud as she was of his greeting, although it probably seemed odd to Clara and Emily. But they just smiled at Fen's brother.

"Hi, Alex!" the two girls said together.

"I like your sneakers," Emily commented. "I really like the frogs on them with the blinking eyes. They're so cool!"

"It's nice to meet you, Emily," Renee said quickly, taking the focus off Alex so he would feel more relaxed. He was smiling, but flapping his hands and rocking back and forth in agitation.

"It's nice to meet you, too, Mrs. McCullough," Emily said, shyly. She knew that Fen's mother was a well known lawyer in town. Emily's dream was to go to law school and eventually do legal work for environmental causes.

"And it's nice to see you again, Ms. Perkins." Renee smiled and turned to Clara. "How is Lily doing?"

"She's doing really well, Mrs. McCullough. Thank you for asking."

"They're helping Hack and me with the drill team routine," Fen said, happily.

"Wow! Now that takes generosity and lots of courage!" Renee laughed as Fen's cheerful expression turned into a scowl. "I take it practice went a little rough today, dear?" Renee asked.

"That's an understatement," Fen muttered. "Mr. Willy won't let us perform if we don't get better and fast."

"But don't worry," Emily broke in. "With enough practice Hack will be great. He's so smart."

"Um, I think that's an overstatement!" Renee chuckled. "But I like the optimism! Well, Alex needs a snack and I have to get out of these work clothes and get into real work clothes, if you know what I mean." Renee pulled at her A-line skirt and lifted one leg up, letting her high-heeled shoe dangle off her toe.

The girls laughed. They turned as they heard a truck pull up the McCulloughs' driveway. It was Emily's big brother, Eddy, ready to take the girls home. Country music was blaring from the open windows of the truck. Eddy's girlfriend was nearly sitting on his lap, playing with his hair and whispering in his ear.

"Ugh," Emily said. "It's the new one. He changes girlfriends like babies change diapers. I can never keep track. He can't either. He calls them all 'babe' so he doesn't mess up and say the wrong name. Oh, well. Time to go, Clara. We'll see you tomorrow morning at the fairgrounds, Fen, and we'll come over again in the afternoon. Let's practice every day till the rodeo. Okay?"

"Great!" Fen replied. "Thank you guys, so much, for what you're doing."

"Hey, we're a team!" Clara smiled.

They gave each other a group high-five as Emily's brother honked the horn and rolled his eyes. Fen watched them go, happy she had Alex for a brother and not one like Eddy. Thinking back over the day, Fen realized it had begun as a disaster, but ended up being a lot of fun. She also knew that her chances of staying on the team were slim. Fen hung her head as she headed for the paddock to get Scooter. They still had work to do on their barrel maneuvers. It didn't matter that she was tired and just wanted a hot shower, a big sandwich and a plate of cookies. Fen briefly wondered if all the time, energy and emotion would be worth it.

Scooter jogged over to meet Fen at the gate, lifting her spirits. He was always there to make her feel better. Fen realized that she now had two friends of the people sort, as well as her horse friends and it seemed that all of them were not ready to give up on her. The thought made her feel happy and proud. She hoped her feelings would stay that way as the rodeo drew closer. It was a huge event and she didn't want to embarrass herself, her family, her friends or her horses. Maybe Scoot and Hack couldn't understand all the complexities of human emotion, but she knew they would sense her mood in their own horsey way if things went badly.

It seemed to Fen that horses had a sympathetic soul that lay deeper than humans could comprehend. Hack and Scoot knew her in a way that people could not. They were giving and forgiving. They wouldn't wallow in her mistakes or their own. They lived in the pleasure of the moment, savoring food, sleep and shelter. They valued companionship, affection and a place they knew as home. Fen understood that these were the important things in life. At the heart of it all, horses weren't so different from herself. The difference was horses didn't let little things get in the way of remembering the important things in life.

Chapter Twenty Seven

Sitting at the dinner table, Fen was half-listening to the adult conversation while going over the drill team pattern in her head. Clara was proving to be a strong rider and had already mastered the program. Fen felt envious, but realized this was not a competition and they all wanted the team to look their best. She was very grateful that a former opponent, as well as her new friend, Emily, were helping out with the routine. Fen's thoughts suddenly returned to the adult conversation when she heard her father mention Crescent.

"Are you sure that's necessary?" Renee asked, looking at Mack with a frown.

"Buck hasn't made enough progress with him, even with all of his time and training," Mack replied. "He's too wild and stubborn. He's dangerous around the other horses, not to mention people. That stallion's a powder keg ready to go off any minute and I don't want that kind of animal around Alex or Fen. We just can't keep him."

"What?" Fen asked, quickly. "Where are you going to take him?"

"No where, honey. I can't sell him. He's got to be put down."

"Put down? No! Buck just needs more time with him!"

"Buck doesn't have more time, Fen. There are too many things to do around this ranch, as it is. Besides, Buck could get hurt and that would be no good for him, us or his family. The horse has got to go, Fen. I'm sorry."

"It's all Frank's fault!" Fen exclaimed in anger. "He put the whip to him and yelled at him. He didn't do what Buck told him to do. Frank used his own methods and scared that poor horse to death. It takes time and trust to get over that kind of treatment. And who knows how he was treated before we even got him?"

"Exactly," Mack replied, staring at Fen. "And whose idea was it, by the way, to have Frank work with that horse? Next time, maybe you'll be more careful about what you ask for and why, young lady."

Fen glared at her father, slammed her fist on the table and stomped up the stairs to her room. The tears were streaming down her face before her head hit the pillow. She could hear Alex's high pitched squeal, knowing he had gotten up from the table and was spinning in circles with his hands over his ears. It was the beginning of a terrible tantrum. People thought Alex didn't understand adult conversation. But Fen knew he understood a lot more than they gave him credit for. Fen knew he loved that horse more than anything.

Fen's mother opened the door and sat next to her on the bed. "Honey, I know it's hard, but your father is right. The risk is too great."

"You don't understand! Horses in the wild act like that all the time. It's how they communicate. We just haven't learned how to communicate with him," Fen said between sobs. "Frank's brutal ways made the stallion mistrust all of us. It's not fair!"

Renee rubbed her daughter's back, not knowing what to say. She agreed with Fen, but also understood her husband's feelings about the stallion. He was dangerous and Mack was only trying to protect his family and employees. Besides, decisions about the horses on the ranch were ultimately made by Buck and Mack.

"I don't want to talk about it. Nobody understands." Fen turned her head to the wall and hugged Ringo. For the first time, the stuffed horse just wasn't enough to stop her tears. Fen knew that Crescent didn't mistrust all of them, but she couldn't tell her parents about what Rosie and Alex had been doing everyday. It wasn't fair to Rosie. But it wasn't fair to Alex, either. By not telling the truth, she was allowing them to take away her little brother's only friend. She was so confused about what to do.

"Oh, Fen," Renee sighed. "I wish I could help. I'll be here if you decide you want to talk about it." She kissed Fen on her cheek, got up and softly closed the door behind her.

Feb sobbed into her pillow. She hated Frank for all of his mean ways. She was mad at her father for deciding to have the beautiful horse put down and she was disgusted with Pete, who didn't stand up to her father and tell him to fire Frank. But most of all, Fen hated herself because she knew it was all her fault. She had put Frank and her father up to the challenge to prove a point. She knew Frank would be fired when he would, inevitably, get impatient and be caught mistreating the horse. Her plan had worked too well and now a horse that had become her brother's only friend was going to be killed. Fen decided she did want to talk about it and she knew who would understand. She picked up the phone and dialed his number. Clancy picked up.

"Clancy, we have to talk," she said between sobs.

"Hey, Fen. What's up?"

"They're going to put down Crescent."

"Oh, no. That's too bad, Fen. I really thought Buck could turn him around."

"Buck can turn him around, Clancy." From his sympathetic but casual tone, Fen could tell Rosie hadn't even told her son about Alex's daily meeting with the horse. "Buck just hasn't had enough time to undo all the damage Frank did, on top of whatever happened to him in the past."

"Well, Fen, sometimes horses get to be too dangerous. You know that."

"I know. But not this one, Clance. He's something special and worth the effort."

From the hallway, Rosie had heard part of the conversation and had come into the kitchen. She knew something was wrong at the McCulloughs' house. Her instinct told her it had something to do with the stallion, which meant she would have to get involved, like it or not. Clancy looked over and caught his mother's anxious expression.

"Just a minute, Fen. My mom's here." He took the phone away from his ear and told Rosie what was going on.

No, Clancy!" Rosie exclaimed in an angry voice. "They can't do that!"

"Mom. Hold on. You know how these horses can be. You know that sometimes they just aren't trainable."

"Not this one, Clancy. Alex adores that horse. It would be devastating to him to have that horse disappear and not know why."

"Alex? How did he get attached to the stallion?"

Rosie sat down and sighed, putting her hands flat on the table. "Every morning Alex cuts up two apples, a red one and a green one. He takes them out to Crescent's paddock and carefully places the apple pieces on the fence. The horse comes over and slowly eats them, chewing them carefully, one by one, just like Alex eats his food. When he's finished eating, Alex puts his hands out and Crescent licks them." Rosie's voice caught with emotion, thinking about their daily ritual. "Alex rubs Crescent's face and neck and the horse just melts like butter. That stallion and that boy have hearts as big as the sky and no one knows it. All on their own they have learned to trust someone, Clancy, and neither of them have had the chance or the courage to do that before." Rosie looked out the window and wiped her eyes.

Clancy sighed and returned to the phone. "Fen, tell your father to wait. We'll be over tomorrow night to talk. My mom can explain. It sounds like that horse and your little brother have found their way into each other's hearts. Maybe that stallion can be trusted and maybe there's a way to find your little brother, if we can sort through this mess. But your father is going to blow his stack at my mom, for good reason by the way, and that's not going to be good for any of us." Clancy glared at his mother, but Rosie didn't see her son's expression. Her face was hidden beneath her hands, already dreading the confrontation with Mack.

"I know my father's going to be mad, Clancy," Fen said. "But your mom does what she does with only the best of intentions. Besides, she knows Alex better than anybody. And they both probably know that horse better than anyone, too. Please don't be angry. She took a big risk and she's going to need our support. After all, she's supported us when we've taken the wrong leap at the wrong time."

Clancy sighed and hung up. He turned around, crossed his arms and looked out the window. He thought about all the foolish things he had done and how his mother had supported him, before and after his dad had died. Fen was right. His mom had been there for Alex. He and Fen needed to be there for her. They all needed to stick together. He sat down next to his mother and took her face into his hands.

"Mom. You did the right thing for the right reasons. And when you talk to Mack tomorrow night you just need to remember one thing. Dad is standing right there with you. It always works for me." Clancy left the house and took a long walk down a dark road, just so that he could cry and not have to explain anything to anyone.

Fen went downstairs. She sat on the floor next to her father who was reading the newspaper. He looked down at her with solemn eyes. He hated to see his daughter sad, but he had a responsibility to the ranch and the people who lived and worked there.

"Dad? I called Clancy. Rosie has something to tell you. Will you please hear her out and give Crescent a second chance? She's planning to come over tomorrow night."

"What's she been up to?" Mack asked in a gruff voice. He looked at Fen, sternly.

"Mack," Renee said, quietly, looking up from her book. "We can at least hear what she has to say. We can wait on the horse one more day." Renee looked at her daughter with soft eyes.

Alex did have a tantrum after Fen went up to her room and Renee's maternal instinct told her it had more to do with that horse than Fen storming up the stairs. Her lawyer mind told her that Fen's sudden inclusion of Rosie in the picture was further evidence of what she sensed in her heart, that Alex was caught in the middle of this.

"Alright, alright." Mack glanced at the newspaper on his lap. "You know, I used to think a man was the king of his own castle. Men were the ones who made decisions for their families, their communities and the nations around the world. We were the inventors, the explorers, the thinkers, the doers, the backbone of the world from the beginning of time. But it seems that either the world has changed or I have been fooled all these years." He scowled at Renee. "And I would like to know something from my two lovely but stubborn subjects," he continued in a gruff voice. "When did this house turn into a democracy where the female majority rules, rather than a gentle dictatorship where I pretend to listen to everyone and then make the decisions myself?" His voice was stern, but he winked at Fen.

Renee smiled at her husband. She knew it was not necessary to tell her proud king that to be loved was far better than to be feared. But she also knew that whatever Rosie had to say could very well cause a split between the two families. She hoped Mack would be open-minded and see that the relationship between Fen and Clancy, as well as Alex and Rosie, would be greatly affected if he acted rashly. Mack could be a dictator at times and it never turned out well when he chose to ignore the feelings of his daughter and son, over his own sense of pride.

It had always bothered Renee that Mack often acted as though his son was not present, as though Alex was just orbiting around the family like a silent moon. Maybe when Buck had named the stallion

Crescent Moon, he had unconsciously presented a foreshadowing of things to come. Maybe there was still a way for Alex and the horse to grow into beings who would become big and bright and awesome, as Buck had pronounced. Renee knew that something remarkable needed to happen for Mack to see his son as a complete human being, rather than a shadow in their house who moved in and out of the corners of their lives.

Chapter Twenty Eight

Scooter was wild the next morning, ripping around the barrels like a doohickey in a video game. Fen managed to stay on, surprising herself and Buck. It left her exhausted but exhilarated. She hopped into Clancy's truck late morning and they headed for the rodeo fairgrounds.

"Thanks for talking with your mom last night, Clance."

"I don't know what she was thinking." Clancy looked at Fen and shook his head. "This little secret of hers could get her fired and we can't afford that."

"My father wouldn't fire her, Clance!"

"I would. She was going against his numero uno rule, putting his child in a potentially dangerous situation." The two friends were silent until they reached the fairgrounds.

"Clancy?" Fen said, quietly. "I knew what your mom was doing. I just trusted her judgment and I thought it was good for Alex. People are always protecting him. When is he going to be allowed to spread his wings and try new things?"

Clancy turned off the engine and shifted in his seat to look at Fen's face. He often had this feeling that she had a mind of a forty year old woman trapped in a teenager's body. If he could be certain about one thing in life, besides his love for his family and friends, it was that Fen knew a lot more about people's emotions than he did. He realized it was important to listen.

"Sometimes I feel like Alex lives in a bubble because he wants to," Fen said. "But maybe we all let him stay there because we're afraid of what will happen when the bubble bursts." Fen returned Alex's intense look. "I want Alex to have a life of adventure and fun and doing crazy things with people he trusts, just like we do. I think Rosie is trying to pop the bubble Alex lives in, but do it early in his life so that we'll be there to catch him when he falls."

Fen put her hand on Clancy's shoulder as he turned to look out the front window. She knew her friend might get angry at her next words, but she had to take that risk. She remembered what Rosie had said about friendship. Through time and experiences and being who you really are with each other, you become true friends. You know and trust each other so well that you can always say what needs to be said, but know the love is still there and the bond between you will never be broken.

"After your dad died, how would you have felt if your mom treated you like people treat Alex? What if she had protected you, hovering over you like a lioness who wouldn't let her cub roam, never out of sight or scent? You understand why your mom doesn't want you to bull ride, but a part of you will always resent her for stopping you from doing what you love." Tears slowly rolled down Fen's face, but she didn't turn away from her friend who was holding her hand. "What if Alex resents all of us because we won't let him be who is, always interfering with his attempts to develop his own relationships on his own terms? In this case, it happens to be with a stallion, who probably knows how he feels better than we do."

"Well, I know how I'd feel if someone tried to put me in a bubble and protect me from myself," Clancy said, quietly. "And you're right. I understand my mom's feelings about bull riding and I am a little resentful, but I have the ability to understand her feelings. If I didn't, I'd move out and go on the professional circuit and ride until I died, as they say." Clancy put his hands on the steering wheel. "It sounds pretty stupid when I say it out loud. What a dumb way to look at life. Anyway, Alex doesn't have the ability to see things from someone else's point of view. He wouldn't understand why his family is taking away his best friend." Clancy looked at Fen. "I get it. You're right, as usual." Clancy sighed. "I was just worried about my mom and me, not thinking about how all this affects Alex."

"I know," Fen replied. "My father does the same thing. Sometimes he acts as though Alex doesn't know what's going on or have feelings about what happens around him or to him. I worry about you and your mom, too. But your mom is smart and strong. She can handle my dad." Fen shrugged and swallowed. "I think." The two friends looked at each other and smirked.

"Right," Clancy said, sarcastically. "Well, if anybody can handle the men around them it's your mom and mine." He paused and smiled at Fen. "And you, unfortunately for me. It's funny how that works with men and women, when I always thought it was the other way around." He rolled his eyes and sighed. "The world sure has changed since the old westerns, when men ruled the west and women were there just to come home to."

"Are you kidding?" Fen retorted. "I do believe Maddie had Rooster Cogburn wrapped around her little finger."

Clancy grinned, reminded of the heroine in the movie, *True Grit*, who turned a ruthless, rebellious law man into a hero with a heart. "How come you always have something to say to prove me wrong?" Clancy laughed.

"It's because girls think faster than boys," Fen chided. "And we both had better move faster if we want to participate in this rodeo, which I'm not so sure I want to do, but now that we're here I don't want to look gutless by leaving."

They got out of the truck, unloaded the horses and went to their respective arenas, promising to meet at the snack stand for lunch. They both looked forward to eating the greasy fries and dried out hamburgers that always looked like the bulls had stampeded over them.

Drill team practice went slightly better and Mr. Willy decided Hack could keep trying, with the stern note that he needed to improve daily to stay in the game. The girls agreed and thanked Mr. Willy for his patience and understanding. He walked away smiling but wondering if he was doing the right thing. After all, the whole point of allowing children in the performance was to improve their skills and confidence. If Fen could succeed in this event, he would be doing his job well and giving the girl a chance to earn respect in a different venue.

Fen was already well known for her barrel racing and roping. Clarence knew she had opted out of the roping this year so that she could participate in the drill team, knowing that it was going to be a challenge for herself and her horse. It was admirable and he wanted to honor her spunk. Besides, he was getting a kick out of watching Hack prance around like a Thoroughbred. The horse had as much confidence as his owner and Clarence liked to see that in a horse, as well as in a girl.

After having lunch with Clancy, the girls squeezed into his truck for a ride home. They practiced all afternoon at the McCulloughs' ranch. Fen was happy with her friends and the practice but worried at the same time, thinking about the inevitable confrontation between Rosie and her father. She loved Rosie, Clancy and her father and she strongly believed that Crescent and Alex needed this chance. How could it all work out?

Dinner came and went all too soon and the adults were sitting around the dining room table drinking coffee. Buck and Pete had stayed for dinner and the discussion. Fen sat on a rocking chair by the wood stove with Boss in her lap. She stroked him and waited in silence, feeling like she was going to burst. Alex was sitting with a pile of books next to him near Fen's feet. He had selected ten of Fen's horse books and had found three new horse magazines from Mack's study, flipping through each one, looking at the pictures and words for a long time.

Finally, there was a knock on the door and Rosie and Clancy came in. Mack stood up and welcomed them, much more formally than usual. Renee smiled at them and went to the kitchen to get Rosie a cup of coffee and Clancy a glass of milk. Fen noticed that Pete gave Rosie a sympathetic smile. Fen hoped that meant he would support her, maybe performing his first pre-emptive strike. Fen smiled to herself at the thought.

"Please, have a seat," Mack said in a quiet voice, sitting in his usual place at the head of the table. Clancy and Rosie sat at the other end of the table, to the left and right of Renee, while the others took their places.

"I understand that you have something to tell me about the stallion," Mack said, looking directly at Rosie.

"Yes. I'll come right to the point, Mack." Rosie shifted in her seat and wrapped her hands around her coffee cup. "Shortly after Crescent came, Alex kept wandering over to his paddock. I made sure that he stood far away from the fence, just as you told me. One morning, Alex went to the refrigerator, took out some apples, cut them in chunks and put them in a bag. I followed him outside and he headed straight for the stallion's paddock." Rosie sighed and shifted in her seat, again. "I was caught in a conflict, Mack. It often happens when I'm with Alex. How much do I let him do on his own, but keep him out of harm's way? How much independence can I give him and protect him at the same time?"

Fen looked at Clancy. He stared back with a serious face, but there was a smile around the corner of his eyes. Fen knew he was thinking about what she had said earlier in the day. It suddenly occurred to Fen that people could communicate without words just as easily as horses did. She and Clancy did it all the time.

"Anyway," Rosie continued. "Alex pulled on my hand with such force that I slowly let him walk me to Crescent's paddock. Alex put the apple chunks on the fence, one by one. I pulled him back a little, although he tried to resist. Crescent was across the paddock and standing calmly. I know horses, Mack, and he was not showing any signs of aggression. He was standing with a hind foot bent and his head and neck relaxed. His ears were up but his eyes were soft. I had never seen him look so calm."

Mack put his hand up to stop Rosie and turned to Buck. "Buck, can you look at that animal and predict what he's going to do?"

Buck shifted uncomfortably in his seat. He didn't like to be put on the spot. He agreed with Rosie, but didn't want to go against his boss. He took a sip of cold coffee and grimaced. Renee got up and took his cup to the kitchen for a refill.

"Sometimes I can predict what he's going to do. When he's standing in the position and showing the behaviors that Rosie described, I'm confident that I can move around him safely. When I ask him to do something he doesn't like to do, then he's unpredictable." Buck glanced at Mack then looked at Rosie.

Fen silently blessed Buck for showing Rosie support, without creating conflict with Mack. That was not an easy thing to do and Buck communicated what he had to, quickly and calmly, just like he did with the horses. Mack looked back at Rosie and nodded.

"We did this every day," Rosie continued. "It became part of Alex's morning ritual. You know how he is about doing things the same way at the same time each day. But it was more than that. He clearly loved seeing that horse and I know Crescent anticipated their time together. If we were a few minutes late, Crescent would whinny before we turned the corner of the barn where he could see us. I swear, Alex and that horse are so much alike . . . ." Rosie's voice trailed off as she looked down into her cup.

Everyone was tense, waiting for Rosie to continue. The sounds of the clock ticking, the dogs shifting and the turning of pages as Alex flipped through his magazine seemed so loud in the quiet room. Finally, Rosie looked up at Mack.

"Every time Alex put the pieces of apple on the fence, Crescent would walk over and eat each chunk, one by one. He would chew them slowly and then walk down the fence line to the next one. At first, I made Alex stay back when the horse came over. But, at some point, I just knew that it would be okay. After eating the apples, Crescent would put his head over the fence and stretch his neck out towards Alex. It just seemed the natural thing to do, to let the boy and horse smell each other. Alex loves horses, Mack, as much as anybody here. I thought it was only fair to let him have the chance to interact with Crescent."

"He interacts with horses all the time." Mack's voice rose. "He goes into the fields and paddocks with Fen and grooms and feeds them everyday. How much more interaction does he need?"

"How about riding? How about training? What about developing a bond with a horse, like all of us have had the chance to do?" Rosie glanced around the table, pausing to look at Pete. She wanted his support and wanted him to know it. "I think every person has a horse that they need and that needs them. Just like every person needs another." Rosie bowed her head, knowing that she had said more than she should, but believing that even Mack couldn't deny her words.

"You had no way of making that kind of decision with an Autistic child and a crazy stallion!" Mack exclaimed.

"Mack," Renee spoke quietly, but sternly. "Alex is a child with Autism, not an Autistic child. Remember? He is a child first and then someone who has challenges to face, just like we all do."

"You don't have to remind me of what I've been told," Mack demanded, his voice getting louder. He was angry and everyone was stiffening in response.

Rosie sat in silence. She had been patient, listening to Mack, trying to understand how he was feeling. She had been thinking about the situation the previous day and had lain awake all night, staring at the ceiling, looking at the problem from Alex's perspective, as well as Mack and Renee's point of view. They had entrusted her with the care of their daughter and then their challenging son for so many years. She was a knowledgeable horse woman who had ridden and trained horses for years. Why were they doubting her now? Since her husband had died, had they come to think of her as just a waitress, a maid and a babysitter? Rosie was hurt, confused and downright mad.

"Mack," Renee said. "Rosie knows Alex better than anyone. She also knows her way around a herd of horses. She is saying the horse is calm around him. The horse has shown no aggression towards Alex. It seems reasonable to think that Alex and Crescent may be forging a bond."

"Reasonable?" Mack yelled. "Rosie displayed a terrible lack of reason when she allowed Alex to do what he did. She put our child in a dangerous situation and that is completely unacceptable! She has shown herself to be irresponsible with our child and I cannot let that continue!"

Everyone bowed their heads, knowing that Mack was firing Rosie. Pete started to say something but Rosie interrupted him. From her perspective, he had waited just too long to get the chance to defend her now. Besides, she didn't need anyone else to justify her own actions.

"Now just one minute, Mack!" Rosie stood up as her voice rose. "I am just as competent and confident a horse person as all of you sitting at this table. My instinct about their intentions and actions are as finely tuned as yours. I am also extremely knowledgeable and skilled at the art of taking care of children. You are accusing me of putting your child in jeopardy without trusting my judgment. How many years have you given me the responsibility of watching your children? Have you questioned my judgment all that time? If so, then YOU are the irresponsible person here, not me!" She pointed her finger at Mack and they locked eyes.

They all stared at Rosie. She was such a sweet, gentle soul who had such a calming effect on Alex. But it was becoming clear that Clancy had gotten his bold, stubborn streak from someone and that someone was standing over the table, speaking to Mack with vinegar in her voice and glaring at him with fire in her eyes.

"That boy needs someone, just like we all do," Rosie continued, her voice becoming more calm but no less confident. "That horse needs someone, too. How can you stop a relationship that could bring both of them into the world, into our world, into a world that is full of understanding, patience, compassion and adventure? I'll go, if that's what you want. But the only ones you will be truly hurting are a beautiful horse with a huge heart and your little boy, a child who is locked up inside himself just because we won't trust him to follow his own inner compass and forge his own relationships!"

When Rosie headed for the door, Pete stood up. "Rosie, wait." He looked at Renee and Mack. "Something needs to be worked out here. I don't know the answer, but I do know that letting Rosie walk out on Alex and all of us is not the right thing to do."

There was silence as Rosie hovered by the door. For a long moment, all that could be heard was the ticking of the clock and the heavy breathing of Boss, asleep in Fen's lap.

"Agreed," Mack said, finally. "Please, Rosie. Come sit down."

It was quiet again, except for the sound of Phoenix's paws clicking on the hardwood floor as she left Pete's side to lie next to Alex. Even the sound of pages being turned by the boy had stopped. No one could deny that Alex had been listening to his grown-ups, feeling their anxiety and knowing that things were not as they should be. But he couldn't understand enough of what was going on to fix it, to make it right, to make things feel like they were supposed to feel. It was as if he saw some of the pieces to a big, complicated puzzle, but didn't have enough of the pieces to see the big picture and finish it so everyone would be happy again.

"I have an idea," Buck announced, a little too loudly. Everyone looked at him in surprise. "Why don't Rosie and Alex join me in my sessions with Crescent? They can stay behind the fence but where the horse can see him. Alex can offer treats when Crescent is calm and obedient. I don't normally use treats to train horses, but I don't think it's the apples the horse wants. I think it's Alex's presence. The offering of apples will allow them to continue to connect in the way they have been. I think Crescent will find comfort in that connection and Alex's attention will serve as a reward for being obedient."

Everyone sitting around the table looked at each other. Fen stopped rocking in her chair. Alex began humming and stroking Phoenix along her back. She slowly rolled over and lifted her two legs, offering her belly for a good rubbing. Mack let out a sigh and glanced at all the people sitting around the table. He looked at Renee, sitting at the other end of the table. He had relied on her for so many years to help him make decisions when it seemed there were too many pieces to a problem and the puzzle wasn't taking shape in his mind.

"What do you think, Renee?" Mack asked, looking at his wife.

"I think you should ask the other two people in this room who haven't been heard from yet." Renee raised her eyebrows and curled her hands around the cold coffee cup.

Mack look surprised for a moment. He suddenly realized that Fen and Alex had been sitting behind him by the wood stove during the conversation. Why was he just now realizing that they hadn't been part of the conversation? He looked at Renee. Her brow was furrowed and she looked sad. He looked at Clancy, sitting across from his mother at the table. Clancy returned his gaze, the dark eyes confident yet gentle. He was so much like his mother. Mack turned around and looked at Fen and Alex, sitting by the wood stove.

"What about it, Fen? Alex? Do you both think it's worth the risk?"

"I think it's worth a try," Fen said, quietly. She looked at Alex, who had returned to calmly flipping pages with one hand and petting Phoenix with the other. "I think my brother would agree."

"Alright." Mack looked at Rosie. "If you are willing to stay after my outburst, I will allow the plan to proceed until you or Buck decide it isn't working. Agreed?"

"Agreed," Rosie said.

Fen wanted to burst with relief and happiness, but she sat quietly, patting Boss and watching Alex rub Phoenix's outstretched belly. In that moment, Alex looked like any other six-year-old boy and no one could have known the trauma and near tragedy that the wolf-dog had experienced as a pup, if Pete had not been there to rescue her from the wild fire. Fen realized that both the dog and her brother had been victims of circumstances beyond their control, but they were also blessed by the gift of second chances.

"Hey, little brother," Fen said, quietly. "You've got a job now. You have a horse to train."

Alex looked up and started humming softly, off-key, with no rhythm. It was the most beautiful music Fen had ever heard.

Chapter Twenty Nine

"**H**ack! I've had it with you!" Fen yelled for the tenth time in an hour.

They had two days until the rodeo and Hack was acting like an annoying teenage boy. The three girls had been practicing in the ring for almost a week now and Hack had taken a particular liking to Majesty. Today, he was following her around the ring, nibbling on her bottom, rather than following Fen's cues to do his part in the routine. Hack didn't seem to care that Majesty kicked him every time he came within striking distance. It almost seemed to make him want to be with her all the more. Clara ignored Hack's advances and kept Majesty on track, but it was really irritating and they were all getting frustrated.

"Are you sure Hack is a gelding?" Emily asked Fen.

"Yes. I watched the process," Fen replied, shivering a little with the memory.

"Yuck," Clara remarked, covering her face.

"In that case," Emily suggested to Fen. "You have to be more assertive with him."

"You try being assertive with a fifteen hundred pound beast with a mind of his own when you can only use one arm!" Fen shouted. Fen's sling had been removed, but the doctor had made it clear that she still couldn't use the arm.

"I know. I know. I'm sorry," Emily said.

"No. I'm sorry, Emily. I'm just worried we'll have to quit," Fen replied with reluctance.

"No, we won't!" Clara declared. "We'll just keep trying and do the best we can. It's probably my fault for having a mare with such a cute back end!" She smiled and smacked Majesty on her rump.

They started the routine for the last time and Fen yanked on Hack's reins every time he started to get off course. It helped a little, but he still had trouble staying on task when Majesty walked across his path.

"How about using a reward system, rather than punishment?" Emily suggested.

"How are we going to do that?" Fen asked.

Emily dismounted and headed for her backpack outside the gate, with Rhumba following close behind. She pulled out a bag of carrots and headed back into the ring. She tied Rhumba to a post and directed Fen and Majesty to start working around the course. Every time Hack did a maneuver correctly he was rewarded with a chunk of carrot. It worked well until they ran out of carrots. The girls decided to stop so that Hack wouldn't go back to following Majesty's swishy tail around. Just as the girls were riding out of the ring, Clara's father pulled up in his truck.

"Hi, girls! Is your father at home, Fen?"

"Yes. He's working with Pete in the paddock out back," Fen replied.

"Thanks." Dale paused. "How's it going with the routine?"

"Unfortunately, Hack has developed a crush on Majesty and she's not too happy about it." Fen laughed. "But who can blame him? She's a beauty and he's a beast! By the way, congratulations on Lily's puppies! I can't believe she managed to have ten perfect pups with all the stress she had. It's so great!"

"We are very happy, indeed," Dale replied. "The pups are worth quite a bit and we have already had numerous calls from people wanting to purchase them. And we're happy that Lily went through the whole thing so well. She's turning out to be a wonderful mother."

"You guys have to come over and see the puppies," Clara said, proudly. "They are so adorable. You should bring Alex, too. He is so good with your dogs and the horses. I'm sure he'd love them."

"Yes," Dale added. "You are all welcome, anytime. Well, I need to see your father. Good luck, girls. Don't give up!" Mr. Perkins disappeared around the house.

The girls headed to the barn to untack and give the horses a treat and a bath, knowing they would end up getting wetter than the horses. Both the girls and the horses thought bath time was much more fun than practicing their routine. Hack leaned into whoever was bathing him so the girls took turns. When it was their turn, they stripped out of their clothes down to a bathing suit, all ready to get soaked.

"Mack! Pete!" Dale called when he saw the two men leaning on a fence, watching a paddock full of horses.

"Dale! You're just in time!" Mack called back.

"Can I help?" Dale asked.

"Are you kidding? Join the party!" Pete let out a laugh.

The three men spent the next two hours giving all the horses health checks, hoof work and shots. Renee finally called everybody in for dinner. She invited the girls and Dale to join them.

"I want to thank you all, again," Dale said, "for saving Lily. Not only are she and her pups worth a lot of money, but we all love that dog. Did you know she saved Clara's life once?"

"No!" Renee gasped, turning to Clara. "What happened?"

"A cougar was after us on a trail ride. He stalked us for a long time. Both Lily and Majesty were spooked and I was scared to death. I knew the cougar was just waiting for the right time to strike. I think Lily finally got fed up with the stress or maybe she was trying to cause a distraction so that Majesty and I could get away. Anyway, she took off after the cougar. At first, the cat just stood his ground and snarled, weaving and dodging like a snake ready to strike. But Lily kept going at him, barking and snapping. Leaving Lily with the cougar was really hard because I knew she could easily be killed. But I took the chance to get away, knowing I had to save myself and Majesty. I had just lost my first horse to colic." Clara paused for a moment, remembering her friend. "Rumsey was a super pony. He was my best buddy for years." Clara stopped talking and put her head down.

Everybody sitting around the table understood her sadness and stayed quiet for a few moments. They had all lost a friend or two and knew that the feeling of loss doesn't ever really go away. The sadness just finds a place to settle in a corner of the heart, only to pop out every now and then.

"And what about Lily?" Renee asked. "It looks like she came through it alright."

"Oh, yes." Clara took a bite of steak and chewed slowly. "Lily showed up at the house hours later, wounded and worn out, but the vet was able to sew her up as good as new."

"I know how you feel about losing Rumsey," Fen said, sympathetically. "They just seem to become part of yourself, part of who you are. They certainly know the best and worst of us." Fen rolled her eyes. "Hack is definitely seeing the worst of me these days!"

"Yeah," Emily said. "But all fifteen hundred pounds still follows you around like a little puppy dog!" They all laughed as Renee and the girls started taking dishes to the kitchen.

"I want to thank you again, Dale, for helping us out today," Mack said. "It sure made the job go faster. Which reminds me, whatever happened to Frank and your ranch hands?"

"Ha!" Dale responded. "They are being dealt with by the Federal Government, thank you very much! Not only did they not know that I had a license to round up wild horses, but they acted without the consent of their employer and, thus, are being nabbed for stealing, among other things. Apparently, Frank is also wanted for abandoning his wife and infant without paying child support and assaulting a guy in a bar who owed him money. I needed ranch hands so badly I didn't check references before I hired him. What an idiot I was."

"Well, then, we're both idiots because I didn't check Frank's references, either," Mack said.

"Then idiots come in threes," Pete added. "I knew he was a bad apple and didn't pressure Mack to fire him." They all laughed and shook their heads.

"Are you having a hard time finding new hands for the ranch?" Mack asked Dale.

"I am. I want to be really careful this time and it seems there aren't as many capable men around as I thought."

Renee had come back into the dining room with mugs of coffee for the adults. The girls had gone into the adjoining living room to check out horse thrills and spills movies on the computer. Alex sat on the floor with his ten books and five magazines. Fen had added to his collection of literature when he wasn't looking. Alex would get upset if she took anything out of his pile, but Fen knew that adding new pictures and words would be good for him.

"Well, all of that is unfortunate," Renee said. "But I have a proposal that might help us all out." She sat down at the end of the table, facing Mack, with Pete and Dale on either side. They looked at her expectantly, knowing she had been doing some silent scheming for awhile.

"Uh, oh," Mack said. "This usually means she has a great idea that takes a lot of work, time and money."

"Like getting Sir Prize and starting this ranch, you mean? And suggesting we have children?" Renee smiled at her husband, coyly.

"Yes." Mack cleared his throat and scowled. "All three were great ideas, if not costly. But it's all been worth it, so plunge ahead, my dear."

"Well, we have too many horses for three men to handle. Dale, you don't have enough horses to keep your ranch going. I know you've been using the traditional way of training horses because that's the method your ranch hands had been taught to use. So, why don't we give half of our horses to Dale and share the cost and time of Buck? He can train the horses while we actively look around the country for men and women who are trained in the natural horsemanship techniques. There must be a lot of trainers in the east who would love a chance to visit the west. We also have Clancy and Fen who know a lot already. They could work with the horses that are almost at the point of selling. And there's a new trainer in town, Don Lacey, who is looking for a job."

"Yeah," Dale added. "I've talked to him about coming out and seeing the horses I've got. He's interested in starting up his own business, but maybe he'd work for us for awhile. It would allow him to get to know the area and the people a little better."

"Perfect!" Renee said. "With all of that going for us, hopefully we can attract good ranch hands to join the team. I can put the word out via computer and let it go nationwide."

"Training horses the way Buck does takes a lot of time and money," Dale commented.

"But we do have Clancy," Pete spoke up. "He learns fast, he's great with horses and he knows a lot about natural horsemanship, already. He trained Bo and Bandit and look how well they turned out. We could offer him a full-time job in the summer and he could work around his class hours during the school year. It would get Rosie out of debt and give Clancy a great start in a career." They all nodded in agreement.

"It will take time," Renee warned. "We'll have to think of it as a long-term investment. What we do know is that people want horses that have been trained by 'horse whisperers'. They're better horses and we can get more money for them. In the long run, it will be worth the investment. We could even offer a place for young people to come to learn the methods from Fen and Clancy. They could hold clinics for teens, take them out on trail rides and show people from the east what the real west is all about."

"It's starting to sound like a dude ranch, Renee." Mack frowned and slurped his coffee.

"Not if we specify the level of expertise clients need to have to be invited," Renee replied. "We can think of it as a five-year plan. If we join forces, in five years we'll have more trainers, more horses and more clients. You know as well as I do that there are thousands of horses out there just sitting around in backyards and places much worse than that, waiting to be trained and ridden. We could save some animals while reducing the need to take horses from the wild."

The men looked at each other for a moment. Suddenly, Mack was surrounded by three excited girls who had heard every word the adults had said.

"Hey, hey, hey!" Mack yelled over the squealing and pleading of the girls. "I thought you were watching a movie or something!" He gently shoved them away, but chuckled softly at their enthusiasm.

"We were," Fen said. "But remember. We are the generation of multi-taskers! We can watch, talk and listen, all at the same time!"

"I've noticed," Mack said with a sideways glance at Fen.

"Dad, we can help! We're all good riders and trainers. We can help with the clinic as well as getting the chores done. Please think about it?" Fen pleaded.

"I suppose you'll be wantin' payment for your work?" Dale asked, pretending not to smile.

"Well, yeah!" the girls said in unison.

"It's certainly something to think about," Mack said.

Renee smiled and put down her coffee cup. "Funny, that's what you said when I first suggested getting married, then having children, then building a ranch."

Pete slapped his hand on the table. "Well, then, I'd say it's a done deal. When do we start?"

Chapter Thirty

Fen was sweating like a horse after the Kentucky Derby, washing and grooming Scoot and Hack the morning of the rodeo. Hack was leaning and sighing, which is why the girl had jumped out of bed and slipped into her bathing suit at six o'clock in the morning. Fen stood back and looked at her horses. They were radiant in the morning sun. She was proud of her horses for working so hard the past few months. All she could do now was cross her fingers and toes and pray for a good day.

Everybody helped load the horses in assorted trailers. Pete and Buck both looked cool as cucumbers, even though they were competing in the roping events. Pete also rode in the bronc-riding events. Buck always opted out of those. He chose that time to get lunch because he didn't like watching the horses used in that way. Yes, he was a western man, but some of his ways were just different than the other cowboys. Everyone accepted it because they respected him so much. And he respected that this was part of their culture and he wasn't going to try to change it.

Rosie and Alex stayed home and waved as the trucks pulled out of the driveway. Alex couldn't stand the crowds and noise and Rosie couldn't bear to be part of the event that had killed her husband. She was finally feeling healthy and happy again and didn't need bad memories to seep in.

Fen and Clancy headed out first, anxious to get there. Clancy looked over at Fen who was all decked out in her western finest. She was wearing brand new jeans, polished boots and a glittery shirt her mother had made as a surprise. Her hair was done up in a French braid and she looked about eighteen-years-old. The constant nail-biting was a distraction, however.

"Fen?" Clancy glanced at her. "Are you going to be alright?"

"Yeah," she replied, tentatively. "I just don't feel ready. I mean, Scoot is doing really well and I can almost use my arm again if I had to, but Hack is still being naughty. I really think he knows what to do, but it seems like he's playing with me, like he wants to do it wrong on purpose."

"Maybe he wants to make sure you don't ask him to do a drill team performance again." Clancy laughed. "I mean, it's kind of like asking me to take ballet, ya know what I mean?"

"That's not a pretty picture." Fen grimaced.

"That's what I'm saying. His body and mind were not designed for this type of thing."

"Do you think I'm being mean, making him do this?"

"Not at all. It's good for horses and people to learn new things, especially when they work as a team. He'll be fine. He won't look like Majesty or Rhumba or Sir Prize, but he isn't them. He's Hack. He'll take you anywhere you want to go, at the speed you want to go and he'll always be there to save you. There's nothing better than that in a horse."

"I know. I really love him." Fen heaved a great sigh.

"You even sound like him." Clancy chuckled. "You also sound like a woman in love." Clancy looked at Fen with a grin and batted his eyelashes, imitating the women he had seen in the movies they had watched together.

"Oh, please," Fen said, sarcastically, and rolled her eyes. "But you are right. The probability of me falling in love with a horse is much greater than me falling in love with one of your species, thank you very much."

"You say that now," Clancy replied with a wink. "Maybe I'll just have to remind you of that in a year or so."

"Well, don't hold your breath," Fen smirked.

"No, I guess I'm smarter than that," Clancy sighed.

He pulled up to their spot on the fairgrounds, they got out of the truck and joined the usual chaos, confusion and crowds. Renee and Mack got settled on the bleachers and saved room for Buck's wife, Tracy, and their baby, as well as for Pete and Buck so they would have seats when they had finished their events. Renee knew Fen and Clancy would be hanging out with friends between their events. She was so happy that her daughter had finally found some girlfriends that she liked and respected. Despite Fen's difficult two years in middle school and the recent problems with Frank, Renee knew it was the beginning of a good summer. She looked forward to their crazy adventure of joining Dale and Susan Perkins in a business partnership.

At the end of their competitions, both Pete and Buck were in champion positions, beating out the other cowboys with the roping contests. Buck did a demonstration of using natural horsemanship to calm the wildest horse in the county, who had been selected by the judges of the rodeo. The crowd was amazed and gave Buck and the horse a standing ovation. Typical of Buck, he took off his hat, bowed once and walked out of the arena. The stallion calmly walked next to Buck's shoulder, the lead rope hanging over his neck. Renee had a twinkle in her eye, knowing this would mean a good start to attracting clients to their new horse business. She briefly contemplated what they should call their ranch. The McCullough Ranch was just not catchy enough.

It was time for the drill team performance. Fen tacked up Hack and gave him a carrot for good luck. He looked calm. He looked almost too calm. It made Fen nervous, as if he was up to something. They had worked on Hack's final maneuver so hard. She prayed that he would remember how to do it. She met Clara and Emily as they entered the gathering area. They all high-fived and rolled their eyes.

"Well, as my grandfather used to say," Emily started when Fen joined in, 'Sometimes just showing up is good enough!'" The two of them laughed, but they were surprised to see Clara laughing, too.

"My dad says that all the time!" Clara exclaimed. "It must be an old person thing that's been handed down, generation after generation."

"Old people are all the same," Fen smirked. She looked at Clara and Emily who started laughing.

"And now we're saying the old person thing!" Emily exclaimed. "Oh, no! We're turning into our parents!" The three of them went into a giggling fit, until they saw Clarence Willy heading their way.

"Well, the fun is over, gals," Fen said with a sigh. Hack leaned on her and sighed back.

Mr. Willy came over, quickly formed lines and barked out final instructions. He walked over to Fen and patted Hack on his neck. "Just do the best you can, honey."

"Yessir." Fen momentarily wondered if he was calling her, 'honey', or Hack. It didn't matter. They were a team, come what may.

The music started and the performance began. Hack was calm, but a little bit too fast and bouncy, as usual. He was prancing and sashaying around like a gorilla in a tutu, but Fen was pleased that he was actually following the routine! He did have some trouble slowing his momentum at times, bumping into a few hind ends. The few kicks he received didn't seem to bother him or the riders, so there weren't any mishaps, just chuckles from the audience. He got out of position once and Fen made him do a quick turn on the forehand to get back in place, but the crowd just applauded. At one point, Hack caught sight of Majesty across the arena. He tried to cross the path of an oncoming line of horses to sneak a quick nuzzle from his true love, but he changed his mind with one quick yank on a rein from Fen. He looked back at her as if to say: Alright, alright, as long as I can get some alone time with her after this dumb thing is over.

At the finale, when the horses had to stay at a halt for one minute longer than Hack thought necessary, he started to lean into the horse next to him, who started to push into the horse next to him. Fen yanked on his rein and Hack straightened up, saving the beautiful row of halted horses from turning into an equine game of dominos.

The drill team received a standing ovation with lots of "bravos" and "yeehaws" and "yahoos". The horses marched out of the arena with Hack hanging back, as though he forgot where he was supposed to be in the line. At the gate, Fen slowly turned Hack around. He gracefully went down onto one knee, stretched his other leg out in front of him and bowed his head. The crowd went wild, stomping their feet, clapping their hands and waving their hats. Then a roar of laughter went up as Hack elegantly picked up his front end, turned his back end to the crowd and exited the arena, his long, black tail swishing with pride.

Renee, Mack and Tracy clapped until their hands were sore and Pete laughed so hard he nearly toppled off the stands. Through the entire performance, Buck had been sitting with his back against the bleacher behind him, his arms crossed in front of his chest. He could tell the minute Fen and Hack entered the arena that they were ready. He watched Hack's elegant bow and sarcastic exit with a small smile on his face. Buck had put Fen up to the challenge, but he knew she and that horse had the courage, diligence and confidence to pull it off. People said he was the best trainer around and he was. Buck knew that if you wanted to be a good trainer you had to know your riders and their horses and trust them to follow their instincts.

Fen was relieved that the drill team performance was over, even though she had to admit it had been really fun. She had shown people that Hack was a smart horse and could do more than just hack. But mostly, she was proud that he had hung in there with her through all the practices and the performance. He was a winner in her eyes. Everybody from the team, including Clarence Willy, surrounded them with hugs and praises.

Barrel racing was the final event of the rodeo. Fen was the twenty-fifth girl in a line of thirty girls, all competing for the blue ribbon and a lot of money. Clara was waiting right behind her. They smiled and nodded, Clara giving her the thumbs up sign. Finally, the announcer introduced her.

"Next up is Fen McCullough from the McCullough Ranch! She's the girl to beat, grabbing the blue ribbon for three consecutive years at the first rodeo of the season! Here's Fen and her boy, Sundancer, a.k.a., Scoot!"

The bell rang and Fen and Scoot were off and running. He shot out of the gate like a bullet from a pistol. Fen hung on for dear life with two legs and one arm. Her sling had been off for some time, but the crowd could see that she had her arm tucked up next to her stomach. It still ached when Fen held it loose for balance. Renee held her hand over her mouth and started to close her eyes. Mack gave her a hard nudge and she opened them again. Pete and Buck sat like posts on the bleachers, knowing the risk involved. The crowd was silent.

Scoot cleared the first barrel with no room to spare. He tore around the second barrel, knocking it slightly but it stayed up. He galloped for the last barrel and rounded it cleanly, but just as he started to straighten up for the run home, Fen slipped in the saddle. She hadn't straightened up as fast as Scoot and she was falling. The crowd let out a gasp, watching Fen falling head first to the ground. But Scoot felt her unbalanced weight and quickly leaned, pushing Fen back up into her saddle.

The spectators let out one loud, long sigh of relief. Fen regained her balance in less than a second while her horse went ripping for the gate. Scoot looked like he had taken flight, his mane and tail flying behind like a streak of gold flashing in the sunlight. Fen's eyes blurred with tears, partly from the speed but mostly from the sweet release of control, giving it up to her horse for the final run for home and first place.

The crowd was on its feet, clapping and cheering. Renee and Tracy were crying, Mack was grinning from ear to ear and Pete and Buck were slapping each other on the back. The announcer was yelling over the din.

"That, my friends, was the ride of a lifetime for a fifteen-year-old girl! Everybody sing 'Happy Birthday' to our amazing cowgirl, Fen McCullough, and her incredible horse, SCOOT!"

The crowd laughed and sang 'Happy Birthday'. Dismounting from Scoot, Fen was in shock. She had forgotten it was her birthday! In all of the excitement and tension of the last two months, it had slipped her mind. For the first time in her life, her birthday had become less important than all of the events around her. Clancy came up from behind, picked Fen off the ground and put her on his shoulders. Fen waved at the crowd from the gate, smiling and blushing like a spring rose.

"For Pete's sake," Fen said to Clancy in a loud whisper. "Put me down!"

He put her down and gave her a hug. They quickly left the gate and headed to the fence to watch Clara and the last of the riders. Clara did an amazing job, ending up in tenth place. She was so happy with Majesty's first performance in a rodeo. The Perkins family and McCullough gang all met at their trailers to untack, groom, water and load the horses.

"You're all invited to our house," Susan Perkins said. "We're having a barbecue to celebrate. Rosie and Alex are already there preparing the food and waiting for our arrival."

"Yahoo!" Clancy yelled. "Food!"

"Food, yeah, but I can't wait to see those beautiful puppies!" Fen exclaimed, smiling at Clara.

"I do have to tell you," Clara said, suddenly solemn. "One of them is really sickly. He won't move and hasn't eaten for two days. I don't know if he'll live. He's the smallest and Daddy says the runts usually don't make it. We tried feeding him with a bottle but he just turns away. He sleeps most of the time in a corner of the box by himself. It's been really hard to watch the poor thing."

"That's so sad," Fen said.

"Yeah. Dad says these things happen and we have to let it go and move on."

"Adults love to say stuff like that." Fen rolled her eyes. "It's like when you become an adult you forget to wish on the first star and put pennies in fountains and have dreams with happy endings. They get all full of gloom and doom and expect the worst. Come on," Fen said cheerfully. "Let's go see that little runt and pray for a happy beginning." Fen put her arm around Clara and they headed for Clancy's truck.

"Oh, I forgot," Clara said, suddenly. "I met this really cute guy during the rodeo. He's going to drive me to our place. There he is!" She pointed at a tall, muscular boy walking towards her. He was dirty from tying up calves in the arena, but smiling at Clara through the dust on his face.

"Okay," Fen laughed. "I guess I'm being rejected for a handsome boy. I better get used to it! See ya there!" Fen walked off and met Clancy at his truck. "It looks like Clara has found a friend of the male sort."

"Really?" Clancy smiled. "Thank heavens. I'm off the hook!" He winked at Fen and she smiled back.

"Let's get to the Perkins' ranch," Fen said. "We have a problem to solve there."

"What's up now?" Clancy looked concerned.

"You'll see. We need to create a happy beginning to a story, but I think only Alex can pull this one off."

Chapter Thirty One

C lancy and Fen pulled up in the truck at the Perkins' ranch. Pete was already there handing out glasses of lemonade to everybody. Susan and Rosie were busy putting platters of food out on picnic tables and Dale was at the barbecue pit with beef ribs, hamburgers and hot dogs simmering on the grill. Mack was trying to tell Dale how to cook and the two men were already in a friendly debate about the best way to grill meat, western or eastern style. Clara and her new friend were sitting on the double swing, hanging on the porch. They were both watching everyone else and smiling a lot, but not talking much.

"Where are Mom and Alex?" Fen asked Mrs. Perkins.

"Oh, they're out back with Lily and her puppies. I understood from your mother that Alex doesn't like crowds but he loves animals, so I kept the gathering to a minimum and put the puppies out back where Alex would have a quiet place to be."

"Thank you, Mrs. Perkins," Fen replied, but she let out a little sigh. She was always concerned about how people would react to Alex's disability. It seemed most people were respectful and tried to be sensitive to his needs. But Fen was tired of Alex being treated like another creature that you put somewhere to protect him from the rest of the world.

"I invited Emily, too," Mrs. Perkins continued. "I know you three girls have become quite good friends. I asked her if she would like to invite her parents, but she said they're out of town." Mrs. Perkins looked over Fen's shoulder. "Oh, here she is now."

"Hi, Fen! Hi, Mrs. Perkins!" Emily greeted them with a wave and parked her bicycle against the porch.

"You didn't bring your brother, Emily?" Susan asked.

"Are you kidding?" Emily exclaimed. "It's my one chance to get away from Mr. Creep! He's been bossing me around all week with my parents gone and his new girlfriend has been hanging around the house like a slobbering puppy. It's making me crazy! I needed the time with normal people who know how to have fun."

"Speaking of puppies and people who are having some fun," Susan laughed. "You'll find some of both around back."

Fen and Emily went behind the house to find Renee and Alex, who was happily covered in yapping, tumbling, furry, soft bundles of energy. The puppies were licking his face, pulling on his Velcro shoe straps and tugging at the zipper on his shirt. Alex was giggling so hard he finally fell over and the puppies jumped all over his sprawled out body.

"Mom? Maybe we could move Lily and her box of puppies to the side of the house so that Alex can see everybody, but not get too overwhelmed by the commotion. He seems kind of, well, out of it back here."

"That's a good idea, honey," Renee said. "Give me a hand moving these bundles of fluff off your brother!"

Buck came around the back of the house in time to help with the big puppy move. While Fen and Emily led Lily to a spot beside the front porch, Renee and Alex followed, each carrying a puppy. Buck hefted the big box with the rest of the puppies and gently put them next to Lily, who had been barking incessantly, watching her puppies being carried off without her.

"Congratulations on a great rodeo!" Buck said to Fen when Lily had quieted down and Alex was settled back in with the puppies. "Now I can tell you my secret, as long as you promise not to blab!"

"Oh, no," she smiled. "It's a good thing I can keep secrets."

"A friend of mine said he saw your wild herd, the dun stallion, mare and foal, over the mountain in the next valley. He was on an all day hack and just happened across them in a secluded meadow. He said the filly's getting pretty tall. She's got real long legs and a beautiful face."

"No! Seriously?" Fen couldn't contain her excitement. "Oh, Buck! Are you going to hold me to that secret? I have to tell Clancy!"

"Well, I figured on that. He's excluded from any secret of mine that you have to keep." He winked and walked away.

Dale and Susan had invited a local band and the fiddles and banjos began playing with gusto. It didn't take long for people to start dancing and everyone was in high spirits. While Clara's new friend hung out with the other men, she held Buck's baby and showed Emily and Fen around the farm. They had fun finding chickens' eggs in all sorts of strange places, petting the goats and giving some slop to the pigs.

During their tour, the girls disappeared around the barn for awhile. All of a sudden, there were shrieks and loud cries for help. Everybody turned to see the three girls running around the yard, two tom turkeys on their heels. Buck's baby, still clutched in Clara's arms, was the only one giggling, happily waving her arms and legs around, while the girls were scampering around like wild goats fleeing a wolf.

Dale laughed. "Those are the meanest turkeys I will ever have the pleasure of eating. Susan carries an umbrella around the ranch, just in case they ambush her. I swear they sit and wait for an innocent passerby and launch an attack, just for fun."

"Girls!" Dale called. "Stop running, turn around and yell, time for the freezer, boys!" Dale turned to Mack. "Works every time."

Emily, Fen and Clara stopped running and turned around. "Time for the freezer, boys!" they yelled together.

Dale was right. The two birds turned tails and ran as fast as they could to their coop, gobbling all the way. Only Buck's baby was disappointed when the turkeys disappeared around the barn. Fen consoled her with a piece of corn on the cob.

"And people say turkeys are dumb," Dale muttered to himself as he locked the birds in their coop so that no further mishaps would occur. He was a little concerned that the turkeys might go after Alex.

After everyone had danced and stuffed themselves with good homemade, farm raised food, Susan asked Emily and Clara for some help in the house. Emily went to the box of puppies and squatted down next to Alex, whispering something in his ear. He got up and followed her into the house. Fen and Renee were sitting at the picnic table having a serious conversation about what the summer might hold, which included a lot of work from both of them.

Susan, Alex and the two girls came out of the house carrying a cake and singing "Happy Birthday". Everyone joined in and a loud applause went up at the final note.

"Thank goodness that's over," Dale laughed. "We sounded like a choir of barn yard animals!"

"With the exception of Rosie," Pete added. He had been standing next to her, enjoying the only beautiful voice in the din.

Fen was so surprised and embarrassed by the attention she was getting about her birthday that she didn't know what to say. She made a wish, glad that she was still young enough to believe it would come true, and blew out all fifteen candles with one breath. Everyone clapped and cheered. They all ate a piece, saying it was the best cake they had ever eaten. Soon after, the inevitable moaning and groaning started up, everybody complaining about how much they had eaten. The men lay down on the grass, put their hats on their full bellies and talked about the new business. Fen noticed that Alex had gone back to playing with the puppies.

"Where's the little runt?" she asked Clara.

"Oh. He's in his own little box in the shade. He won't eat or drink and we're afraid he'll get dehydrated in the sun. We don't know what to do with the sweet thing. He just lies by himself and whimpers.

Fen found the scrawny puppy and brought him to Alex. Clancy and the girls rounded up all the other pups and put them back in their big box. The runt lay in Alex's lap and whimpered. Alex began humming and stroked the pup gently from the tip of his nose to the end of his tail. He put his finger to the little, pink mouth. The pup started to lick Alex's finger and then he tugged on it. He pulled the boy's finger into his mouth and started to suck. Alex giggled. Susan gasped quietly and disappeared into the house. Moments later she came out with a warm bottle of milk. She gave it to Alex and showed him how to hold it. Within minutes, the puppy was greedily sucking on the milk.

Everyone crowded around and smiled, watching the runt finally willing to take nourishment. After some hearty guzzling, the puppy stopped eating and climbed up Alex's belly to lick his face. Alex giggled and stroked the puppy who put his brown paws on the chest of his new friend. The runt was mostly black with small white and brown spots all over his body. His head was all black with one distinctive white marking right between his eyes.

"Well, we know who gets the first puppy!" Dale exclaimed.

Fen sat down next to Alex. She stroked the puppy for a moment. "What should we name him?"

Alex looked up and stared at Fen's hair. He reached up and stroked her curly locks, which she had removed from the French braid after the rodeo. "Fen," he said.

Renee gasped and put her hand over her mouth, hearing Alex say his sister's name for the first time. Fen smiled and tears started streaming down her face. "Yes, Alex. I'm Fen."

"Fen," he repeated, still stroking her hair.

Clancy squatted down next to Alex and touched the puppy. "What's the dog's name, Alex? Dog's name?" Clancy shrugged his shoulders and put his palms out as he asked the question.

Alex stroked the puppy. He took one finger and gently traced the outline of the marking on the pup's little face. Alex put his hands up and made the gesture in sign language that only Rosie knew. She started to cry softly, knowing that Alex was saying something new, something he had learned at school but had never used anywhere else. Every rainy day, the teachers would take Alex to the window and make this sign with their hands and say the word it represented.

"Rain," Alex said.

"Just like the foal," Fen said to Clancy.

Clancy just smiled. The families and friends stood around Alex and his new puppy, Rain. Renee and Mack were standing arm in arm. Buck was holding his baby with his arm around his wife. Susan and Dale were hand in hand and Pete slipped his arm around Rosie's shoulder. She smiled and leaned into him. Clara and her new friend stood close to each other and sighed. Fen was suddenly overcome with relief and happiness. She leaned into Clancy and started to cry. He pulled her to him in a strong but gentle hug. After a few moments, Fen pulled away and looked at Clancy's shirt.

"I got your shirt really wet," she sniffed.

"No wetter than in a blinding rain storm at night." He smiled and pulled her back into a hug. He started to think that maybe he might not mind a little complication in his life. Clancy's gaze rested on Pete who still had his hand resting on Rosie's shoulder. Pete winked at Clancy, knowing they both felt a sense of contentment. Clancy was new at this, but Pete felt he had finally been given a second chance to be with the one he had always loved. Somehow he knew Rosie felt the same way.

Chapter Thirty Two

The next morning, Fen woke up to a quiet house. She got out of bed and leaned out her open window. The distant mountain peaks were clearly etched against a bright, blue sky. Fen's heart pounded as she thought about her father's promise. When she was fifteen, he would take her and Hack into those mountains, following paths that wild animals had taken for centuries, trails that settlers had used to make their own difficult journeys. Now it was her chance to wander through those rugged passes and across the jagged cliffs she had seen from her window all these years. It was her chance to look down at their ranch from somewhere so distant that her home would look like a tiny raft floating on a vast sea of grass.

Fen took in one long breath of sweet summer air and then turned away from the window to get dressed. She was surprised not to hear Alex outside her door, humming and bouncing his ball. Just to make sure she hadn't been dreaming for three months, she pinched herself.

"Yup. I'm awake and it's all real." She went downstairs and found her mother at the stove making breakfast. "Where's Alex?" Fen asked.

Her mother turned to look at Fen. There were tears in her eyes. She nodded towards the mud room adjacent to the kitchen. Fen found Alex in the corner of the room, sitting next to a box with a blanket inside. He had Rain in his lap, the puppy guzzling down milk from a warmed bottle. Alex was humming a tune no one would recognize, but one that Rain had already learned meant food, warmth and comfort.

"Good morning, Alex," Fen said, quietly. She didn't want to startle the puppy from his meal.

"Fen," Alex replied. He looked up and gazed over his sister's left shoulder. He looked back at the pup in his lap. "Rain."

It was one moment of connection but it was enough for Fen. She went back to the kitchen, hugged her mother and wolfed down breakfast, chugging milk so fast it spilled out of the corners of her mouth. Renee watched Fen in silence and just smiled. Her daughter was fifteen and still ate like a two-year-old. She guessed Fen had an agenda for the day and nothing was going to get in the way. Two minutes later, Fen was calling Clancy.

"Hey, are you ready for a really, really long trail ride to a hidden valley?"

"Hmmmm. Do you know something I don't know?" he replied.

"It's a secret."

"Some secret. Remind me never to tell you any more of mine."

"Buck gave me permission."

"Ah. The secret is beginning to make some sense." Clancy laughed. "I'll be ready when you get here."

"Pack a lot of food and water!" Fen hung up the phone.

"Are you off on another crazy jaunt with that good for nothing young man?" Renee glared at Fen, trying to sound disapproving.

"Crazy jaunt? I would never do such a thing. It's called an adventure!"

Renee laughed as Fen ran out the door. Her ponytail was flying like a horse's mane in full gallop and she had one boot on and the other one in her hand. It took no time to get Hack tacked up and ready to go.

"Well, boy, we're back doing what we both love to do and what we were made for. We're going on one long trail ride." Hack leaned on her and sighed.

While Clancy and Fen were on their adventure, Alex started on his own. With Buck at his side, he began working the stallion in the ring at the front of the house. Having watched Buck and Fen train horses, Alex quickly learned how to hold the longe line and whip. Through his body positions and eyes, Alex asked Crescent to walk, jog and lope with easy transitions. The horse snorted and let his tail flow back and forth in an easy manner as he moved. With one eye the stallion gazed at the far fields and distant mountains. With the other eye he watched Alex, waiting for messages given without words. Crescent was learning to be at ease in the space between his body and the boy's gently guiding hands.

When the work was done, Alex sighed, let his hands fall to his sides and Crescent came to an easy stop. He turned his head and looked at Alex with both eyes. Alex returned the horse's gaze and the two walked toward each other, meeting halfway between Crescent's space and Alex's space. Alex walked over and unclasped the longe line from the horse's halter. The boy stroked Crescent's nose and rubbed his neck, then turned to leave the arena. Crescent was free to go where he wished. Buck stood and watched as Crescent followed Alex to the gate.

Instead of leaving the ring, Alex started walking around with Crescent following at his shoulder. The horse stopped when the boy paused, walked when Alex walked and jogged when the boy trotted. Alex walked in circles and serpentine patterns and Crescent followed, like a shadow, like an echo, like a reflection of the boy's being. Finally, Alex stopped and turned toward Crescent. The horse bowed his heavy head, rested it gently on the boy's small chest and closed his eyes, breathing in the smell of his friend. Alex scratched the horse's ears, rubbed his face and hummed.

Buck knew that, for the first time, he was watching the boy and the horse do what came naturally to them. They were beginning a bond that would last a lifetime and doing it of their own free will. With all the books, poems, movies and songs of love ever created by man, none was more powerful than this moment to this cowboy. Buck knew this was a relationship born of freedom, for they could each be who they were with no tethers, no reins and no expectations. It was to become a bond that would only ask them to try their best, trust each other and have that be enough.

Epilogue

The old mare was lying under a large tree, dozing in the shade. Her grey dapples were getting harder to see as she turned whiter with each passing year. She put her head up to watch her last foal challenge another yearling in a game of bite and run. The filly with the raindrop star had grown up to be strong and tall, her chestnut color radiant in the sun. The old mare knew this horse was ready to compete for the position of alpha mare. She was strong enough to protect her own foals from predators and men on horseback, just as the old mare had done for so many years. But she knew her time had passed. It made her happy to just graze in the sun and watch her foals grow up, knowing they would continue to make the wild herd strong and healthy.

The old, dun stallion had left his mares and foals long since their escape from the river valley, having lost a challenge by a young, strong red roan. The old stallion had joined a bachelor band and was living out his days in the protection and company of this male herd. His wounds had been numerous, but only a few scars remained from the worst of his battles. Sometimes, when the rain came down hard and thunder boomed and lightening flashed, he would find protection under a tree. He would stand, safe and dry, remembering the night that his herd had been left corralled in the open, confused and terrified in a storm that raged around them.

The stallion had been uncertain of their fate that night until he heard a loud "clank" and a long squeaking sound. He had peered through the darkness and rain, saw an opening and headed for it, whinnying to his herd to follow. He quickly rounded the fence and headed for a trail that wound up through the woods, rather than retrace their hoof prints back to the valley where the men on horseback had captured them. The stallion had led his herd to a remote canyon where few would venture, where his wild horses could once again be free. The stallion had always done his best to feed, protect and care for the herd who had depended upon him. He knew that was enough for one lifetime.